# Beginning of Tomorrows

Chronicle of Ceres, Book 1

CL LaVigne

For permissions, contact:

CL LaVigne

cindy@cllavigne.com

Cover Designed by MiblArt

Beginning of Tomorrows

(Chronicle of Ceres, Book One) - 2nd Edition

www.cllavigne.com

www.facebook.com/CLLaVigneAuthor

ISBN (paprback): 978-1-7322933-5-9

ISBN (eBook): 978-1-7322933-6-6

# Dedication

To my incredible husband, Chris, who endured my sleepless nights, story line and character ramblings, and spent countless hours reading the chapters of all seven edited versions. You are my hero!

# Contents

# Prologue

TED KEMP PONDERED HIS final moment on Earth. How would it feel? What would it look like? He swirled the ice in his Manhattan and stared through the windows overlooking Apollo's Fountain, a once-vibrant portal to the many exotic lands he visited around the world. He consumed scorpions in Asia, jumped with the Maasai in Africa, read hieroglyphics in Egyptian pyramids and even materialized once at the North Pole, a trip gone awry which nearly killed him. Now, Apollo and his four marble horses lie in ruin, obliterated by Stygian and his army.

Ted turned to Darrius, "Will Freda survive her death?"

Ted had known Darrius for almost sixty years and, even though Ted was a human, Darrius respected him like an equal, and loved him like a Cererian brother. "Hard to say. Stygian's plague is a relentless virus, a hybrid organism that is consuming Freda one cell at a time. Prasad and I have stabilized her with our healing powers, but the trip through the portal may be too hard on her fragile body." Darrius placed an arm around Ted's shoulder and looked out the window. "We warned you this day would come. You were too reckless. Your actions invited the eyes of Stygian. Now you're paying the price."

"I don't like your plan at all, Darrius. I love my children even if they aren't really mine. Freda and I were fortunate to have them in our lives; and watch them grow, flourish and display their gifts. But purposely hurting them, pushing them away and now staging our deaths..." Ted trailed off as he heard Freda's hoarse whisper.

"Ted...please dear...please..." Freda lay on the sofa, the only furniture that provided even a modicum of relief from the pain that racked her body. Oozing boils covered her face and torso. Tendrils of green pus seeped from the craters like the undulating arms of an octopus creeping along the seabed searching for prey. The tendrils licked the surrounding skin in search of new places to take root and birth new blisters. Immense pillows cradled her body. A large cloth bib spread across her chest to capture the constant drool flowing from her gaping mouth infested with eruptions on her gums, tongue, and throat.

"Ted...Darrius is...our...friend. Please listen...to him." She winced as the words caught in her throat like shards of glass scraping raw skin. Her eyes misted but she dabbed at them, fearing the salty tears in her wounds would only make the pain worse.

Ted knelt by her side. He was desperate to calm her fears and soothe her pain. He reached for Freda but hesitated. His hands, cupped on either side of her face, hovered inches from her skin.

"My friend, do not touch your wife. You must not get too close or the virus will attach to you as well," Darrius cautioned.

Ted's fingers twitched. The green tendrils sensed fresh skin and whipped up from Freda's face, frantically waving, searching for the new host they sensed was nearby. Ted reluctantly withdrew his hands and gazed into his wife's eyes full of sorrow and pain. He clenched his teeth in frustration.

"I hate to see you suffering, my dear, and it was my foolishness that has brought all this pain and destruction upon our house, upon our family. Darrius can't guarantee you'll survive the portal."

"I...will..." Freda grimaced, struggling to speak the next word. She stiffened, drew in a halting breath and spat the last word out, "...survive."

Prasad entered the room and joined Darrius at the window "We must consider the time, my brother. The portal will soon close and our opportunity will be lost."

"Yes, time is of the essence. Let's escort the Kemps to the patio."

Darrius gently gripped Ted's shoulder. "I know this isn't easy, dying never is, but I will protect your children and ensure they finish the quest that you started," Darrius promised.

Ted hung his head and nodded in agreement, resigned to the fact that Darrius' plan was the only solution. To live, they would need to die. Their demise would save the lives of their children.

Ted grabbed Darrius in a fierce hug. "You've been a good friend," he whispered. "You and I have accomplished so much. With few exceptions, I wouldn't change a thing."

Ted examined Darrius' face—still youthful and smooth after all these years. "You haven't changed at all, Darrius. One day we'll continue our conversation on the Cererian's gift of immortality."

"I look forward to that day," Darrius responded. He studied Ted who, at the age of eighty-five, was slightly hunched, but still possessing the sharp mind and piercing blue eyes that Darrius remembered from their first encounter when he explained how the Kemps were a critical link to the lives of four unique children. "And, I hope we get to play another game of chess."

"It's time my friend," Darrius said as he guided Ted onto the patio where the portal awaited them. A kaleidoscope of colors pulsed and shimmered in the gaping maw of the gateway.

Ted gazed into the spiraling abyss, mesmerized by the swirl of vibrant colors. "Does this mean goodbye?" Ted asked Darrius.

"I never say goodbye, Ted. One never knows where life will lead us. Once on Ceres, Freda will have continued care. Our physicians will be able to isolate the virus."

"Yes, if she survives the trip."

The two men joined Prasad and Freda on the patio. Freda lay waiting on a cushion of air manifested by Prasad. Over the decades, she and Prasad had grown close, sharing cooking, gardening and teaching the children different languages and fine art. While Ted and Darrius traversed the world hiding family relics and artifacts representing the birth families of the children, Freda ran the household with Prasad.

Darrius embraced Ted and whispered, "Don't worry about anything. You and Freda have done an incredible job raising extremely gifted children and protecting them as they grew. Prasad and I will guide the children through the next chapter of their life. The world depends on their survival. When it's time, they will learn the truth about you and your wife."

"You must now leave." Prasad said. With a subtle flick of his hand, he directed the invisible pillow of air carrying Freda toward the portal. Ted followed close behind. Stopping them momentarily in front of the gateway, Prasad pressed his hands together in front of his chest and then raised them to his temple while bowing toward the couple. "I wish you safe travels on your journey," he said. He jerked his hand and Freda's bed of air advanced toward the portal.

The entranceway widened as the Kemps approached. Multi-colored clouds rotated clockwise within the maw. Spiraling faster, the puffy strands soon blurred. Ted watched his wife disappear into the colorful fog. He locked eyes with Darrius and walked backwards into the unknown. A brilliant flash engulfed the patio and the Kemps were gone.

The portal closed. On the other side of the gateway, Darrius's Cererian friends awaited the arrival of Ted and Freda Kemp. They would keep them safe and beyond Stygian's reach.

Darrius and Prasad stood together, witnesses to the lie they must now perpetuate, the death they must recognize so that the Kemp children would return to the family estate, The Nine Muses, and fulfill their destinies.

"Are the announcements ready to mail?" Darrius asked.

"Yes, all is proceeding to plan," Prasad answered. "I fear Stygian will try to attack again. We don't have much time to prepare the Kemp children for what awaits them."

"There is never enough time to prepare for battle," Darrius sighed.

# Chapter 1

# The Nine Muses

PRASAD THREW THE FLORAL brocade curtains aside in the dining room. Clouds of dust drifted through the sun beams. He gazed disdainfully at the flecks of dirt and thought, *I'm a Cererian soldier, not a housekeeper.*

He peered out the window toward the horizon. A thick cloud cover swaddled the sky like crimson cotton balls. The golden sun barely peeked above the calm Atlantic Ocean.

"A beautiful sunrise," he said. "What's that old saying? 'Red sky at morning, sailors take warning?'"

Darrius Dagda glanced up from reading the newspaper and followed Prasad's gaze. "Yes, that's right and the rest goes, 'Red sky at night, sailors' delight'.

"I'll prepare breakfast," Prasad said as he refilled Darrius' water glass. "Do you feel like anything in particular?"

Darrius glanced up at his friend. "You ask me that question every morning. But despite what I tell you, you always bring me what *you* want."

A generous smile spread across Prasad's face, wrinkles creased his brown skin. "This is true. I would bring you what you request but you never ask for the proper items." He chuckled a rich, throaty laugh. "But I'm hopeful you will eventually get it right."

"In that case, I'll have oatmeal with brown sugar," Darrius responded. He studied Prasad's face, checking for signs that he ordered wisely but his friend's blank expression provided no clues.

Prasad whirled and exited without a word.

The diminutive man padded around the massive kitchen in his bare feet. He detested shoes. He didn't understand the fascination with strapping stiff materials onto one's soles. It was unnatural. Why would someone want to break the energetic connection to Mother Earth?

He moved quietly and easily, gliding along the ceramic tile floor, the bottom edges of his mundu lightly brushing his ankles. He rolled up the sleeves of his simple white cotton shirt and cracked a fresh egg into the frying pan with one hand while sprinkling fresh herbs with the other. The toaster spat out a burnt bagel with a loud *kerchunk*. The fried egg spit and snapped in response. Prasad buttered the bagel and set it on the plate leaving enough room for the over-easy egg. He snatched a ruby red grapefruit from the refrigerator and sliced it open. A faint citrusy aroma mingled with the savory and burnt odors swirling around the kitchen. Placing the halved fruit in a small bowl, Prasad grabbed the plate and headed back into the dining room.

He placed the breakfast in front of Darrius. "This is what you should have requested," he said. The corners of his mouth bowed in a wry grin. Grabbing the grapefruit, Prasad sat cross-legged in a chair and carefully sectioned the fruit as if performing intricate surgery.

"Thank you. This is the perfect meal for me," Darrius admitted. This was his response to Prasad's amusing ritual every morning.

Darrius had known Prasad for over one thousand years, and he never tired of his friend's style of humor—a playful display few people witnessed. Since arriving on Earth, the two men had learned to embrace the emotions and idiosyncrasies that developed within their host bodies.

A thousand years ago Cererian Harvesters were unaware that the DNA they collected from human cadavers would combine with Cererian lifeforces in an unpredictable manner. Each explorer evolved into a hybrid who exhibited the traits of his human donor. While Darrius and Prasad grew into kind and gentle individuals, many of their companions developed ill-natured personalities. The Cererians were a peaceful and non-threatening race; and, now, some of them were becoming barbaric murderers because of the DNA's effect.

This unfortunate development troubled the Cererian High Council, especially when the Yfel Brethren formed. This evil group of soldiers refused to adhere to the mission's directive of peace and non-interference. Compelled by their evolving human emotions which urged them to destroy, these brothers learned that that they could become powerful if they killed the magical people and consumed their energy.

The killings began a thousand years ago. That action forced a wedge between Cererians—those that supported the peaceful directive and those who craved dominance over others.

The bond between Prasad and Darrius flourished on the mutual belief that they must do everything within their power to protect Earth's magical populations and to protect the chosen ones—the magicians who would restore peace to the world.

"What is the arrival schedule for our guests today?" Darrius asked.

Prasad slowly chewed a grapefruit section and replied, "Mr. Chance Kemp will be here at two, Mr. Kai Kemp will follow at three, Ms. Fenna Kemp will arrive at four, and Ms. Hilliard Kemp is due at five."

"Excellent. It will be nice to have the entire family in the house again, minus their parents of course. The last time we saw them was in 1992. I'm sure they've changed a lot."

"I'm more curious how the siblings will react to each other, and to the reading of the will."

"Yes, indeed. Keeping the secret about their true identities was easier than expected. But we must prepare for the repercussions once the Kemps discover who and what they are." Darrius gazed out the window, lost in the storm clouds. He mulled over how the siblings might react to the news.

Prasad abruptly stood. "I must leave you, Darrius. Much needs to be done before the Kemps arrive." He carried the breakfast plates into the kitchen, and placed them in the sink. Raindrops tapped against the window, and he gazed at the gray clouds rushing by.

*The storm is coming.*

Prasad placed a vintage brown vase filled with fresh daffodils on the dresser and walked to the window. He pulled the heavy curtains open to reveal a panoramic view of the Atlantic. He hefted one window open a few inches. The old wooden sash had swelled from the rain and wouldn't budge any higher. A chilled breeze slid through the opening and swirled the musty essence of the bedroom.

The room had not been used in twenty years and it showed. Prasad placed fresh cotton sheets and a goose-down comforter on the four-poster bed, spritzing lavender water between each layer. He haphazardly dusted the furniture, the platoon of toy soldiers and the model planes with a worn feather duster that shed aged feathers with each pass. He plugged in the vacuum and crisscrossed the worn Oriental rug in a hurried, uneven pattern. Before leaving the room, he placed an envelope in the middle of the bed. On it, the name "Chance Kemp" was elegantly hand-lettered in dark purple ink. Prasad glanced at his pocket watch.

Eleven o'clock.

He glanced out the bedroom window. All hints of the morning sun had been replaced by a blanket of gray clouds. Precursors to the storm that brewed off the coast.

He pushed his housekeeping cart to the next bedroom and repeated the same ritual. It was critical that he finish all four rooms before the arrival of the first guest: Chance Kemp.

# Chapter 2

# Chance

CHANCE LEANED TO THE right and farted loudly. A sour cabbage stench filled the car and swirled around his head like cigarette smoke. He grimaced, "Ewwwie, that's a bad one."

He chuckled as he thought of Janet, his wife of twenty years. If Janet was sitting beside him, she would be fanning the air with her hand and wrinkling her nose in disgust. She didn't appreciate the fine art of passing gas. There was a finesse in creating the right sound and producing that perfect smell that could drop an elephant in its tracks. Chance had devoted his life to developing both.

Years earlier at a family reunion, after devouring ten deviled eggs, Chance excitedly gathered his cousins—a pack of pals eager for fun. "Wait for it!" he said like a magician preparing to reveal an amazing trick. The men leaned in. Chance squeezed his eyes, bent his knees and clenched his fists. His cousins gawked, wide-eyed in anticipation.

Sweat poured down Chance's brow as he strained. Like a bottle of soda that's been shaken in the hot sun, the flatulence sputtered like a moped straining uphill. When Chance leaned right, he surprised everyone with a booming goose honk finale. The nuclear blast of digested eggs showered everyone in a sulfur fallout. His cousins stared in shock, tears streaming down their faces. Chance bowed low before his amazed audience. No one spoke for several minutes. Most were overwhelmed by the noxious fumes.

"Well?" Chance asked, his arms outstretched. "What do you think?"

The cousins exchanged glances and then yelled in unison, "That was awesome!" Chance beamed at his adoring fans. It had been one of his best.

"Can you do it again?" one cousin asked.

"Come on, Chance, do it again!" another urged.

Chance grinned at the memory. He could always count on his cousins. Janet simply didn't get it. Farting was like his chosen sport. Like an athlete, he had to keep training and that meant eating and passing gas as often as he could. His goal was to achieve perfection much to his wife's chagrin.

The stench lingered inside the car. "I'll give this one an eight," he mused aloud, "It had a rich, loud noise and the smell is long-lasting but it could be just a little more putrid." He chuckled again.

He needed a good laugh. He was driving toward hell.

Silly memories would sustain him as he headed for The Nine Muses: a sprawling mansion on the Massachusetts coast. An image of the cold and dreary manor popped into his head; and dread shivered up his spine.

Built in the 1700s, the house, constructed of white granite, perched on a cliff overlooking the Atlantic Ocean. Ten lush acres surrounded the main house and three out-buildings. A classical Greek fountain split the circular driveway. The remote land was surrounded by a ten-foot-high black iron fence.

A cold, unfriendly house, The Nine Muses protected a dark secret.

It had once been Chance's home.

A wave of nausea boiled up from his belly. He rolled down the window and spat. The loogie flew into the wind and whipped back to smack against the side of his face. "Shit!" he yelled, scooping the spittle off his cheek. He cursed his stupidity and The Nine Muses. He wished he was back in Asheville drinking a double bourbon and warming a stool at his favorite hangout, Flanagan's Pub.

He had fond memories of Flanagan's.

He had met Janet at the pub. She bounced in with her girlfriends one Tuesday night to sing karaoke. Her blonde hair, sculpted high on her head thanks to an entire can of hairspray, barely moved as she ran to the stage. She wore a red leather mini skirt with matching red boots. Her friends were dressed in similar outfits and they promoted themselves as the Teasing Trio. Chance was intrigued. He ordered another drink and leaned against the bar.

Janet and her friend Cissy were backup singers to the real star, Bethany. Bethany grabbed the mike and belted out the words to Donna Summer's "Last Dance." Chance and the other patrons winced. Bethany's pitch was better applied to horseshoes than music. What the poor girl didn't have in voice, she made up for in enthusiasm. After all, who wouldn't want to see a young woman bounce around the stage in a see-through blouse and much-too-short mini skirt that revealed her bouncy bottom every time she bent over? After the performance, the crowd went wild.

Bethany never lacked for drink invitations, but Janet and Cissy always found themselves forgotten, a performance afterthought. But, not this time. As men rushed toward Bethany, Chance strode over to Cissy and Janet. Tipping his hat, he drawled, "Howdy!" Cissy rolled her eyes and walked away.

"What a bad accent." Janet giggled, "You really need to perfect your style."

"Damn, I was trying to be so cool."

"Just be yourself. That's all you need." Janet walked to the end of the bar and motioned for Chance to sit with her. They spent the rest of the night chatting about everything and anybody. She was twenty-eight. He was thirty-four. They married three years later on her father's ranch near Hendersonville.

Chance sped down the Yankee Division Highway in Eastern Massachusetts. His stomach churned. Going home after twenty years made him nauseated. *Home* wasn't the right word. It was a house owned by people who tricked him by claiming to be his parents. Now, he was being coerced into coming back. The last thing he wanted was to go back to those painful memories. But he was obedient. He always did what he was told.

Mom and Dad had died. As he did in life, his father summoned him, only this time from beyond the grave. Chance grimaced as he remembered being contacted by Mr. Darrius Dagda, Executor of the Kemp estate. The order came in the form of a certified letter.

> *"It is with great sadness that I inform you of the death of your father and mother, Theodore and Freda Kemp. You are required to attend the reading of the will on Friday, April 27, 2012. Only you may attend, no family members or friends may accompany you. You are required to arrive on Thursday, April 26, 2012 at precisely 2:00 p.m.—no sooner, no later—or you will forfeit your entitlements to the estate and any inheritance."*

Recalling the rigid terms in the letter Chance clenched his jaw and mashed the gas pedal to the floor. He had been forced from his home once, and now, he was being blackmailed to return to it. Chance gripped the steering wheel, forcing his knuckles white.

In 1992, his father summoned him, demanding that he come home immediately for a very important announcement. "I need you to come to The Nine Muses. I can't stress how important it is for you to be here for me and your siblings."

"Dad, I've just started a new job. They won't give me time off." Chance reasoned with his father, "Can't we manage this over the phone?"

"Be here or don't bother calling me again because I will disown you! I'm serious."

The car flew through the countryside as Chance blinked back angry tears. He hated his father and now the bastard was dead. He should be happy but he only felt sadness and regret.

There had been happier times. As a child, he admired his father's job, which took him around the globe. Chance was fascinated by the souvenirs from each location. His favorite was an authentic camel saddle dyed red. It was embellished with a small brass bell wound around the horn with a red leather strap. Dad brought it back from Egypt by dismantling it and carefully packing the pieces in his suitcases. His father reconstructed the saddle in time for Chance's birthday. Chance fantasized that his father stole the magical saddle from an emir.

When Chance was sixteen, he experienced a nastier side of his father. It had been just past midnight and Chance couldn't sleep. He wandered downstairs hoping to raid the refrigerator when he heard voices coming from his father's office down the hallway from the kitchen. The voices grew louder and angrier. Chance tiptoed closer so he could hear. He reached the open door and carefully peered through the crack.

His father and another man stood nose-to-nose screaming at each other, taking turns jabbing their index fingers into each other's chests as if to emphasize their respective viewpoints.

"You have no fuckin' business coming to my home in the middle of the night," Dad barked.

"You're getting reckless, Ted, and it's being noticed by the others!"

"I don't fuckin' care what the others think. It's my fuckin' life and I'll do what I want!"

"You can't do what you want, and that's the point! So many lives depend on what you do. The world's survival was entrusted to you."

Chance stiffened. What were they talking about? He leaned closer, pushing his ear almost into the crack. The hinges complained with a loud *squeak.*

"Shh. What was that?"

Chance bolted. The two men ran out of the office as Chance slid into the kitchen, running back to his bedroom.

"Chance, stop," his dad yelled.

Chance continued up the staircase and his father bellowed a second time, "Chance, STOP! NOW!"

Chance froze midstride. His father continued, "Chance, come here, please."

Head hung low, Chance obeyed like he always did and turned around. He walked back to his father. "What did you hear?" Mr. Kemp asked.

"Nothing," Chance lied.

"Ted, I've got to leave now," the other man interrupted, "And, for the sake of others, stop what you're doing. Please, please consider your actions." The man peered at Chance and scurried out the front door leaving Mr. Kemp and Chance in silence.

They stood there for several minutes before Mr. Kemp spoke, "Chance, you must forget what you saw and what you heard tonight. Is that clear? I don't want you to tell anybody else. Pretend that this never happened. You're a good boy and you always do what you're told, don't you?"

"Bastard!" Chance spat out the word as he recalled that long-ago exchange with his father. "Yes, I always do what I'm told, Dad!"

Back in 1992, Chance called in sick and hurried home for his dad's big announcement. That's when his world fell apart. Nothing made sense anymore. The past and the truth, as he knew it, no longer existed. He left the house with a basket full of lies, deceit, and anger toward his parents and his siblings.

"Shit!" Chance realized he was flying down the road at almost one hundred mph. Suppressed anger raged through his body and reached his foot, which smashed the gas pedal to the floor. He couldn't risk the police pulling him over and making him late. He eased his foot off the pedal, and scanned the side and rearview mirrors. No blue lights, all was clear. "Take it easy, Chance," he muttered aloud. "Just a quick visit, and then you'll be out of there for good!"

Chance eased onto Summer Street which led to the entrance of the family estate located on Coolidge Point. A cold rain had fallen since he reached Manchester-by-the-Sea, and he was thankful Janet packed his goose-down jacket. Asheville was immersed in spring when he hit the road to come home, but Massachusetts welcomed him with a chilly reception. He smiled at the irony.

He already missed his wife and children. He felt grounded around his family and felt safe in the peaceful North Carolina mountains. He sought refuge there in 1992, after Mom and Dad destroyed his life.

Chance shivered. It wasn't the cold rain. He was getting close to the house; and the memories reached out to him with icy fingers from a tortured past. He jerked the steering wheel and stopped the car on the shoulder. White knuckles gripped the wheel as he lowered his head. Anxiety seized control: his heart raced, he panted, and sweat trickled down his face. He feared he might pass out unless he talked himself down from the escalating panic attack.

"Calm down. There's nothing there that can hurt you." He hoped saying the words aloud would trick his mind into believing them. He glanced at his watch.

Almost two.

"Gotta get going. I can't be late." He breathed deeply several times. An image of Janet popped into his mind. She had convinced him to join meditation classes at their local yoga studio. He hadn't expected much, but was pleasantly surprised when he learned how to control his anxiety through proper breathing. He loosened his grip on the steering wheel and swiped the sweat off his face with the back of his hand. His heart and breathing were slow and steady. Janet would have been proud. Easing the Ford Escape back onto the road, Chance proclaimed, "Ready or not, here I come."

# Chapter 3

# Kai

KAI KISSED HIS HUSBAND and hugged him tightly.

"You're squishing me," Jeff teased.

"You know I hate flying," Kai said softly. "I wish you could come with me."

Jeff caressed Kai's face. "As much as I would love to see your family's palatial estate, I'm fine chilling with our friends this weekend. Besides, I need to keep an eye on your exhibit this Saturday. That snobby Beatrice Brandy will be by to opine about your technique." They both giggled.

Beatrice's last name was actually Bradley, and she fancied herself to be Sedona's authority on abstract paintings even though she couldn't tell a Malevich from a Pollock if her life depended on it. Her greatest love, other than sharing her opinion on art, was for Hennessy brandy. She would often arrive to opening nights heavily snockered. Hence, the reason many locals affectionately referred to her as Beatrice Brandy.

"Maybe I'm the lucky one," Kai joked. "Be nice around Beatrice. It's been a while since I've had a show at one of the main galleries and I want to make an impression even though I won't be there."

Jeff shook his head. "I still can't believe Mr. Dagda couldn't be flexible on the date for reading the will. Your exhibit is a big deal! The fact you need to arrive on April 26th at 3:00 p.m. is crazy. Does he even understand how airlines work nowadays? I don't even want to talk about the logistics of the rental car and the Massachusetts traffic."

Kai hung his head. Tears filled his eyes as he remembered the chaos of 1992. He came out to his parents during their annual New Year's party. His mother, Freda, had always known he was gay and was his biggest supporter when he wanted to take art classes instead of trying out for football as his father desired. Influential in the Boston art scene, Freda introduced Kai to many of her creative friends who visited the estate and invited Kai to participate in their plein air painting weekends. Outdoors, the elements of nature influenced his unique style as he combined bold strokes with the natural paint splatters created by the ocean breeze.

Coming out to his father was met with awkwardness but was not totally negative. He was prepared for what his dad might say thanks to his friends who shared their own 'coming out' stories.

"Well, that explains your interest in art," his father said upon hearing the news.

"Dad, there are gay football players as well. I just prefer to paint my grass on canvas and not with my face after being tackled," Kai said with a big grin on his face.

After a few seconds, Mr. Kemp broke into a huge smile. "You could always make me laugh, Kai. No matter what trouble you were in, you could make me chuckle and make the world right again. I love you and nothing will ever change that."

The rest of the year soon unraveled. Not long after the New Year's party, his father unexpectedly called insisting he come home immediately for an important announcement to be shared with Kai and his siblings. The accepting father he had known in January was now threatening to disown him in March if he didn't come home right away. Kai had hopped on a red eye to Boston and caught a taxi to make it home on time. Nothing could have prepared him for what his parents shared that night. His life was turned upside down and inside out as if he had been thrust into a washing machine.

"I shouldn't have gone. I should have let my father disown me," Kai sobbed, "At least I would still have wonderful memories and not feel as though my entire life has been a huge lie."

Jeff hugged Kai. "Please stop talking about it. It upsets you so much and you've come such a long way since '92. To hell with your parents and your siblings! Fuck them all!"

"I'm so glad you're in my life." Kai smiled weakly at Jeff, "I can do this. All I need to do is go home one more time, and then I'm done. I'll come back to you and we never have to talk about the Kemp family again!"

Kai abhorred flying. He didn't like relinquishing control to people he didn't know. To ease his fears, he paid extra for the comfort of a first-class seat and enjoyed a couple of vodka tonics before easing into a restless sleep during the five-hour flight. He jolted awake when the pilot announced they were preparing to land in Boston and that they were on time.

Kai was a genius at packing a multitude of clothes into two carry-on totes. Once the plane landed, he grabbed one bag from the overhead and lifted the light bag onto his shoulder before exiting the plane. First class had its benefits.

Once inside the terminal Kai readjusted his clothes. He smoothed his straight-legged jeans and re-rolled the sleeves on his blue-checked dress shirt. It was chillier in Boston than in Sedona so he threw on the black leather jacket Jeff had purchased for him just before the trip. *Jeff thinks of everything.*

He walked briskly through the airport to the car rental level and gave his reservation number to the clerk at the booth. The young blonde woman cheerfully greeted him and checked his reservation on the computer. "Oh, dear," she exclaimed.

"What? Is there a problem?"

"I'm afraid there is an issue. Because of the bad weather many of our cars have been delayed in returning to the airport. I don't have a car for you. I'm so sorry." Kai calmly stared at her and she at him.

Tense moments passed until Kai broke the silence. "And, you intend to do what?"

"I'm sorry, sir, we don't have any cars."

"I'm aware of that, but I made a reservation with you and you're not making good on that promise. Good customer service would dictate that you find a solution to my predicament."

Visibly shaken, the clerk sputtered, "Let me get my supervisor."

"Thank you."

Soon a young man strode to the counter and stuck out his hand to shake Kai's. "Mr. Kemp, I'm Brandon. I understand that we don't have a car for you."

Kai narrowed his gaze and prepared for a fight, "Yes, that's right and I have an important meeting in Manchester-by-the-Sea at three. I can't be late by even a minute. It's a matter of life and death."

"Manchester-by-the-Sea," Brandon repeated. "That's quite a distance from here. You'll need to get on the road right away to arrive at three." Turning toward the young woman, Brandon asked, "Marcy, would you call Mr. Stanton for me?"

Marcy handed the phone to Brandon. After a short discussion, he hung up. "Mr. Kemp, I apologize that we don't have a car for you; and to correct that situation I have my manager's approval to have our service car take you to your destination."

Kai relaxed. "A service car?"

"Yes sir. We hope this will resolve this unfortunate situation."

"This is excellent customer service," Kai exclaimed. He shook hands with Brandon and then Marcy.

Gesturing toward the automatic doors, Brandon advised, "The car will pull up to those doors behind you within five minutes."

"Thank you," Kai said as he gathered his bags. "Thank you so much." He dashed out the doors just as a black stretch limousine pulled to the curb.

Puzzled, Marcy looked at Brandon. "I didn't know we had a service car."

Brandon watched as Kai climbed into the vehicle. He then turned toward Marcy. "We don't, but Mr. Stanton does and he's a collector of Mr. Kemp's art."

"That guy was an artist?" Marcy asked.

"Yes, I recognized him when I walked out. He got his start right here in Boston, but he now lives in Sedona. He's a humble guy and doesn't like attention. Otherwise, I would have asked for his autograph," Brandon gushed.

The chauffeur stood beside the open door. "Mr. Kemp?"

"Yes." Kai handed a note to him. "Here's the address and I must arrive by three o'clock. It's a matter of life and death."

"Yes, sir." The driver tipped his hat. "I'll have you there on time."

Kai climbed into the darkened back seat and slid against the far window. Easing against the plush leather, he closed his eyes, and exhaled in relief.

"Hello, Mr. Kemp!"

Kai jumped and pressed against the window. He thrust his hands in front of him, defending himself against the unknown. A deep gloom caused by the tinted windows swirled in the cavernous back seat of the stretch limousine. He hadn't noticed that he had company and peered into the shadows, searching for the owner of the voice.

*Click.* The overhead light suddenly illuminated, temporarily blinding Kai.

"Don't worry, Mr. Kemp. I won't hurt you."

Kai squinted as his eyes adjusted to the brightness. Several seats away perched an older man. Small in stature, the stranger sported a full gray beard and a meticulously waxed handlebar mustache which he stroked between the index finger and thumb of his left hand.

"Who are you?" Kai demanded.

"I'm Mr. Stanton, the owner of this car."

"What are you doing here?"

"When Brandon told me about the rental car situation and how it impacted my favorite artist, I knew I had to make things right. Of course, I also wanted to meet you."

*This is kind of creepy*, Kai thought as he slowly lowered his arms.

"I followed your work when you were in Boston, but haven't been able to attend any of your exhibits in Sedona," Mr. Stanton continued. "Why did you leave Boston?"

Kai ignored the probing question. "Well, I certainly want to thank you for your generosity in providing your car."

"My pleasure, Mr. Kemp." Mr. Stanton grinned as he crept closer to Kai. His Cheshire cat smile of yellowing, jumbled teeth reminded Kai of candy corn. "It will take about an hour to reach Manchester-by-the-Sea. May I offer you a drink? I believe you prefer vodka tonic, is that correct?"

*This guy knows too much about me,* Kai thought.

Unsure about his strange companion, he responded, "No thank you, but I could use some water. I feel a little dehydrated."

"Absolutely! My pleasure! By the way, please call me Melvin."

Kai took the bottle and leaned back into the seat. He sipped slowly, taking his time so he didn't have to speak with the strange little man.

"All of this may seem so odd to you," Melvin began. "I must seem like a stalker. But it's just that I adore your work so much and have loved visiting your exhibits here in Boston. That's how I know what you like to drink. You always had a vodka tonic in your hand on opening night, and you wore a scarf, a different color to match the theme of the exhibit. You're not wearing one now. Why is that? My favorite show, by far, was the *Tortured Soul* display. I really identified with those paintings. I have quite a lot of those in my collection. What was your favorite?"

Kai studied Melvin as he fired questions without pausing for a breath. The little man wore a dark gray suit, tailored meticulously for his small frame. A blood-red tie sat perfectly at his throat against a bright white, dress shirt. Melvin crossed his legs and Kai noticed the Italian leather shoes with a shine so brilliant he could see his reflection. The expressive, energetic man waved his hands to punctuate his statements, and that's when Kai noticed the diamond-studded gold rings on each finger.

"Mr. Kemp, did you hear my question?" Melvin repeated.

Kai lurched out of his musing. "Sorry, I'm tired, and didn't get much sleep on the plane."

Embarrassed, Melvin blurted, "My apologies! Here I've been chatting incessantly. Please forgive me."

"No, I should apologize. You've been a gracious host and I've been boorish."

"Are you sure you wouldn't want a vodka tonic?" Melvin smiled his crooked smile.

"Sure, that sounds wonderful," Kai relented.

"Excellent! Now, sit back, enjoy your drink and tell me what brings you home."

Kai considered the question while he slowly sipped his alcohol. He eyed Melvin over the rim of the glass. The little man's eyes danced and jumped in anticipation of whatever Kai might say. He was obviously smitten with Kai and now had a captive audience all the way to Manchester-by-the-Sea.

"I'm heading home because my parents died and the reading of the will is this weekend."

"Oh, no!" Melvin dramatically grabbed his throat. Placing a hand on Kai's knee, he continued, "I'm so sorry for your loss. It's never easy losing a parent, or so I've been told. My parents passed when I was only eight. Car accident. I had no siblings, just a guardian who tried his best to rob me blind!" Melvin chuckled at the memory. "I learned at an early age how to hang on to what is mine."

Melvin abruptly changed the subject. "Are your siblings coming?"

*What an odd question,* Kai thought. Melvin knew a lot about Kai as if he had researched every detail of his life. An uncomfortable feeling descended and his intuition poked his gut with a warning. He'd play along for now. But The Nine Muses couldn't arrive fast enough.

Kai didn't think about his siblings often. He didn't care if he saw them or not, but chances are they would be at The Nine Muses. And, he would need to deal with them. "Yes, I imagine they will be there. We haven't really kept in contact. We all have our own lives."

The last time all of the children were together was when Dad had summoned everybody to the estate for the announcement. They may have been a close family before that night, but they departed as broken individuals.

"I wouldn't know about family, I don't have any yet," Melvin said with a twisted little grin. "I always dreamed of having a family. It gets very lonely sometimes." Shyly he looked into Kai's eyes and emphasized, "Very lonely."

Kai blushed at Melvin's clumsy flirting and gazed out the window. "Having a family is not always beneficial. Family can be an anchor that weighs you down so much so that you feel like you're drowning."

"Mr. Kemp, we are almost at your destination," the driver interrupted.

The limousine eased into the left path of the circular drive. Kai gawked at the remains of the once-magnificent fountain. "What the hell happened here?" Kai mouthed.

"All good things must come to an end," Melvin chirped, oblivious to the destruction outside the window. "I enjoyed our conversation. Perhaps you'll have time to visit before you go back to Sedona."

"I enjoyed our time together," Kai said with feigned enthusiasm. "You are the perfect host. Unfortunately, I have other plans."

Melvin brightened. "What if you had an exhibit in Boston? You could stay with me and I could show you around the town."

"Let's see what the future brings," Kai replied, careful not to commit to anything.

# Chapter 4

# Fen

FEN CALCULATED THE DISTANCE to Manchester-by-the-Sea, Massachusetts from Stone Mountain, Georgia. Over seventeen hours on the road, not counting any construction delays which seemed ever-present on all the interstates.

She wasn't looking forward to a long road trip, but she abhorred flying since her close call in 1992 when the plane had skidded off a Boston runway. She was hurrying home to see her parents and a late nor'easter lashed the Eastern Seaboard. While in the air her intuition had poked at her, warning her of misfortune and tragedy. Her instincts had always been right in the past, and Fen feared something horrible was going to happen.

And, it did.

Everything went wrong—the plane, her parents, her siblings, her life.

That trip home twenty years ago had left a gaping hole in her heart, a pain that was worse than when she lost her husband, Lance, to cancer. Her entire world shattered into a million pieces when her parents had calmly told their children that they were not who they think they are.

She and her siblings had been living a lie concocted by deceitful people who claimed to have their best interests at heart. Her memories and her past were not hers to claim. Time stopped for Fen.

She read the letter again. *"You are required to arrive promptly at 4:00 p.m., April 26, 2012—no sooner, no later—or you will forfeit your entitlements to the estate and any inheritance."*

She shuddered. She really didn't want to go. She no longer had the energy to deal with that house or her siblings who she had not contacted since that long-ago night.

She had started a new life in a small town where nobody knew her or Lance. Stone Mountain offered them a simple life, free of drama, where they could create happy memories and make new friends.

Her eyes misted. Fen had loved her parents, especially her father. He possessed all the traits she desired in a man: loyalty, compassion, strength, protection, sense of humor. The words in the letter called to her again.

*"It is with great sadness that I inform you of the death of your parents, Theodore and Freda Kemp."*

Lance had been very much like her dad, especially his sense of humor. He had loved surprising Fen by hiding a small Buddha statue in different parts of the house and garden. She found Buddha in the shower, in the pantry, in the bed and was particularly surprised when Buddha, looking cool in sunglasses, appeared behind the steering wheel of her car. She missed Lance. She missed her dad.

At forty-nine, she was getting too old to pull all-night road trips, so she grabbed a marker and plotted her route on an old map. She didn't like using GPS. The damned thing had gotten her lost too many times and she didn't want to risk being late. She preferred depending on her intelligence and knowledge of the areas through which she would drive. She found the perfect route, doable in three days as it offered frequent breaks and lodging. That would allow her a stress-free ride and ample time to arrive at the estate at four o'clock.

Fen had been the organizer of the family. She thought of every detail needed for an event or outing, sometimes to excess. There was no doubt the family had everything they needed whenever Fen was involved.

This trip home was no different. Her Toyota RAV4 was stuffed with boxes and suitcases, each with its own purpose: cold-weather clothes, warm-weather clothes, electronics, toiletries, shoes, books, puzzles and boxed snacks. A small cooler rode shotgun and contained bottled water, oranges, carrot sticks and pecans (which were her favorite). Her favorite navy-blue cardigan was slung around the seat, within easy reach, and her purse was carefully tucked out of sight. Sliding a water bottle into the cup holder, she adjusted her seat, tightened her seatbelt, checked the mirrors, and then turned the ignition.

She needed one more thing before she backed out of the driveway: mood music for the long trip. She slid her favorite CD into the player and smiled as John Denver's "Sunshine on My Shoulders" floated from the speakers.

Time to go home, again.

Fen awoke and stretched her arms above her head. She blinked in the sunlight filtering through the slightly parted curtains. She absently raked her fingers through her hair, scratching one side into a wild thatch. *That's the best sleep I've had in a long time,* she thought.

*Where am I?* She scanned the hotel room trying to make sense of where she was. Her eyes struggled to focus and one was sealed shut by sleep sand. She dug a knuckle into the corner of her eye and rubbed.

*Ah, that's right...the Lakeside Inn.* She smirked at her momentary lapse of memory. She had pulled into the Lakeside just past five o'clock the night before. As she crossed the border into Massachusetts the car bucked as if it had hiccups. She was mad at herself from not having the car serviced prior to travelling. She had so many other things to do and that little detail got lost in the chaos. After three days on the road, she reasoned the car was just cranky from all the driving.

Now that she was in the home stretch, Fen relaxed, proud of what she had accomplished. All the preparations were paying off. But an element of fear darkened her lighthearted mood. The Nine Muses. She bit her lip and trembled as she conjured an image of the mansion.

The Lakeside Inn was a simple, clean hotel. The price was great—only eighty-five dollars for the one night—and it offered a free breakfast. She showered and got dressed.

She swept the curtains apart and watched the clouds race by. It had rained all night but was now sunny. She touched the glass, it was still chilly outside, but not cold enough for snow or ice. The inn was only thirty minutes from The Nine Muses and would allow her plenty of time to arrive by four o'clock driving at a comfortable pace, especially since the drizzle was expected for the rest of the day. She didn't want to risk being late for any reason. She unfolded the map and checked her itinerary again. Her organized planning had brought her this far and it comforted her to recheck the details.

Her stomach growled. Immersed in the particulars of the trip, she had forgotten about breakfast. Throwing her sweater around her shoulders, she took the elevator to the lobby. Delightful aromas teased her nose as she passed the check-in counter, and she imagined what she might eat. As she neared the breakfast bar she stopped and gawked, her mouth wide open. Almost every station had been picked clean. The hotel was full and the available food had dwindled at the hands of travelers eager to get on the road early.

*Shit,* she thought. *I should have come down earlier.* Fortunately, she found an orange and a biscuit, which was cold but not too hard. *This will taste great with a cup of tea.* On the way back to her room she poured hot water into a paper cup and snatched two English breakfast tea bags.

In the comfort of her room she laid her sparse meal on the end table and sat cross-legged on the bed. As the *Today* show played on TV she peeled the orange and rechecked her calculations to The Nine Muses.

Fen recently started limiting the time she spent watching television or playing on her laptop or smartphone. She felt she was wasting too much time watching others enjoy their life instead of doing something about her own. It was a gallant effort to pull herself out of the hold depression had on her since Lance passed, and although it might be short-lived, the video embargo provided her a feeling of accomplishment. The *Today* show was different. This is how she stayed in touch with the world.

Her second-floor room faced the parking lot and her car. Being able to keep an eye on her property was crucial to her mental wellbeing. The compulsion to control elements of her life ramped up when Lance fell ill and he relied on her to get things done like the shopping, car and home maintenance, financial matters and, in the end, funeral arrangements. Maintaining control was second nature to her now. When she wasn't in control, her life was utter chaos.

Fen's cell phone rang, and she glanced at the screen. It was her friend, Phyllis. Fen didn't feel like talking to anyone, but Phyllis was a great friend especially when Lance fell ill. She was dependable, helped with chores and never complained. She seemed too nice sometimes.

Fen knew it would be better to answer now rather than call later. She sighed and cheerily answered, "Phyllis, how good of you to call!"

"The weather is so nice here. Looks like it might be raining up there. Is everything okay?" Phyllis had a reputation for being overly chatty, but Fen didn't mind since she didn't like talking to people anyway. It was a good friendship match.

"It's sunny now, but a cold drizzle is expected for the rest of the day." Fen took a bite of her biscuit and lied, "I just finished breakfast."

"Oh? Well, be careful when you get back on the road. I had this weird dream that you got in a bad accident. I ran up to the window on the driver's side and found you staring at me. There was pure terror in your eyes, Fen. The door wouldn't open. You shoved and I pulled, but it wouldn't budge. Smoke spewed from the engine and we just kept banging the windows..."

"Phyllis! All is okay," Fen interrupted. "I'm relaxing until I leave a little after three. How are the cats? Are they causing you problems?"

"Something is up with them. They must miss you. They've been caterwauling at night and chasing each other into the early morning hours. But I love them like kids. They're doing fine. So the car *is* okay?"

Fen grimaced. Phyllis had a way of pushing too far on some issues. "The car is fine. It was sputtering a little bit yesterday when I crossed the border, but it will be okay today. It had a nice rest overnight."

"Don't forget that you have AAA. I know you like to do things yourself, but if something happens, call them," Phyllis said. She lowered her voice to a serious tone. "Promise me you will."

Usually Fen hated when Phyllis fussed over her but today she realized Phyllis' motherly doting was exactly what she needed. Fen didn't want to drive to the estate. She wanted to stay at the hotel, watch movies, eat popcorn and drink wine. She wanted to do anything other than go to the house and see her siblings. *Anything* would be better than listening to the reading of her father's will.

"Fen, are you still there? Hello?"

"I'm here. I really appreciate your concern. You're such a good friend, Phyllis."

They continued chatting. First, it was the latest gossip from their hometown, and then it turned to Fen's plan for the day.

"Are you still on schedule?" Phyllis asked. "I was impressed with that plan of yours with every detail color-coded."

"Yes, today I leave at three fifteen to drive to the estate. The ride should take about thirty minutes, but I've given myself extra time. I'll leave for home Monday morning and get home late Wednesday night."

Phyllis added, "Don't forget to call me with updates. Don't worry about the time of day. I'm here for you. This is so rough for you, and I want you to know that you can depend on me."

"Thanks, Phyllis. I appreciate that."

"Gotta run, Fen. Keep me posted, and I look forward to when you get home. Toodles!"

Fen imagined Phyllis bustling around the kitchen where she kept the landline phone. *Yep, Lance and I chose the right town. It's full of friendly weirdos just like Phyllis.*

As if a light switch had been flicked, shadows darkened the room as the weather abruptly switched from sunshine to a heavy drizzle. Fen glanced outside. "I hope this lets up by the time I leave," she mused aloud. Drowsy, she leaned back into a stack of pillows she had piled on her bed. It wasn't long before she drifted into a deep sleep.

*Beep. Beep. Beep.* The phone alarm startled Fen from her nap. Thankfully she had pre-programmed multiple alarms into her phone—a new habit warranted by a a history of missed appointments because she fell asleep all too easily.

Fen hurriedly packed her bags and paused. She considered staying at the hotel for the rest of the day. A bottle of wine and movies sounded like a great Plan B. But she had to face whatever was at the estate. If she didn't go now, she would have to deal with it later. She didn't want another woulda, coulda, shoulda situation. Her past was already littered with many of those.

Fen checked out and stood in the hotel entrance. The drizzle eased up a little allowing her to dash to her car. She hated umbrellas. They were messy things and left puddles either in the car or in the house. The duffle bag thumped against her side as she trotted to the car. The raindrops hit her face like tiny cold fingernails jabbing her sensitive skin. She pressed the key fob to open the door. Nothing happened. She squeezed it again. The door remained locked.

"Shit!" Fen hated when things went awry. "Damn this friggin' car!" She jammed the key into the lock and yanked the door open. Throwing her bags onto the front seat, she slid in and slammed the door. She sat in silence while water trickled down her face. "Shit!"

Luckily Fen dressed in layers. She whipped off her soaked sweatshirt, tossed it into the back seat, and grabbed her favorite cardigan that was wrapped around the front seat. Although the wool sweater had spent the cold night in the car, it was dry and warmed her in no time.

She glanced at her watch. Time to leave. She slid the key into the ignition and turned it slowly to the right. The tired engine groaned, *chugga, chugga, chugga.*

"Bitch!" Fen yelled as she slammed the steering wheel with both hands. "Of all the damn times to die on me!"

Fen gritted her teeth, turned off the heater, unplugged her phone charger, and tried again.

*Chugga, chugga, chugga.* The engine sputtered and died.

"Son of a bitch!" she screamed.

She closed her eyes and inhaled slowly trying to calm her nerves. "I'll try one more time," she threatened. She wrenched the key to the right. After one loud cough, the engine finally purred to life. Fen depressed the gas pedal and raced the engine proving it was alive. A triumphant grin spread across her face.

Fen switched on the heater and re-plugged her phone into the charger. She checked her map one more time, careful to note key exits and landmarks. Finally satisfied, she slid the stick into *reverse* and backed up. The car bucked in disagreement but finally submitted with a low metallic groan as she threw the gear into *drive* and eased onto the highway.

Traffic was not too bad this time of day and Fen relaxed despite the intermittent rain. This route was familiar, and her mind wandered. As children, she and Kai had joined their mother, Freda, on trips to Boston.

Her mom introduced them to strange and fascinatingly creative people. Kai explored painting with different media while Fen read novels, many with forbidden language. When Freda went into town everybody requested an audience with her. Once Kai and Fen were busy playing, Freda would close their door so she could have private conversations with her friends, debating topics such as politics, religion and the magical arts. Within this circle of close acquaintances, Freda felt safe to discuss the unusual lives of her adopted children.

Fen had never questioned the actions of her mother or father, but as she drove down the freeway toward Manchester-by-the-Sea, the pieces fell into place, signs she should have noticed. How could she be so stupid? She had a wonderful, happy childhood, but her father's later announcement had placed a foggy filter on all those fun memories. Her reality was flipped upside down. She had been trying to rebuild her life since that night.

The car gently bucked as Fen drove onto Summer Street. "Come on, stay with me, we're almost there," she implored.

The drizzle slowed and sunshine illuminated the tree-lined driveway like a landing strip toward home. She approached the circular drive and stopped. Fen gripped the steering wheel and gaped. Ahead lay the crumbled fountain and tortured vegetation. She and her siblings had played in the cool waters of that basin. She remembered looking up at Apollo and wondering if she would ever meet such a man in real life, a man who also had horses.

She surveyed the destruction and shook her head with disbelief. "My goodness, what happened?"

Realizing the time, she urged the car forward up the left spur of the circular drive, but it responded with a violent buck before stalling and dying with a strangled death gurgle.

"Damn! Damn! Damn!" Fen pushed the door open and marched away from the car with her hands on her head. Her life was in chaos, not going according to plan, and her anger rose from the pit of her stomach. She glared at the car, balled her fists and assaulted the tires with well-placed kicks. Despite her rage, her logical mind knew that kicking the rubber would at least not hurt as bad as kicking the metal parts of the vehicle.

A cool breeze shifted her focus. She stared up at the sky, dark rain clouds had returned. *Great! Now the rain is coming.* Her world was spiraling out of control. Her well-orchestrated plan didn't allow for disruptions such as these.

*Think, Fen. Refocus. The first priority is to get yourself to the house on time. You can always deal with the car later.* Armed with a new plan, she sprang into action.

Always prepared, Fen grabbed her backpack of essentials, swung it onto her back, and shouldered the larger duffel bag that held her winter clothes. Thank goodness she took the time to separate clothes by climate conditions.

Walking on the slick gravel was neither easy nor comfortable, and Fen struggled to the house. She had not been very active since Lance died, and she always intended to establish a regular exercise routine. "Looks like I'm beginning one, now!" she quipped as she walked fast to the overhang.

# Chapter 5

---

# Hilly

THE PURPLE FORD RANGER Splash pulled into the gravel parking lot of the Old Corner Inn in Manchester-by-the-Sea.

"Hilly, I don't know about your scheme. The letter said no one could come with you," her husband, Curtis, cautioned.

Hilly frowned. "Don't be paranoid. You won't be with me at the estate. You'll be down the road in this quaint bed-and-breakfast. If something goes wrong, I'll hop in the truck, pick you up and we'll skedaddle out of here."

They climbed out of the truck and surveyed the area. Ancient Atlantic white cedars, some almost seventy-five feet tall, surrounded the inn like a natural windbreak to the coastal breezes. A rock garden featured near the front of the building exploded in daffodil yellows, tulip reds and crocus purples. A quaint curio shop was across the street and featured a cutout of a black crow swinging from a sign that read: *The Black Crow Gifts and Collectibles.*

"This is a perfect place for you to hang out," Hilly exclaimed. "It's quiet here and you can explore the town while I'm enduring a boring will reading at the estate."

"I think I'll have a much better time than you," Curtis chuckled.

Hilly closed her eyes and recalled the vivid dreams that had haunted her every night for the last week. Often prophetic, her dreams usually hinted of cheery future events. Lately they had been dark and disturbing. Something evil was coming and she knew it awaited her at The Nine Muses.

In her recurring dreams, she stood on a beach scanning a turbulent sea while a violent thunderstorm raged overhead. She wore heavy armor stained red with blood, and she held a four-foot long broadsword. Each flash of lightning illuminated a creature, black as oil, flying closer to shore with each beat of its leathery wings. Was it the storm gales or the beast that pierced the night with a high-pitched shriek? Or did the scream come from Hilly?

She always awoke before the beast reached the shore. Thankfully, Curtis never stirred, allowing her time to settle down. Sitting on the edge of the bed in the twilight, she placed her hand over her galloping heart. Focusing on its wild thumping, she inhaled a slow breath through her nose, held it for several seconds, and softly exhaled out her mouth. She repeated the exercise until the blood pounding in her ears abated. Her raspy throat surprised her. If she had been screaming in her sleep, why didn't Curtis awaken? A warm saltwater gargle quickly remedied the soreness.

Her dreams also provided snapshots of moments frozen in time, and of places that she had not visited, but soon would come to know. One such vision was the Old Corner Inn. She instinctively knew this old Victorian house would be safe and no harm would come to Curtis. Her intuition was reliable and she learned long ago to trust it. If she was to confront evil, she needed to be sure Curtis was protected and safe. The inn was perfect. It sat on an energetic ley line, which would enhance her protection spell.

"Hilly! Hilly, you zoned out on me," Curtis teased as he unloaded the truck.

"I was breathing the fresh salt air," Hilly lied. "It's so peaceful here. Maybe I won't go to the estate tomorrow. I'll just stay here with you and Mr. Spatz!"

A loud yowl yodeled from the truck. "Speak of the devil," Curtis quipped. "Here he is!"

Mr. Spatz, weighing almost twenty-five pounds, wasn't overweight, he was just huge, almost the size of a small bobcat. Curtis set the pet carrier on the tailgate. Shiny black fur, punctuated by two orange eyes, filled the entrance. Upon seeing Hilly, Mr. Spatz thrust his bright-white paw through the wire, desperate to get her attention and spring him from his prison.

*Yowl!*

The cat had appeared on their doorstep three months earlier. A thunderstorm had flooded the yard, and the bedraggled cat found refuge in a planter on the front porch. Initially Hilly thought the mournful sound was from the storm. Upon further investigation, she found the soaked cat precariously perched on her flattened petunias, his white paws waving in the air to get her attention. She had smiled at the pitiful sight. Before long, he was inside the house warming himself by the fire and eating some of Curtis' chicken dinner.

Hilly decided to bring him along on the adventure so he wouldn't be lonely; and was grateful to find that the Old Corner Inn accepted pets for an extra fee.

"Let's check out this burg since you don't need to be at the estate until five tomorrow afternoon," Curtis said.

"That sounds great! Let's enjoy this town while we can," Hilly eagerly replied. "I have a feeling tomorrow night won't be as much fun."

# Chapter 6

# The Arrival

THE NINE MUSES LOOMED cold and foreboding as Chance drove slowly along the poplar-lined driveway leading to the three-story mansion. He stopped just as the road split into a large circular drive which encompassed a tangled green space. "I'll be damned," he said staring ahead at what used to be an impressive marble fountain. Now it was a bramble-snarled wild area.

As a boy, he loved splashing in the water of the marvelous fountain. Apollo straddled a chariot pulled by four white horses. Each horse pawed the air in a different compass direction and spewed frothy water from its mouth. The spills of water then tumbled into a circular collection pool surrounded by lush evergreen bushes. Chance gawked at the destruction. The heads of Apollo and the horses were obliterated as if missiles had struck from above. Large chunks of marble lay everywhere inside the basin, which was now home to weeds and dirt. The arbor vitae grew tall and unkempt.

Chance steered the car down the left drive, pulled up to the porte cochere and parked underneath. A man stood on the middle step in front of the double wooden doors. He glanced at his pocket watch and cheerfully acknowledged Chance as he exited the car.

"Good afternoon, Mr. Kemp. You are right on time. I am Prasad. So nice to see you on such a dreary day."

Chance inspected the old, brown-skinned man with bare feet, thinning hair and full gray beard. He approached him and stuck out his hand.

Prasad ignored his hand and continued, "Please unload here and then park your car in the carriage house straight ahead." He pointed to his left.

Chance stared at his hand hanging in midair. Already exhausted from the drive, he was in no mood for bad manners. He eyed Prasad who continued pointing toward the carriage house. "I've got four bags. Will you help me with these?" he asked as he moved back to his car and grabbed a gray duffel back from the hatch.

"I don't transport luggage, Mr. Kemp," Prasad replied impassively. "You'll need to manage by yourself. But, please hurry, we're on a very tight deadline." Prasad turned and opened the door. The ten-foot tall wooden door easily swung open without a sound.

Chance shouldered three bags and dragged the wheeled suitcase behind him toward the slate steps. A black cat darted out of the open door and startled him. The feline ran between his legs and jumped onto the stacked stone wall supporting the overhang. A smudge of white swam in the middle of its forehead like a third eye. It stared at Chance with emerald-green eyes.

"That's Pyewacket," Prasad noted. "He's lived here all his life. He's a curious cat, almost *too* nosy for his *own* good." Prasad narrowed his gaze at the cat and it responded with a loud *yowl!*

"I can remember black cats living on the grounds when I was kid," Chance said. "Is he an offspring from one of those?"

"I wouldn't know, Mr. Kemp. We can't waste time talking about cats. We have a tight deadline. Please follow me."

Chance frowned at Prasad's brusqueness and grudgingly followed him into the house. The suitcase complained with a loud *ker-plunk* as it climbed each step. Prasad grimaced at the noisy intrusion. He stepped aside and motioned for Chance to enter.

The two men traded tense glances as Chance entered the home, passing with inches of Prasad. The air was just as chilly in the two-story foyer as it was outside. Chance set his bags down on the marble floor and scanned the interior. Dusty memories skulked in every corner of the room. A shiver raced up his spine. "Nothing has changed," he said quietly. "Nothing at all."

"Mr. Kemp, you will need to move your car into the carriage house before I take you to your room. Please be so kind as to do that now." Prasad swept his hand toward the open door and managed a weak smile.

"Er, sure...right now...okay," Chance sputtered. An unsavory mix of anger and embarrassment brewed inside. For a second he considered grabbing his bags, tossing them into the car and speeding back to Asheville. He could endure a will reading for parents he detested or stay in a house full of painful memories, but he didn't have to tolerate the antics of an insensitive boor.

He recalled Janet's words, *You can hang on for three days, hon. You can get through this.* Chance bit his lower lip as he mulled over her words. She was right. Just three days.

Chance moved toward the door.

"You may need this, sir," Prasad said as he offered an umbrella. "A cold drizzle has begun to fall."

Chance angrily snatched the umbrella without a word and bounded down the steps. *Who the hell is this guy? He's the worst host I've ever met.*

Sliding into the front seat, he cranked the engine and glanced back at Prasad who pointed to the his pocket watch. "Tight deadline, sir!"

"Shit," Chance said, mashing the pedal to the floor. The wheels squealed as the car jerked forward. "I don't like this dude one bit. He's just like Dad—too goddamned demanding."

Prasad watched Chance drive away. "Just like his father," he muttered.

Larger raindrops fell cold and heavy. A chilly mist swirled around Chance as he trotted back to the house. Prasad patiently waited for him and took the damp umbrella, fanned it several times and set it into the brass holder by the open door. "This way, sir," he said, gesturing toward the staircase. "I'll lead you to your room now."

Chance hefted the bags onto his shoulders and viciously grabbed the wheeled suitcase. Once they reached the bottom of the wooden staircase, Prasad stopped and added, "Please pick up your luggage, sir. We don't want to mar the wood, do we?"

The two men stared at each other—Chance seethed while Prasad maintained his stoic gaze. Tense moments passed before Chance slammed the handle into the bag and seized the strap. "This *would* be easier if you helped me," he snapped.

"This way, sir. You'll be pleased that you're staying in your old bedroom," Prasad responded cheerfully, ignoring Chance's harsh words. He padded to the second floor and waited as Chance grunted and complained all the way up the stairs. The old floral carpet spread down the hallway like a field of faded autumn blooms welcoming the return of their young master. The two men walked in silence. "Here's your room, sir." Prasad pushed the door open and stepped aside.

Chance slid through the doorway into the chilly bedroom. An unusual scent of fresh lavender mixed with the mustiness of the old curtains and furnishings.

"Nothing has changed since I left. It's like a museum here. Look at all my soldiers and my models," he said as he touched the miniature planes gently swaying in the breeze by fishing line tacked into the ceiling. Chance dropped his bags in the middle of the floor and walked to the dresser. Yellowing snapshots peeked out from the mirror's wooden frame. He lightly touched the old prints as memories resurfaced. One photo, in particular, pulled him back to the past. It was a shot of him standing with his siblings when they were much younger...much happier. He was about sixteen and stood bare-chested on the sandy beach with his arms curled upward like a strongman. At his feet were Kai, Fen, and Hilly giggling and staring up at Chance in mock fear. The sky was an electric-blue and the sea was calm.

"That was a nice day," he mused. "Fun times." He continued looking at the old collectibles on his dresser when he noticed the fresh daffodils. He touched the blooms gently and gazed toward the Atlantic. "A symbol of new beginnings. A new start is exactly what I need."

"Sir," Prasad interrupted, "Cocktails will be served promptly in the study at seven o'clock and will be followed by dinner. We ask that you not leave your room until that time. These rules are tied to your parents' will so we ask that you observe the instructions to the letter."

"I can't even explore my own house?"

"That is correct, sir. We ask that you follow the rules for this evening. At dinner tonight, more will be revealed and you will have more freedom to explore. We appreciate your understanding."

Prasad glanced at his pocket watch. "If you'll excuse me, I have a pressing engagement and must leave you. There is a card on the bed. It is important that you read it." Prasad exited the room closing the door with a soft *click*.

Chance stared at the door in disbelief. *Rules, rules and more rules,* he thought. He glanced toward the bed. A crisp white envelope with dark purple lettering lay in the middle of the comforter. He lifted it and studied his name penned in elegant calligraphy. He turned it over and untucked the flap which had not been sealed, and removed a white vellum card. In the same stylish penmanship a simple poem read:

> *Keeper of the records, a warrior stands.*
> *From Amesbury the bugles blow*
> *And, the light casts its shadow on bluestone.*
> *The time is nigh. The battle approaches.*
> *Gather the troops and reclaim the forgotten throne.*

Chance stared at the poem. "What the fuck is this?"

The limousine pulled under the porte cochere just as a man stepped out of the house. He glanced at his pocket watch and smiled toward Kai.

The driver exited and opened the passenger door. Kai gathered his bags and climbed out. He turned back to Melvin who had pressed up against the open window.

"Thank you again, Melvin. You made this trip enjoyable."

Melvin beamed and grabbed Kai's hand with both of his. "I will miss you!"

Kai watched the service car drive away and then approached the man who stood on the slate steps. "Hello, I'm Kai Kemp."

"Yes, sir, I know who you are. And, you're on time."

A loud *yowl* interrupted the two men. Kai turned and found a large black cat sitting under the overhang where the car had been parked. "Hello, who's this?"

"That's Pyewacket, sir. He's our resident cat and welcomes all our guests."

"I love cats," Kai said as he stepped toward the feline with an outstretched hand. "Do you like to be petted?"

"Sir, we have a tight deadline," the man interrupted.

Agitated by the gentleman's statement, Kai scowled at him and turned away to pet the cat. But it had vanished. Puzzled, Kai scanned the driveway.

"That was odd. The cat disappeared in a flick of a second."

"Sir, please follow me. We need to stay on our schedule," the man urged as he opened the door and motioned for Kai to step inside.

"I'm sorry, who are you? I missed your name," Kai said as he walked into the foyer.

"I am Prasad, sir. I will show you to your room upstairs."

Kai surveyed the foyer. Nothing had changed since his last homecoming twenty years ago except for a fine layer of dust covering everything as though a bag of flour had exploded. Wispy cobwebs fluttered from the crystal chandelier which cast a dim light throughout the cold, unwelcoming room.

He grabbed his bags and followed Prasad up the staircase.

"Are you the only one here?"

"No, sir."

Kai pressed, "So, who else is here?"

"You'll soon know all, sir. Turn left here and the third room is yours."

"My old bedroom," Kai exclaimed.

Prasad unlocked the door and invited Kai to enter.

"Wow! time stood still in my room." Three paintings from Kai's childhood welcomed him from their perches on wooden easels. Lace curtains, tinged ivory from age, lifted in the cold breeze sliding through the small window opening. Wafts of ancient oil paint and stale bedroom air swirled. "I'm glad I brought this leather coat," Kai mentioned sarcastically as he gazed out the window at the ocean. "Don't you have the heat on?"

"We are checking on the furnace, Mr. Kemp," Prasad replied.

Kai noticed a crystal vase containing purple crocus and gently cupped the blooms, breathing in their scent. "Such beauty in my hands, the flower of cheerfulness and glee. Exactly what I needed today!"

"Sir, cocktails will be served promptly at seven o'clock in the study and will be followed by dinner," Prasad announced. "We ask that you not leave your room until it's time for cocktails. These rules are tied to your parents' will, so we ask that you observe the instructions to the letter."

"Okay, I'll do a little exploring around the old home in the meantime."

"No, sir. You are not allowed to leave your room until it's time for cocktails. All will be revealed tonight. We appreciate your understanding." Glancing at his pocket watch, Prasad continued, "I must leave you now as

I have a pressing matter to attend. There is an envelope on your bed. It is very important that you read the contents." Prasad hurried away.

Kai stared at the bedroom door musing about his encounter with Prasad. *I might have fun with that man before this weekend is out.* Then he shifted his attention to the room—his boyhood sanctuary where magic revealed itself in his paintings. He strolled to the bed and retrieved the envelope lying on the comforter. The bold purple lettering appeared to jump off the crisp white envelope. He carefully untucked the flap and removed the card. In elegant penmanship was a simple poem:

> *Keeper of the keys, a warrior stands.*
> *Shasta beckons the mystics and the shamans.*
> *Electric, magnetic and balanced, the vortex opens.*
> *The time is nigh. The battle approaches.*
> *Gather the troops and reclaim the forgotten throne.*

Kai's eyes sparkled with excitement. *Yes, this will be quite an entertaining weekend after all.*

With her car dead on the driveway and a deluge imminent, Fen trudged toward the house as fast as she could manage. Shielding her eyes from a sudden storm gust, she noticed a diminutive old man standing on the steps of the house. He glanced at his pocket watch, and Fen panicked. She jogged several steps before her lungs and knees protested, forcing her to abandon that gait for a more sedate shuffling stride.

With the weight of the duffle bag slamming her hip as she lumbered along, she imagined she must look like Quasimodo on his way to ring the bell. She reached the protection of the porte cochere just as a chilled wave of rain sheeted down.

"Hello, Ms. Kemp," the man said coldly, unfazed by her efforts struggling up the driveway. He looked at his pocket watch and then back to Fen. "You're a few seconds off, but we'll ignore that won't we?"

"You saw me laboring to get up the drive, Why didn't you help me?" Fen asked angrily, her face flushed from the final push to reach the house in time. "My car broke down by the fountain and that's about one hundred yards away!"

"I don't transport luggage, Ms. Kemp and *you* were responsible for arriving on time, not I." He eyed Fen from head to toe and continued, "I'm Prasad, and I'll show you to your room."

"What about my car?" Fen challenged. "I need to call AAA and have it fixed."

"We'll deal with your car, Ms. Kemp, when we've got you settled in your room." Prasad glided up the steps and opened the front door. He gestured for her to enter. "We have a tight deadline to observe, please come inside."

Still panting from her laborious journey up the driveway she mouthed "asshole," and slowly walked toward Prasad.

"The name is Prasad," he said wryly.

Fen entered the chilly foyer. She sweated profusely from her jog and the chilled interior only made her colder. "Do you believe in heating the home?" she said sarcastically.

"We are working on the furnace, Ms. Kemp. Please follow me up the staircase to your room."

"The staircase!" Fen exclaimed. "I'm almost fifty and just ran up the driveway. You now expect me to climb stairs?"

*YOWL!*

Fen's eyes enlarged as she looked at Prasad, thinking the noise emanated from him.

*YOWL!*

Then she saw a large black cat trotting down the stairs toward her. The brilliance of his emerald-green eyes snatched her attention. They shimmered and flashed like a strobe light. Mesmerized, Fen leaned forward and peered into the feline's face. Her world tilted and she felt as though she occupied her past, present and future all at the same time. Disoriented, she lurched toward the railing.

Prasad caught her arm. "Are you okay, Ms. Kemp?"

Fen stood up. "There's something about that cat's eyes," she muttered.

"That is Pyewacket. He's usually not allowed inside the house, but he's been taking certain liberties lately," Prasad said as he and the cat exchanged glances.

"Kitty, kitty, kitty," Fen cooed as she extended her hand toward the cat's head. She was eager to delay her tortuous climb up the stairs.

"Ms. Kemp, we are on a tight deadline," Prasad emphasized. His tone was clipped with impatience as he waited on the landing. "If you want to participate in the reading of the will, you *will* join me up the stairs and come to your room."

Fen glared at Prasad.

Prasad squinted back at her.

An impish grin bowed on Fen's face as she turned away to stroke Pyewacket. But the cat had vanished. Fen frantically searched the steps for the kitty but it was gone. *That's odd,* she thought.

"Ms. Kemp!" Prasad said loudly.

His sharp tone jolted Fen back to reality. She abandoned her search for Pyewacket and reluctantly leaned down to pick up her duffel bag. She grumbled under her breath and silently mouthed, "asshole."

"As I told you before, Ms. Kemp, my name is Prasad," he said continuing up the stairs, a beguiling smile on his face.

Prasad waited patiently on the second floor, his hands folded in front of him, his face expressionless. Fen adjusted the bags—the backpack slid easily over her shoulders and she clutched the duffle bag with her left hand.

Gripping the bannister, she pulled herself up one step, paused, and then climbed another. She continued her arduous journey one cautious step at a time as the duffle bag thumped a rhythm on her hip.

Fen paused on the landing, readjusted her bags and restarted the ascent to the second-floor summit. She reached the final step, dropped her bags, and leaned against the wall panting.

"I had faith in you, Ms. Kemp!" Prasad chirped as he strode down the hall.

Fen glowered as he padded away. She imagined devious methods to push him down the stairs and make it appear like an accident. She giggled as the graphic images fluttered through her mind.

"Come on. We have a tight deadline."

Fen sighed. She would have to plot Prasad's demise at a later time. Getting to her room and lying down was more important. She grudgingly followed him down the hall.

"My old bedroom," she whispered, a hint of excitement in her voice.

"Yes, ma'am. Please enter." He held the door open as Fen limped into the sanctuary, her angry joints demanding rest. A faded, pink floral rug puddled under a single bed which was covered in a matching pink comforter. Dolls of all shapes and sizes crowded the simple wooden shelves and stared at her with unblinking eyes. Porcelain, plastic and stuffed figures gazed at their mistress, a diminutive audience who had waited patiently for the return of their star, their dancer, their singer.

"Nothing has changed. I've just traveled back into time," she said as she surveyed the room.

"I'm sorry, Ms. Kemp,  I couldn't open the window to allow fresh air into the room," Prasad apologized.

"It's cold enough in this room, I don't mind that the window isn't open," she replied as she stepped toward the dresser. Something special had caught her eye. "Pink tulips! I love pink tulips," she squealed as she picked up the plain white-milk vase holding the blooms. "This was Mother's favorite flower, too. She told me they meant good wishes would soon arrive."

"Ms. Kemp," Prasad said, "Cocktails will be served promptly at seven o'clock in the study. Dinner will follow. We ask that you not leave your room until it's time for cocktails. These rules are tied to your parents' will so we ask that you observe the instructions to the letter. Now, I must leave you for a pressing engagement."

"Fine, I want to take a long soaking bath and a nap," Fen replied. "Oh, about my car..."

Her words were never heard. Prasad had already left.

"Asshole!" she yelled at the closed door.

She sighed and fell back onto the bed. A pointy object poked into her fleshy upper arm. "Ow!" she yelled as she sat up and rubbed the wound. It was then that she noticed a bright white envelope addressed to her in deep purple cursive lettering.

"What's this?" She slid the flap open and removed the card. Her eyes widened as she read the poem.

*Guardian of peace, a warrior stands.*
*The Big Wheel turns again.*
*Healing, atonement and visions, the quest begins.*
*The time is nigh. The battle approaches.*
*Gather the troops and reclaim the forgotten throne.*

"Now this is *very* interesting," she mused.

"That woman is impossible. She muddled my mind and now I'm running late." Prasad muttered to himself as he hurried down the stairs. It wasn't until he reached the foyer that he remembered he neglected to tell her about the card on the bed. "That woman confuses me! I never forget details. I'm sure she can cope, I've got a more important thing to manage right now." He padded quickly to the front door and yanked it open.

"Well, hello there." A young woman leaned against the cab of her truck and waved.

"My apologies, Ms. Kemp, I was delayed by an unfortunate matter."

"I thought being on time was of the utmost importance." Her eyebrows arched and she flashed a sarcastic grin.

"Yes, you are correct. My apologies again for making you wait," Prasad said as he pressed his hands together at heart level and bowed toward Hilly.

"No harm, no foul," she proclaimed as she bounded toward Prasad to shake his hand. Unsettled by her sassy behavior, Prasad froze and stared at her hand dangling in the air. "I'm Hilliard Kemp but you can call me Hilly." She wiggled her fingers in front of his face and then shoved them toward his hand. "And, you are?"

Exhausted from his encounter with Fen and overwhelmed by the short-haired fireball of energy waving her hand in front of him, Prasad awkwardly pushed his small brown hand toward Hilly. "I am Prasad, and I will show..."

"I'm so glad to meet you!" Abruptly cutting him off, she wrapped both of her hands around his and shook enthusiastically. "You know, there's a RAV4 stalled in the middle of the drive down by what's left of the fountain. Geez, what happened to that poor thing? Looks like a bomb exploded on it. Anyway, I have a hitch on my truck and some rope, I'd be happy to haul it up to the house if you want."

Prasad drew in several long breaths. Although Darrius had cautioned him about the unusual energy that surrounds the Kemp children, he was not prepared for Hilly's explosive aura. His heart had quickened since Hilly uttered her first word, and now it thumped at a furious pace. He needed to center himself before he passed out.

*I must regain control of the situation,* he thought. "Ms. Kemp, we are on a tight deadline and I need to show you to your room."

"Well, that time schedule isn't exactly etched in stone, now is it," Hilly teased.

"If you'll unload your bags here and park in the carriage house over there, I'll be glad to show you to your room." Ignoring her comment and sticking to his well-rehearsed script, Prasad hoped to seize command of the conversation.

"What about the stalled car?"

Prasad closed his eyes and sighed. Hilly was unnerving him. "That's okay Ms. Kemp, we'll deal with the car later. I appreciate your offer."

Hilly grinned at Prasad. Her eyes danced with mischief.

Prasad scowled. His eyes drooped from weariness but he was determined to stand his ground.

"Okay, you win Mr. P., I'll get my bags and park the truck."

"It's Prasad. Not Mr. P."

Hilly threw a tote on the pavement, looked up and said, "Sure it is." She tossed two more bags onto the ground, climbed into the truck, and glanced at Prasad. "Are you sure you don't want me to get that car now? It will only take, at most, thirty minutes."

"I'm sure, Ms. Kemp. If you'll park in the carriage house, I'll wait for you here."

"Whatever." Hilly shrugged her shoulders. She drove forward and parked beside a Ford Escape with North Carolina plates. "Hmm, someone else is here from Carolina? Sweet. I wonder if it is Chance, Kai or Fen?"

Hilly had not been in contact with her siblings since the family meeting in 1992, but she bore them no ill will. What was done is done. She was ready to move on and she hoped they were, too.

She recalled the dream she had the night before. It was more horrifying than the previous ones. The black-winged dragon had grown more heads, each screeching at a different ear-piercing pitch. It pumped its massive wings against the roiling black thunderclouds swirling around it.

Something was different this time.

Hilly did not stand alone on the shore facing the beast. This time she was joined by three more figures—helmeted knights standing with her against the dragon. Together, they withdrew their massive broadswords and raised them into the sky, the tips touching. Hilly faced the figures and asked them who they were. Without a word, they encircled her and lowered their weapons to hip level, the tips pointing toward Hilly. As a flash of lightning illuminated the beach, the knights thrust their swords through her body, the blades emerging on the other side.

Hilly awoke screaming and clutching her chest. Her wild eyes searched the room for the phantom images seared into her mind.

Curtis bolted awake; and soothed and cradled her. He smoothed her matted hair, soaking wet from sweat. "This was a bad one, honey. You're with me now. Everything is okay." He rocked her back and forth while she sobbed quietly.

"Oh, Ms. Kemp!" Prasad yelled.

Hilly jerked back from her daydream. "Yes, Prasad, I'm just locking up now." Heavy raindrops pounded the ground as she dashed to the porte cochere. "Ha! Barely wet at all," she boasted.

Prasad opened the door and motioned for her to go inside.

Hilly gathered her bags and marched up the steps. She stopped in front of Prasad and gazed into his ice-green eyes. Prasad held her stare. His stone face cloaked the irritation he felt inside. After several moments Hilly winked and entered the foyer.

*I don't understand these Kemp women,* Prasad thought. *How are they going to save this family?*

Hilly dropped her bags and gasped. "Wow, it's like travelling in a time machine. Nothing has changed!"

A large painting over the marble fireplace grabbed her attention and she moved closer. As a little girl, she had been told the figure in the scene was a long-forgotten ancestor. The androgynous warrior held a large broadsword and wore stained and pitted armor. The figure stood on a beach surrounded by crashing waves pushed by the gales of a ferocious storm. Dark hair billowed from the helmet.

Hilly shivered and turned back toward Prasad. "It's freezing in this house. Why isn't the fireplace lit?"

"We are working on the furnace, Ms. Kemp."

"But this is a gas fireplace, you can turn this on and make this room toasty in no time! I can help you if you'd like."

Prasad held up his hand. "No, thank you. Please, we need to get you settled as soon as possible."

"Oh, yeah, you have a schedule and a timeline," Hilly mocked.

"This way Ms. Kemp." His patience stretched thin by Hilly's ebullience, Prasad began climbing the stairs to the second floor.

*YOWL!*

A black cat raced down the stairs toward Hilly.

"Who's this?" Hilly asked as she dropped her bags and stooped to pet the feline.

Prasad halted on the landing, and glanced between the cat and Hilly. "His name is Pyewacket," he huffed. Resigned to the unavoidable delay, he folded his hands and waited.

"Hi Pyewacket." Hilly cooed, scratching the cat behind his ears. "I have a black and white kitty, too. His name is Mr. Spatz." Pyewacket snaked between Hilly's legs and head-bumped her hand for attention. Hilly peered into his emerald-green eyes, flecks of yellow and brown swirled like a kaleidoscope while he purred a hypnotizing melody.

The air thickened like a dense fog, yet Hilly felt light and carefree. No fear, no anxiety, only peace and calm. She drifted in the tranquility.

Pyewacket's purr grew louder and louder. Soon it jackhammered on her eardrums.

"Here you go, Ms. Kemp, this is your room." Prasad gestured toward the door.

Hilly blinked and shook her head. "What just happened? I was petting the cat. I don't remember coming up the stairs."

Prasad gently took her elbow and guided her into the room. "You've had a long trip. You must be weary from the drive. Come in and rest."

Once inside, Hilly brightened. "This is my old bedroom. Mother and I painted glow-in-the-dark stars and planets on the ceiling." She gazed upward. The universe had faded but it still welcomed her along with the moon-phase drapes covering the windows. She pulled one curtain back. Angry, dark clouds swirled in the sky, whitecaps exploded on the ocean. "I love watching storms roll in. There's something calming about them. There's a lot energy that propels them forward."

She then noticed the clear glass vase on the dresser. Huge blossoms of purple rhododendron gracefully arched toward her. "The flower of danger," she mused, "How fitting that you placed it in my room, Prasad."

"I wouldn't know about such things, Ms. Kemp. Cocktails will be served promptly at seven o'clock in the study. Dinner will follow. We ask that you not leave your room until it's time for cocktails. These rules are tied to your parents' will so we ask that you observe the instructions to the letter. Now, I must leave you for a pressing engagement."

"Are my brothers and sister here?"

"All will be revealed tonight. Until then, please read the card that sits upon your bed. I must take my leave of you." Prasad pressed his palms together and bowed.

His humble gesture touched her. "Thank you, Prasad, you've been a good sport. I can't wait to see what happens tonight. So many secrets, so many mysteries."

Prasad and Hilly shared a lingering stare. He wanted to say more. He knew so much about her—who she was and what she would become. But The Cererian Prophecy forbade him. Prasad's tired eyes smiled at her with unexpected kindness.

The expression startled her. "What is it Prasad?"

The Cererian abruptly exited.

*That was interesting. I'll find out more later,* she promised herself.

She scanned the room. Dozens of mason jars filled with dried flowers and powerful herbs crowded the shelves of the oak bookcase. Freda had taught her the wise woman method of collecting medicinal plants; and they still retained their color: red rose hips, orange calendula, violet lavender. Mom would be proud of her now. She and Curtis made a decent living making organic health products, made from the plants thriving in their garden.

Hilly noticed the bright-white card lying on the comforter and playfully jumped on the bed. "Okay. Prasad said I need to read this so to make him happy, here I go." She pulled out the card and gasped. Tears welled in her eyes as she read the poem.

> *Guardian of battle, a warrior stands.*
> *Denali rises, ancient and sacred.*
> *The beast rips through the vortex.*
> *The time is nigh. The battle approaches.*
> *Gather the troops and reclaim the forgotten throne.*

# Chapter 7

# Mr. Spatz Disappears

"Don't worry about a thing," Hilly had soothed before she left for The Nine Muses. That was two hours ago.

Despite her words, Curtis did worry.

Hilly was impetuous. He adored her spontaneity and love of life, but thought she was too reckless sometimes. Coming to The Nine Muses was one of those instances when he was sure it was a mistake. Her recent dreams foretold danger and Curtis fought the urge to walk to the estate to ensure she was safe. Reluctantly, he would stick to their plan. Hilly was a clever, strong woman, and if anything went wrong, she would jump in the truck and race to the inn.

At least, that's what Curtis hoped.

He was restless. The relentless cold rain dampened his efforts to explore Manchester-by-the-Sea so he prowled the darkened rooms of the the Old Corner Inn. There were no other guests and the innkeeper, Mrs. Ferguson, had gone to the market. The cozy sitting room near the front of the house had once been a formal parlor in its younger days; and had witnessed many fancy tea parties and recitals. Curtis entered the cheerless room which was now a cluttered repository for books, games and movies available on DVD and VHS. He shuffled through stacks of old board games and thumbed the selection of vintage hard-cover books where he found *Adventures of Huckleberry Finn* nestled beside *Lady Chatterly's Lover*.

The television snapped and popped with static interference from the storm. "No English soccer today," he muttered to himself as he turned it off, and headed for the entrance hall.

The impressive two-story foyer reminded him of a small chapel. The space featured two massive, mahogany hall trees standing opposite each other. Each piece was accented with tarnished brass hooks of all sizes that spread outward like the rack of a bull elk. A large stained-glass window installed above the front door showered a rainbow of muted colors across the tile floor. *On a sunny day, I bet this place is gorgeous,* he thought.

His stomach grumbled, and he instinctively patted his belly as he headed for the kitchen. Before she had left that morning, Mrs. Ferguson reminded Curtis to help himself to anything he fancied. This was her humble way of repaying Curtis' kindness when he fixed the bathroom door that had jumped off its hinges.

A yeasty aroma lingered from the sourdough bread baked fresh that morning. His stomach growled a greeting. Scrounging in the fridge, he found a plate of cheddar cheese. After slicing off a hunk of bread, he grabbed the cheese and a can of soda; and trotted up the old staircase which groaned in protest with each step.

The bedroom door creaked loudly, its rusty hinges complaining about the wet, dreary weather. Curtis placed the plate on the small wooden table by the open window. A chilly breeze lifted the cotton floral curtains up toward the ceiling. Curtis called out, "Let's eat, Spatz! Spatz? Where are you?" The tiny room was full of antiques and plenty of spaces for a curious cat to hide. He persisted. "Mr. Spatz. I've got cheese, your favorite."

No response.

He frantically looked under each piece of furniture, and checked the wardrobe and dresser. No cat. Hilly would kill him if Mr. Spatz escaped. He ran to the window and inspected the screen, gently pushing on each section. Then he found it. A bent remnant, easy to miss for a human but not for a sneaky cat. *Could that fat cat get through there?* Curtis pushed the screen, it lifted further away from the windowsill. "That damned cat escaped!" he cried out.

He peered down to the flower garden almost twenty feet below. He didn't see a cat, but he couldn't miss the flattened tulips, hanging limply to one side as though a giant jumped onto the garden. "Damn you, Spatz," Curtis growled as he quickly scanned the nearby lanes and gardens. "Hilly's going to kill me!"

# Chapter 8

# The Reunion

CHANCE LINGERED UNDER THE bedspread.

After Prasad departed, he had showered and climbed into the comfort of his boyhood bed. The familiarity soothed him.

As a teenager, his room had become his sanctuary, a place to escape his family and lose himself in his model airplanes.

And, now as an adult, the space still offered him protection. For the time being he was sheltered from the distasteful events of the weekend. He leaned against the pillows and conjured happy childhood memories as he reread his old 1960s comic books. As he thumbed through the pages, he imagined fighting crime with Superman and Batman like he did when he was a kid.

He glanced at his watch. Half-past six. Time to get ready for the dreaded cocktail hour. Chance heard voices throughout the afternoon and presumed his brother and sisters had arrived. He still didn't understand all the mystery surrounding the meeting. It was just a will reading. How covert could that be?

He pulled on a fresh pair of jeans and a long-sleeved, navy-blue T-shirt with a small Biltmore emblem embroidered on the left breast. After donning a dark gray pair of socks, he slipped his feet into his loafers. Standing in front of the dresser mirror, he combed his hair and grinned at his reflection. At fifty-seven, he still had a muscular build and thick, sandy-blond hair.

*Buff beach boy ready for inspection.* Chance grinned. The nickname was lovingly bestowed upon him by his wife.

Despite his trepidation returning home, happy childhood memories resurfaced as he scanned the fading photos tucked into the mirror frame. He and Kai had relentlessly teased their younger sisters, annoying them until they shrieked. But Fen and Hilly had always found clever ways to retaliate—unexpected attacks which induced peals of laughter from everybody. The siblings had forged strong bonds in their youth.

But deceit and betrayal would later fracture those close relationships.

Chance recalled the night when he unwittingly overheard the argument in his father's office. Dad had warned Chance to remain silent about the incident. Chance had kept his promise and told no one. But now he wondered if his life would have been different if he had told at least one other person, like Kai. Would they still be a happy family?

Chance considered Prasad's caution about exploring the house. He had twenty minutes before cocktails. *Close enough*, he thought as he gathered his wallet and glasses. He carefully opened the door, looked to his right, then left. Nobody was out and about. He slid through the opening and quietly closed the door. The servants' stairs to the kitchen were to his left. Like a naughty child, he slowly crept away on his pre-cocktail adventure, and sneaked toward the stairwell.

He heard voices and clattering pots from the kitchen below. He recognized Prasad's voice. It was loud and frustrated. "I'm *not* a chef. They'll get what I make for them!"

"Come along, dear friend, I'll help you in any way I can, but can we really expect to serve them soup on their first night back? They're accustomed to substantial meals like roasted meats, potatoes and vegetables. Are you sure you can't make something like that?" Chance didn't recognize the other male voice.

"Darrius, I'm not a magician. I can't wave a wand and make a meal appear out of thin air. And that's exactly what we have. Nothing! You should have had some food delivered."

Chance heard the name "Darrius" and realized that the executor who had sent his parent's death announcement was the man in the kitchen with Prasad.

"You're right, my friend. I'll have some groceries delivered tomorrow. Tonight, we'll have comforting vegetable soup and bread. Did you set out the alcohol in the study?"

"Yes, I put out several bottles each of vodka, bourbon, and red and white wines. Do you think that's enough?"

"It's a good start. It's been my experience that humans drink a lot of alcohol."

Chance stiffened. *Did he say humans?* He inched closer.

Chuckling floated up from the kitchen. Chance frowned as he wondered what the two men found so amusing.

"This will be an interesting night," Prasad said. "The Kemp women completely unnerved me today, especially Miss Hilliard. Her energy is completely different from the others. She walks as though she is enshrouded in bright light."

"Yes, I saw that, too," Darrius agreed. "The power she possesses is intense, and filled with a magic that I've not witnessed in a very long time. Imagine what she'll be able to do once her memories are restored. There may be hope for this family after all."

*Magic? Memories restored?* Chance gripped the railing so hard his knuckles blanched.

"Since you were present when Mr. Kemp informed the family of his decision, what exactly were the siblings told all those years ago?" Prasad asked.

Chance frowned. Darrius wasn't there. Only Mom, Dad and his siblings.

Darrius spoke low and serious. "You have to realize that Mr. Kemp was under duress due to his actions that enraged many individuals. It wasn't until Stygian destroyed his property that Mr. Kemp finally relented and tried to right the wrong. He realized he needed to protect his children at all costs.

"He gathered them together and informed them that they were not blood related. They were legally Kemps but they had all been adopted from different families, families who no longer existed. He insisted that they leave the estate immediately, move to new locations and break all connections with each other. It was imperative for their survival to go into hiding and pretend their siblings, their parents, and The Nine Muses no longer existed. He feared that even their thoughts might be intercepted and used against them.

"The children were stunned. They were confused, angry and sad. Mr. Kemp mustered all his fortitude and shooed them out of the house like scattering butterflies from a flower garden. I remember him crying as he watched them all speed away. He was inconsolable, almost suicidal."

Chance winced as the memory pinched his brain. He vividly remembered that night. They all arrived anxious about the announcement and, one hour later, they all left bitter, alone and in shock.

Darrius added, "One thing he didn't tell the children—"

"It's almost seven o'clock. I need to go to the study and greet the Kemps. Watch the soup and I'll be back," Prasad blurted as he padded out of the kitchen.

Chance blinked angry tears from his eyes. It was evident Darrius knew a lot more. But, how? He wasn't there that night. What else did Darrius know? Chance was going to find out, no matter what he had to do to get the answers.

Chance slowly backed up the stairs, careful not to make any noise. He reached the second-floor hallway and walked fast toward the main staircase that would drop him near the study. A door burst open and a body collided with him.

"What the fuck!" Chance barked before realizing who was entangled in his arms. "Kai?"

"Well, fuck you, too, brother!" Kai responded with a big grin on his face.

"Get away from me!" Chance shoved Kai, remembering Prasad's warning about fraternizing with anybody before dinner.

"I see time has served you well, Chance. Still ornery as ever."

Chance pushed past Kai and continued toward the staircase. "It's time for cocktails. We need to get going, we need to be there by seven."

"Well, it was nice catching up with you, Chance," Kai called after him. "Perhaps we can do this again, say, in a few minutes?" Kai laughed out loud and chased after his brother who bounded down the stairs.

The study door was already open, and Chance rushed in. As a child he was never allowed in this room. The dim lighting enhanced the heavy energy hanging in the air as though the study would soon be the epicenter to something explosive.

"Long time, no see, brother!" Kai slapped Chance on his back. "What do you say that I make you a drink to get this reunion started?" Kai didn't wait for an answer, he strode over to the bar and poured himself a vodka tonic, then reached for the Woodford Reserve, "Bourbon, neat, right?"

Chance's anger subsided as he watched his younger brother's antics. "You could always lighten the mood, Kai. Yes, bourbon, neat. Make it a double." Now that they were in the study, and on time, Chance relaxed. He grabbed the drink and tossed it down his throat. "Ah. Perfect. Another one, please."

Kai refilled his brother's glass and toasted, "To new adventures."

Chance gulped the drink, burped and replied, "I'll drink to that."

"You know, this is my first time in this room," Kai said as he gazed around the dreary study, lit only by a small chandelier hanging from the ceiling.

"It doesn't have a comfortable feeling at all. It's as though we've disturbed sleeping spirits and they're swirling around us, plotting a way to get even."

"You have no idea what ghosts haunt this place," Chance said as he poured himself another drink. He sipped while stewing about the conversation he heard between Prasad and Darrius. "Dad conducted his biz in here. It was off limits to us brats."

"What kind of business? I know he was gone a lot, but he didn't like talking to me about his trips."

Chance stood by his father's large mahogany desk. His fingertips stroked the wood grain, pulling old memories to the surface with each pass. "He did travel a lot. Seems like he visited almost every country in the world." He opened a drawer and a residual scent of apple tobacco teased the air. He closed his eyes and imagined his father puffing a black pipe filled with the aromatic leaves.

"Hey check this out!" Kai called out. He carefully removed a crystal ball and its brass frame from the bookshelf. He placed them in the center of the table and took a couple of steps backward. He swept his arms to either side. "Ta da, behold our future!"

Despite his grumpy encounter with Kai upstairs, Chance chuckled. His brother had a way of brightening the darkest days.

"Look closely into the crystal ball. Come closer and learn the secrets of—."

"Shh," Chance interrupted. "What's that noise? Are those voices?"

Fen studied the clock in her room. It was slightly faster than her watch so she wondered if she should adhere to the *house* time or the *correct* time.

She split the difference.

She opened her door quietly and crept through the opening. She was just closing the door when Hilly burst out of the bedroom next door and hailed her, "Fen! The Fenster! The Fenmeister!"

Wide-eyed, Fen gawked at Hilly, immobilized by Prasad's warning that they were forbidden to contact each other.

"Come on, Fen, crack a smile," Hilly joked as she grabbed her sister in a bear hug.

"Put me down, Hilly. Put. Me. Down!" Fen demanded. "You know we're not supposed to fraternize before cocktails. Just pretend you didn't see me." Fen wriggled out of Hilly's embrace and hobbled toward the staircase.

"Seriously, Fen? Fraternize? We're not prisoners in our own home. Where's your sense of adventure?" Hilly ran after Fen who slowly descended the stairs, fearful her arthritic knees might buckle at each step.

Hilly pressed, "We'll be in close contact this weekend, so get used to the idea that we'll be talking. It's kinda weird that you're ignoring me right now. I know you're listening to me. Aren't you interested in how I've been?"

Fen stopped on the landing and glared at Hilly. "You may have forgiven everything that happened in this house in '92, but I haven't. I'm still mad. I'm confused. I don't even know why I came." Fen's eyes misted. She hated appearing weak. Hilly reached to comfort her. "Leave me alone," Fen snapped as she pushed Hilly aside and limped down the stairs.

Hilly followed her sister, but hovered a few steps behind as Fen ambled toward the study.

Clinking glasses and loud conversation drifted through the open door. Fen stopped, unsure about entering. She wasn't prepared to interact with her siblings. She didn't want to talk to anybody. If it was possible, she would rather find a corner in the room and sit there until it was time for dinner.

Hilly noticed Fen's reluctance. "You don't have to go in, Fen. You can stay here. Look, there's a stuffed chair near the fireplace, the cold, unlit fireplace."

Fen didn't respond, so Hilly shrugged and marched toward the study.

"Hilly," Fen said softly.

Hilly whirled around. "What's up?"

"I'm scared. I started a new life, a good life with a great man. I can't take any more surprises. My heart can't handle more disappointments or bad news. I just know something horrible is going to happen this weekend."

Hilly tenderly held Fen's hands. "We will get through this. I've got your back and you've got mine. We've always taken care of each other and that will never stop."

The air abruptly thickened, and Hilly's world tilted. The image of a winged beast punched into Hilly's mind. She gasped as the black monster from her dreams descended from a thundercloud and flew directly at her. Its jaws opened wide. Rows of sharp teeth glittered like glass needles. She tried to scream.

"Hilly?" Fen asked as she gently tugged her sister's arm. "Are you okay?"

Hilly jerked at Fen's touch. Lost in the tentacles of her daydream, she stared intently at her sister, searching her face for a glimmer of recognition.

"Hilly, it's me," Fen soothed as she stroked Hilly's cheek.

Tense moments passed before the pupils in Hilly's eyes pulsed into focus. As if nothing had occurred, she chattered excitedly, "I'm great. Everything is just fine. Let's get inside and make sure the guys haven't torn up the study."

Hilly hooked her arm through Fen's, and impishly grinned. "One, two, three. We're off to see the wizard—"

The sisters skipped through the open door, and Kai joined them for the remainder of the song, "The wonderful wizard of Oz!"

Hilly released Fen's arm and ran to meet the boys. She stood on her tiptoes and threw her arms around Chance's thick neck. At six-foot-two,

Chance towered over Hilly by almost a foot, and had to stoop to return her affection. "Hi big brother. It's so nice to see you again."

"What about me?" Kai whined.

"Good grief, Kai, you just can't share the spotlight with anybody, can you?" Hilly teased. She hugged him, and then pushed him back to study his face. "You haven't aged at all, Kai. Your luscious dark hair and beard have no gray at all."

"Only my hairdresser knows for sure." He quipped.

Fen remained in the doorway watching her siblings laugh and hug. Her intuition nagged her that something was terribly amiss. Hilly's recent episode outside the study unnerved her. For a while it appeared that Hilly's soul had temporarily left her body, leaving her eyes blank and glazed over. And, the reunion with her brothers felt awkward. She hadn't quite recovered from the emotional upset from their last meeting.

Fen grabbed a chair in the corner. From this vantage point she felt safe and secure. Instinctively she eyed the shadows of the room, convinced she was being watched.

"Aw, come on, Fen. Come join us," Hilly implored. "It's been twenty years since we saw these crazy guys. We have a lot of catching up to do."

An unexpected voice sliced into the conversation, "Good evening, Kemp family." Prasad had remained quiet as the siblings filed into the study, and now he emerged from the shadows.

"Where the fuck did you come from?" Chance snapped. He detested surprises, especially by someone he didn't know.

Prasad stepped further into the room. "My apologies for startling everyone but your reunion was so touching, and I didn't want to spoil the moment."

Chance rushed Prasad, his right arm cocked back with a balled fist ready to strike. "So you thought you would spy on us? Listen to our conversations?"

Kai caught Chance's arm and spun him around. "Take it easy, brother. He didn't mean any harm."

Chance loomed over the barely five-foot-tall Prasad and glared into his mesmerizing, icy-green eyes. The diminutive man stood his ground and peered back, his face expressionless except for his eyes which flashed like a strobe light. Chance couldn't break away from his stare, and soon became lightheaded. He drifted and tilted as though bobbing in an ocean wave. His eyes opened and closed slowly. He yearned to sleep but willed his eyes to stay focused on Prasad who smiled gently and raised a hand. A trail of tiny sparks followed Prasad's fingers as he reached toward Chance.

Hilly's faraway voice called out, "Guys! Stop it!"

Chance blinked and he was back in the dimly lit room. "What just happened? Did I go somewhere?"

"What are you talking about?" Kai asked. "You've been here the entire time. You and Prasad were locked in a staring contest for a few minutes. Look, I've made you another drink." Kai shoved the glass into Chance's hand.

"Speak of Prasad, where is he?" Chance demanded as he gulped the bourbon.

"I'm here, sir," Prasad answered as he emerged from the shadows. "It's time for dinner. If you'll please follow me into the dining room."

"Hell no! We're not going anywhere until you tell us what's going on," Chance bellowed. "Why all the secrecy? Where's that Darrius fellow? And, why is my glass empty?" Chance waved his glass at Kai.

"Mr. Dagda will join you for dinner and will answer all of your questions then," Prasad calmly replied.

"You're very kind, Mr. P., and we appreciate everything that you do," Hilly uttered as she stepped between Prasad and Chance. She glared at her brother who nursed another bourbon Kai had shoved into his hands. "My brother has our best interests in mind. But we're all a little on edge considering the events of our last reunion. Kai, please pour a glass of

Malbec for Fen and me. And, you might want to lay off those bourbons for Chance. At least for a little while."

Fen hovered near the entrance to the study. She jumped to her feet when Prasad entered but dared not get any closer. Her little voices screamed at her, and her brother's rage frightened her. Prasad was an irritating man with zero manners and a snotty attitude, but she couldn't understand her brother's hostility toward him.

Hilly grabbed the wines from Kai and turned to Fen, "Come on, Fen, let's get something to eat. This wine will help a little." She took a long sip, smiled at Fen and wiggled the glass. "Yummy."

Prasad opened the door between the study and dining room and stood back. "Please go in. There are name cards on the plates."

Kai shepherded Chance through the doorway. "Come on, big brother. Let's get you something to soak up all that bourbon." Chance glared at Prasad as he passed. Kai steadily pushed him forward. "That's it, Chance. One foot in front of the other."

Fen didn't move.

"Fenster, please join us," Hilly urged. "Wouldn't you rather learn the rest of the story instead of living in fear of the unknown?" Hilly held the wine glass aloft like a lure to a hungry fish.

Despite the warning bells in her mind, Fen reluctantly followed Hilly. She took the wine and sipped it. "Yes, this definitely will take the edge off."

Arm in arm, the girls went into the dining room, followed by Prasad who closed the door behind him.

A large oak table dominated the spacious room. A bank of windows on one wall provided views of the front of the property including the destroyed Apollo Fountain. On the opposite wall, heavy floral brocade drapes framed the windows that faced the Atlantic Ocean, agitated by the approaching storm. Brilliant light from the wall sconces and chandelier illuminated the room as the Kemps drifted around the table studying the name cards on the plates.

Chance staggered to the head of the table and slumped into the captain's chair. He gripped the massive wooden arms, grinned at his siblings and slurred, "As the oldest, this is my seat. If I fits, I sits." He laughed out loud and slammed the tabletop. "Kai, where's my drink?"

Prasad remained in the doorway, his hands folded in front of him. He sighed at Chance's drunken behavior. "Sir, you'll find that chair is reserved for Mr. Darrius Dagda," he said softly.

"I don't give a fuck if it's reserved for the Queen of England. I'm sitting right here!" Chance lurched forward, and then pitched to the side as he struggled to maintain his balance. "Kai! Drink! Now!" Chance barked like a drunken captain on a storm-tossed ship.

"You'll get another drink once you've eaten," Kai calmly replied. "And, don't give me that look, you know I'm right."

Undeterred by Chance's obnoxious behavior, Prasad repeated, "As I said, Mr. Kemp, that chair is reserved for Mr. Dagda."

Enraged, Chance launched out of his chair but tumbled to the floor. He rolled back and forth, barking at Prasad, "This is *my* chair and I will sit here!"

"Brother, technically, you're no longer sitting in any chair," Kai said as he grabbed Chance by the arm, and yanked him to a wobbly standing position.

Hoping to disarm Chance's anger, Prasad acquiesced, "Never mind, Mr. Kemp, you can sit where you please." He abruptly departed.

"Where is that little fucker?" Chance asked as he snapped his head side-to-side.

"He's gone, Chance. Now, sit before you fall again." Kai guided his brother into the chair.

Chance snatched the name card for DARRIUS DAGDA and flipped it into the air. "There, that's taken care of. Now, let's eat," he demanded as he pounded the table with his fists. He abruptly stopped mid-strike. His glazed eyes stared forward, and he blinked slowly as his head gently bobbed back and forth. As his siblings gawked at his unusual behavior, his eyes rolled back, and his forehead slammed the table with a loud *THUD*.

Kai leapt from his seat, grabbed Chance's hair and yanked his head up. "Chance, are you still with us?"

Chance answered with a loud, throaty *SNORT*. Kai lowered Chance's head to the table and gently turned it to the side. "Chance will be taking a short nap before dinner," he joked as he wandered away to the antique sideboard.

Hilly pondered Chance's conduct. Although she had seen him drunk before, the bitterness directed at Prasad was puzzling. The man certainly possessed annoying idiosyncrasies, but nothing that would warrant this level of animosity. *Hmm, I need to chat with big brother later,* she thought. She sipped her wine and glanced around the room. Kai was checking out the china patterns and Fen was staring back at Hilly. Hilly flashed a smile, which prompted Fen to turn away and look at nothing in particular.

"I wonder who will be getting the china?" Kai pondered. "I would love this set if nobody else minds." Kai quickly peeked at his sisters and his sleeping brother. "Great, no objections? So we'll informally say this is mine?"

"Kai, you're like a vulture picking at a body!" Fen snapped.

"Come on, Fen, we'll have to go through the entire estate anyway."

"Not necessarily, Kai," Hilly interjected. "We don't have the will reading until tomorrow. Perhaps Mom and Dad made other arrangements."

The door swung open, and the siblings turned. A young man with short black hair and smooth, brown skin strode into the room as if floating on air. His penetrating green eyes snatched their attention. He flashed a smile. Brilliant white teeth sparkled in his angular dark face. He wore a gray, tailored suit that accentuated his trim build. At his throat, a bright red silk tie spilled down his pressed white shirt. He approached the table, glanced at the sleeping Chance and then gazed intently at Kai.

"Hi, I'm Darrius Dagda," he said as he extended his hand. Kai didn't respond right away. He was speechless, stunned by the beauty of the man who stood before him. Darrius pressed, "Mr. Kemp?"

Kai blurted, "I'm so glad to feel you. Er, see you."

The girls giggled.

Darrius smiled gently at Kai. "My pleasure." He greeted Fen next. "Hi Ms. Kemp, I'm Darrius Dagda. I'm so glad to meet you."

Fen's intuition had quieted. She sensed peaceful energy about the young man before her, and she eagerly accepted his hand. "So nice to finally meet you, too."

Darrius then turned to Hilly who had walked around from the other side of the table. "Ms. Kemp, I've heard so much about you from Prasad. So nice to meet you."

Hilly shook his hand and peered into his brilliant emerald eyes. There was something familiar about him. "Have we met before, Mr. Dagda?"

"Please, call me Darrius, Ms. Kemp. I don't recall meeting you before."

She studied his face. "Interesting. You seem so familiar. No worries. I'll figure it out eventually," she chirped. "Please call me Hilly."

Darrius lightly touched Chance's back, and the sleeping giant roared to life. "What's going on?" Chance demanded. Startled by Darrius hovering over him, he awkwardly pushed away and tumbled onto the floor. "Who the hell are you?" he asked, staring up at Darrius.

"I'm Darrius Dagda. So nice to meet you." He gripped Chance's arm and easily hoisted him back onto his feet. "Are you feeling better?"

Chance shook his head, clearing the cobwebs. "I suppose you want your chair," he said curtly.

"Not at all. If you feel comfortable sitting there, be my guest. I'll join Hilly. I imagine that you're all very hungry after such a tedious day travelling." Darrius rang a small brass bell that lay in the middle of the table. Within a few moments Prasad entered the room. "Dear friend, is dinner almost ready? I believe our guests are famished."

"Yes, the vegetable soup and bread are ready to serve."

"Nice," Hilly said, "I'm vegetarian so that will do nicely." Prasad nodded at her and exited.

Darrius glanced at everyone's empty glasses. "Can I refresh anyone's drink?"

"Better not give Chance anymore for the time being," Kai said. "But, I will have a refresher. I'm sure Hilly and Fen need a refill so I'll help you." Kai collected his sister's glasses before they could protest.

"Very well, Kai, let's go into the study, shall we?" Darrius gestured for Kai to go before him.

Kai ogled Darrius as he passed. *My goodness, he's gorgeous,* he thought as he brushed by Darrius.

"Kai is so damn flirtatious," Hilly said to Fen as they watched the two men leave. He's been married ten years. You would think he would have ditched his dating habits."

"How do you know Kai's married?" Fen asked suspiciously. "We were supposed to break all ties with each other."

Hilly chuckled. "It's hard to keep completely hidden when you're a successful artist. I saw the announcement in an art magazine. That's when I also found out he had moved to Sedona and met his husband, Jeff."

"What do you mean his husband? Is Kai gay?"

"Good lord, Fen. You didn't know Kai was gay?"

"No, I didn't. Does Chance know?"

"I don't know. Let's ask him." Chance had fallen asleep on the table and softly snored through his open mouth. Hilly whispered into his ear, "Chance, did you know your brother is gay?"

"Now, you're being silly," Fen huffed.

"Does it bother you that Kai is gay?"

"No, not at all. It's all such a surprise—that he's married and that he's—"

"I hope you guys weren't talking about us," Kai joked as he and Darrius returned with the drinks.

Hilly and Fen traded guilty glances. "Please, Kai," Hilly began. "Don't you think we have better things to talk about? Like our big brother."

Chance snorted awake. He sat back, rubbed his eyes and tousled his hair. Like a gecko, he slowly opened his right eye and then his left. "What's everyone looking at?" he asked as he glanced around the table.

"Welcome to the living," Darrius said. "Are you feeling refreshed after that well-deserved nap?"

Chance swiveled his head toward Darrius. The two men studied each other for several moments. "So you're the executor, right?" Chance sneered. He hadn't forgotten the conversation he overhead in the kitchen. Darrius was hiding something but he would wait for the right opportunity to get his answers.

Darrius nodded. "Yes. I've been getting acquainted with your siblings. I imagine you're quite hungry."

As if on cue, Prasad burst into the dining room carrying a tray containing a soup tureen and a wicker basket covered with a red gingham cloth. The earthy aromas of carrots, potatoes and onions preceded him. He placed the items in the center of the table and formally announced, "Tonight you have hearty vegetable soup and fresh bread."

"Smells yummy," Hilly gushed. "Do you have butter for the bread?"

"Yes. I'll ladle the soup and then retrieve the butter. Do you need anything else?"

"Don't you have anything good like a big rare steak?" Chance grumbled as he held his head which throbbed from a hangover headache.

"We would love to accommodate your wishes but Prasad worked very hard on this soup and this is what will be served tonight," Darrius answered.

Chance frowned at Darrius who returned his gaze with a serene expression. Exasperated, and too tired to fight anymore, Chance relented, "Fine, hot soup it is."

Prasad ladled the soup and then left to get the butter. Hilly grabbed the breadbasket, took a piece and passed it clockwise to Darrius who then put it in front of Chance. Chance shoved a slice into his mouth and thrust another piece into his soup bowl.

Kai observed the display with a raised eyebrow. "Hey, brother, you still have two hungry mouths over here. If you can jump off the self-absorbed wagon for a few minutes, please pass the bread." Chance grunted and shoved the basket to Kai who offered a piece to Fen. "The beast needs to learn some manners," Kai whispered.

"Darrius, I'm curious about what will happen this weekend. What can you tell us?" Hilly asked.

Darrius sipped his soup and then dabbed his mouth with his cloth napkin before responding. "I'm sure you all have many questions. I'll do my best to answer what I can."

Prasad returned with the butter, grabbed a bowl of soup and sat down near Fen. Fen scowled. She didn't like him and she didn't care if he knew it.

Chance saw his opportunity to get his answers. "I would like to know what you know about our '92 visit here at The Nine Muses." Feeling smug in his questioning, Chance glared at Darrius, daring him to reveal the truth.

Prasad put his spoon down and stared at his soup. An uncomfortable silence followed.

"Yes, 1992 was an interesting year for all of you. Your dad was under a lot of stress and did what was necessary," Darrius responded.

"And, what the fuck do you know about 1992?" Chance could no longer contain his rage. "You weren't there. Or were you? I heard you in the kitchen earlier when you were talking to Prasad. You told him what our father said and how we reacted. And, then you said, and I quote, "One thing he didn't tell the children..."

Chance stood up and pointed at Kai.

"Did you see Darrius there?" Not waiting for an answer, he repeated the question with Fen and Hilly. Everyone shook their heads. "No, nobody saw *you* there Darrius and, yet, you seem to know so much about that day. Please explain. I'm sure we're all curious about how you know so much about us. What exactly did Dad *not* tell us?"

Unfazed by Chance's accusations, Darrius calmly gazed around the table, and evaluated everyone's expressions which ranged from anger to confusion. "Very well, let me start at the beginning. I'll tell you more about myself and Prasad." Prasad issued a soft moan, but Darrius ignored his wordless comment. He rose and faced Chance. "What I have to tell you may seem incredible, but it is the truth. The truth about your parents, all of you, and the efforts of so many other individuals who sacrificed everything to keep you all alive."

Fen became uneasy at Chance's outburst, and now her anxiety compelled her to bolt from the room. She didn't want to hear anymore. She had her memories, and she had made a new life for herself. She couldn't take any more "truths". No more revelations.

Hilly placed a hand on her arm. "Fen, don't leave. Look inside. You know this is what we need. We never got the answers in 1992. Dad told us to leave and never gave us a chance to ask questions. This is that opportunity. Don't walk out on it."

"Ms. Kemp. Fen. Please stay," Darrius urged. "You have no idea how important your role is. And, if you leave, the family will be at a disadvantage."

All eyes were on Fen. Her hand trembled on the doorknob as she struggled with her decision. She had run away from The Nine Muses in '92, and had escaped to a new town and a new life. Dwelling on the past had made her fearful of the present. *Perhaps it's time to stop running away and confront the truth.* "Okay. I'll stay for whatever you have to say. But I won't promise I won't leave in the morning. Kai, please get me another glass of wine."

"Yes, Kai, please refill my glass before we get started. I'm sure I'll need it," Hilly added.

"Kai, don't forget about me," Chance said as he lifted his glass.

"No!" The siblings responded in unison.

# Chapter 9

# The Cererian Truth

DARRIUS SIPPED HIS WINE slowly as he gathered his thoughts. Finally, he set the glass down and folded his hands. "What I tell you may sound fictional, but I assure you it is the truth. A thousand years ago, Prasad and I arrived on your world from Ceres, which is a dwarf planet located between Mars and Jupiter.

"You're aliens?" Hilly exclaimed. "And, you're over a thousand years old?"

Chance snorted. "You're kidding, right? You expect us to believe that you guys are from outer space? This must be a reality show." He bolted from his chair and parted the curtains looking for a camera. Finding nothing, he shrugged at the others before drifting back to his seat.

"This is no joke," Prasad added. "We have observed your family for generations."

"You guys look remarkable for two *really* old guys," Kai joked.

Darrius smiled warmly at Kai. "The explanation is rather complicated but I'll try to answer in terms that you would understand. Prasad and I exist in host bodies that were created by combining our Cererian life force with DNA collected from human cadavers."

"Human cadavers?" Fen squeaked. She imagined ghouls picking at corpses in the dead of night. She shivered and hugged herself.

Prasad turned to Fen. "Our Harvesters—those that collected the DNA samples—were very respectful of the bodies they visited. We consider all life sacred, even those who have passed on to the next realm. Only a small sample was extracted before the corpse was reinterred into its grave. Our Harvesters then prayed over the individual and thanked them for their contribution."

"Then the DNA was united with our energy," Darrius continued. "We were sequestered in a chamber where the host body could carefully develop over several days. This transformation was needed because our original Cererian form could not exist on your planet without a survival pod." Darrius pointed to himself. "In this vessel, we could safely explore your planet while being less noticeable to the rest of the population."

"You mean you came to conquer our world," Chance sneered.

"Let Darrius finish," Kai said. "We asked to hear the rest of the story, so let's hear what else he has to say."

Darrius nodded at Chance. "Yes, I understand your point of view. But our mission was peaceful. We came to your world to collect data on the flora and fauna; and to study the people, many of whom exhibited extraordinary magical powers not unlike Cererians. Our leaders determined that an exploration team should be sent to collect data that might prove our races shared common ancestors.

"When Prasad and I arrived, we found defined groups of humans called tribes, which were led by individuals who exhibited supernatural powers like telepathy, levitation, and shape-shifting.

"Each tribe was composed of several magical families who represented each of the four natural elements including earth, air, fire and water. Wars did not exist in the world since each tribe possessed the same abilities. This balance of power encouraged healthy trade, information sharing, and cultural growth between all the tribes."

Darrius paused and sipped his wine. He scanned the room. Hilly intently gazed at him, absorbing every word. A half smile lingered on Kai's face as he shifted his gaze between Darrius and Prasad. Fen had snuggled beside Kai and laid her head on his shoulder. Straight-lipped, Chance leaned back, teetering on the chair's two back legs, his arms crossed on his chest.

"What we didn't anticipate," Darrius began, "Was the effect the human DNA would have on our personalities."

Prasad stood up and spoke. "We gradually exhibited the traits of the human DNA including the appearance and mannerisms of the donor." He pointed to himself, "I stand before you as my donor would have appeared; and the same is true for Darrius. While many of our comrades remained amicable and friendly, some Cererians developed destructive personalities because their donor led a vicious life when they walked the Earth.

"The Yfel Brethren soon formed. Compelled by human emotions that urged them to kill, these evil Cererian soldiers learned that that they could become more powerful if they killed the magical people and consumed their energy." Prasad sat down and nodded at Darrius to continue.

Darrius cleared his throat. "The murders of magical humans began a thousand years ago. Entire tribes were decimated. Those magicians who escaped the Yfel, fled into hiding and cloaked their whereabouts. Peace was destroyed and the Earth fell into chaos. We realized our interference, no matter how innocent it began, eventually introduced a bad influence to your civilization."

"Let me see if I understand," Hilly said. "You originally came to Earth to investigate if there was a link between our ancestors. The donor DNA affected the Cererians differently with some remaining peaceful and some becoming violent. Those that gave in to their aggressive compulsions began killing humans so they could become more powerful?"

"Yes," Darrius responded.

"How do they become more powerful by killing someone?" Hilly asked.

Darrius tilted the glass and finished his wine. "When a magician dies, their soul seeks the ether. You may know it as the heavens. A Cererian brother discovered that when he inhaled the soul from a dead magician, that soul's energy was transferred to him. The more he killed, the more powerful he became." Darrius shot a quick glance at Prasad.

Noticing, Hilly asked, "Was this a relative of yours?"

Darrius strode to the window and glanced at the ruins of the fountain as his mind traveled back to earlier times. "No. We weren't related. Stygian had once been my close friend. We grew up together. His transformation was tortuous. I witnessed him morph from an affable young man to a brutal tyrant who struggled horribly with the abominable human emotions that urged him to kill. He discovered comrades who also transformed into violent men, and established the Yfel Brethren so they could prowl the world together hunting for magicians."

The room quieted. The siblings looked at each other in shocked silence.

"Is that all?" Chance asked sarcastically. "You're an alien. Your friend sucks the power out of dead magicians. I suppose you're going to tell us that we possess magic."

Prasad huffed. A grin flickered before he quickly covered it with his hand.

Darrius' eyes flashed with excitement. "Correct, Chance."

"What?" Chance uttered dumbfounded.

"Each of you is special in different ways," Darrius started. "Your father told you about being adopted from families that no longer exist. What he didn't tell you is that you're descended from extraordinary lineages comprised of witches, sorcerers and magicians. Your father and mother adopted you out of love but, also, out of duty to sustain those ancient magical families.

"To protect you, most of your recollections were 'clouded'—a technique in which your remembrances, especially of your magical abilities, were overlaid with new memories."

"Wait a minute," Chance barked. "You took it upon yourself to erase our memories?" Angered, he rose from his chair. "I ought to—"

Darrius raised his palm. His pupils pulsed. Chance abruptly halted mid-rise. "If you'll take your seat, I'll explain," Darrius suggested.

Chance sat down. He blinked several times and eyed his siblings. "What just happened?"

"I think Darrius just threw some wicked mojo at you," Kai chuckled.

"Because of your ancient heritage, the Yfel Brethren were determined to find you. They yearned to kill you and consume your magic. Your father requested that Prasad and I cloud your memories. Since Cererians are able to read minds, it was the only way to ensure the Yfel Brethren wouldn't locate you."

Hilly wagged her finger in the air. "I have a question, Darrius. How did you know our parents?"

"Great question, Hilly," Chance agreed. "How long have you skulked the halls of The Nine Muses?"

Darrius walked around the table to Prasad, and laid a hand on his shoulder. "We met your parents in 1956, when we had a critical need for a refuge to house orphaned children with special gifts. The Nine Muses sits on a juncture of ley lines, which creates a web of power. The estate is also located on land comprised of massive slabs of granite, which made this location naturally protected from outside forces.

"Prasad and I are Observers. Along with many brothers around the globe, we monitor and protect the locations of the magical populations. We were always present in this house—when each of you first arrived, celebrated your special occasions, and the day you all left. We remained hidden, observing you from the shadows so that your life in this house would be as normal as possible."

Darrius peered at Chance. "That's how I know what occurred in 1992."

"So, each of us have special skills, and you've removed our recollections of those abilities?" Hilly asked.

"Yes," Darrius said. "Here is an example of a memory we clouded. Chance was almost seventeen. On this particular day, all of you were on the beach while your parents prepared lunch at the house. You took turns batting a volleyball to each other. Only, nobody touched it. Each of you moved the ball back and forth using your mind, using the power of telekinesis. Chance urged the ball toward Kai but it flew into the ocean. Kai leaped into the crashing waves and disappeared under the surface. Unfazed by your brother's actions, the rest of you patiently waited on the beach for Kai's return. The ball shot out of the water, and was soon followed by Kai who hovered in the air for a few moments before landing softly on the sand. You all laughed and resumed playing with the ball."

The Kemps raised their hands and stared at them as if they were foreign objects. Hilly and Kai pushed their palms toward each other. When nothing moved, they looked at Darrius who smiled, amused by their actions.

"I don't remember that at all, does anybody else?" Hilly asked. Her siblings shook their heads. "Darrius, why wouldn't we remember something as fantastic as that?"

"I think this is bullshit!" Chance barked. "The best thing I can levitate is a fart."

"You have your father's temperament," Darrius observed. "You also have his curiosity and stubbornness."

Darrius addressed the room. "Your inherent powers are only a small part of the story. There's so much more you need to know, but if you think we are lying to you, then please feel free to leave. You're not hostages in this house. But if you choose to go, understand danger awaits you. If you're not prepared, you and your family may perish."

Chance rose to leave. Kai grabbed his arm. "Hold up, Chance. Will it hurt you to listen to what he has to say? Afterward, if you still think it's bullshit, then leave in the morning."

Grumbling, Chance sat down. "That's a good brother," Kai said as he patted his arm. "Darrius, please continue."

"Your mother encouraged you to practice your gifts. She wanted all of you to blossom into the magical individuals you were intended to be. But your father was concerned about the attention it might attract. Since The Nine Muses was a natural sanctuary—erected on top of ley lines and powerful granite—your father allowed you to exercise your skills in the house and outside as long as you didn't stray beyond the boundaries of the property.

"To further protect you from possible harm, your father forbade any form of technology. He feared someone might use the devices to find you. This is why there wasn't a security system, television or radio when you arrived. The only connection to the outside world was the rotary phone that still sits in the foyer today. Later on, as technology became more advanced, he banished computers and cell phones. The remote location of The Nine Muses made it impossible to receive cell signals anyway.

"Your father would have succeeded in keeping you hidden had it not been for Stygian following him back from England to The Nine Muses."

The room quieted. Chance chewed his lower lip, his eyes darting between Prasad and Darrius. Lost in thought, Hilly gazed out the window. Fen studied Chance, and Kai closed his eyes.

Quiet moments passed as the siblings processed the information.

"So," Hilly began, "If each of us have certain powers, and those abilities are similar to what Cererians possess, are you implying that you and Prasad have extraordinary abilities as well?"

Darrius and Prasad exchanged glances. They remained quiet, except for an occasional pulse from their pupils.

"You're able to do something with your eyes, aren't you?" Hilly asked as she stood, her finger pointing accusingly at the two men. "Both of you stopped Chance just by looking at him. What else can you do?"

Grinning, Darrius shook his head as he walked to Hilly. "You never cease to surprise me, Hilly. You're very observant, you always have been. But before we discuss magical powers, there's another detail that must be shared. When I sent the notice of your parent's death, it surprised me that none of you inquired about their funerals. Why is that?"

"I can only speak for myself," Fen whispered, "But when I left this place twenty years ago, I hated my parents. I felt betrayed. Why would I care about their funerals?"

"Right you are, Fen," Kai added. "Once we were banished from the estate, I lost all communication with Mom and Dad. If it hadn't been for your notice, Darrius, I wouldn't know my parents had died."

"I see," Darrius commented.

Darrius pushed the curtains aside and gazed out the window. A storm brewed over the ocean. Ominous clouds churned black as distant lightning stabbed the water. Large rain droplets bounced off the glass. He drew in a long breath and faced the Kemps. "There were no funerals for either your mother or father. The history of your planet will always show they died. Death certificates were legally recorded but, in reality, they merely left this planet and teleported to a safe location on Ceres."

"Let's be clear," Prasad continued. "Your parents are not like Darrius and I. They are not aliens as you call us. Their lives were in danger. Stygian and his followers infected your mother with an aggressive virus that was consuming her one cell at a time. He had hoped that your father would divulge your whereabouts to save your mother. When your father refused to comply, Stygian destroyed Apollo's Fountain and the powerful portal it contained. He then threatened to annihilate the house. Darrius and I shuttled your parents to Ceres before Stygian could harm them further. Our physicians are treating your mother and we're hopeful she will recover. With the help of our other brothers we successfully banished Stygian and his followers from the estate."

Hilly raised her hand. She grinned impishly. "If Stygian and his followers are so powerful, how did you banish them?"

"As I mentioned before," Darrius replied, "This house sits atop a convergence of energetic ley lines and a massive slab of granite which lends a tremendous amount of natural energy to this area. We, and our Cererian brothers conjured a magical net which surrounds The Nine Muses and its out buildings. This meshwork is encoded with a protection spell that Stygian and his followers cannot penetrate."

"How did you send Mom and Dad to your planet? A spaceship?" Hilly asked.

"We didn't use a spaceship to transport your parents. We opened a portal." Darrius walked to the window and pointed outside. "It's located outside in the middle of the patio."

Chance followed his gaze. "You mean the fire pit?"

"It's much more than that," Darrius responded. "If you remember, the base of the fire pit consists of a very large stone with carvings all around it. It is known as an Omphalos stone, a very powerful source of energy. Once we activated the portal, your parents simply stepped through the gateway to our planet. There are many portals located throughout the world. Apollo's Fountain contained one of the more powerful portals before Stygian destroyed it."

Hilly quieted. A childhood memory bubbled up when Darrius mentioned the Omphalos stone. She remembered being alone on the patio while Chance played in the surf. Mother had taken Kai and Fen into Boston. The patio was her special, magical place. Purple and white lilacs teased up the sides of the pergola and created a natural tunnel that allowed the cool Atlantic breezes to flow through.

She recalled skipping back and forth over the flagstones while humming a tune. It was a sing-song melody but she couldn't recall the words or where she learned the song. When she reached one end of the patio, she twirled with her hands over her head and then skipped to the other side. Back and forth she danced. On her third pass, she stopped at the fire pit and lifted her hands to the sky. A bright white light arced across the patio. The illuminated portal was ten feet high and just as wide. Even though she was only six years old, she was not shocked to see this burst of energy emanating from the fire pit. She recalled gazing into the brightness, the intensity ebbing and flowing with occasional pops of electrical charges.

She tried hard to peer to the other side, unaware that it led millions of miles away. Curious, she walked toward the opening, her hand outstretched in front of her. She inched closer and closer, mesmerized by the pulsating light. Just as her fingers brushed the liquescent surface, a loud male voice stopped her in her tracks.

"Hilly, STOP NOW!" Hilly wheeled around to find her father running toward her, his face white with fear. As soon as she turned, the portal closed with a slight *hiss*. Ted scooped her up into his arms and held her tight as she sobbed. "Baby girl, please don't do that again."

"Am I in trouble?" she asked her father.

"You frightened me so much. I don't mind you playing here, but don't open the portal again, okay?" He didn't want to scare Hilly, after all, she was only experimenting with her gifts, but he wanted to make sure she understood the seriousness of her actions. He eased Hilly backward so he could search her face, "If you had walked through the light, we would never see you again. I don't know what I'd do if I ever lost you."

"Okay, daddy," she replied softly with a smile on her face. In her mind, though, she was already planning to try it again the next time her parents drove into town.

"Hilly, did you hear me?" Darrius broke Hilly's reverie.

Hilly raised her head and looked around the room. Everyone stared at her with concerned faces. Hilly had walked to the window and placed her palms on the glass facing the fire pit. She dropped her hands and returned to her chair as though nothing had happened. "I'm good, what did I miss?" Hilly sheepishly responded.

"Look at your palms. What do you see?" Darrius directed.

Hilly instantly felt guilty but didn't know why. She thrust her hands defiantly toward the rest of the room and proclaimed, "There, happy?" Kai and Fen exchanged worried looks.

"What the hell did you do?" Chance asked as he rose to look closer. "Your hands are red, no they're *blood* red!"

Hilly looked at her hands and then to Darrius and then Prasad. "Did *you* do this to me? I don't remember anything and now look at me. What special powers did you use on me?"

Fen softly spoke, "Hilly, you went into a trance, walked to the window, and started humming a tune. Don't you remember?"

Hilly shook her head, but the fogginess remained. "The last thing I remember was Darrius talking about the Oompah Loompah stone and I remembered something when I was a kid. But now I can't recall anything." Frustration tears welled in her eyes.

Darrius gathered up her hands, still quite warm even though they had been placed on the cold glass. "You'll be okay, Hilly. The memories will come back. Don't be afraid of them." Darrius rolled his hands over hers. Gradually the color of her palms returned to normal. "There, looking better already."

"I can't listen to any more of this shit until I get another drink," Kai announced. "Does anybody need anything?"

Chance stood. "I'll join you, Kai. I need a break, too."

The boys collected Fen and Hilly's wine glasses before heading into the study. A weak smile flashed on Hilly's face as she acknowledged Darrius. "Thanks, Darrius. All of this is a little too much to absorb in one night."

"It doesn't end tonight," Darrius added. "You'll learn more tomorrow. With a little encouragement, the memories of your original families will return and so will your knowledge of the gifts that you all possess."

Prasad rose and collected dishes from the table. "I'll help you with these," Fen said as she grabbed some spoons and bowls. Prasad protested but Fen continued to gather items, "It makes me feel useful and I want to help."

Prasad pushed the kitchen door open and held it so Fen could pass through. "Thank you, Prasad," she said as she walked into the kitchen.

Puzzled, Prasad glanced at Darrius and raised an eyebrow as if to ask, *What's this all about?*

Fen placed the dishes into the large farmhouse sink and turned on the water. "I'll get the dishes later," Prasad said as he added more dishes into the sink. "I prefer to wash everything by hand anyway."

"Sure, I just wanted to help. Actually, I want to apologize," Fen said softly. Prasad turned off the water and looked at her. "I was rude to you earlier today and I need you to understand that's not really who I am. It was raining, my car died and I had to trudge up the drive, and—"

Holding up his hand, Prasad interrupted her, "Please, Fen, no apology is necessary. I, too, was in a bit of a mood, as you humans like to call it. I'm a very organized person and today has been stressful and much was out of my control."

Fen laughed. "I know exactly what you mean. I'm a control freak as well. And with everything going wrong, it just made me so mad. Unfortunately, you were the recipient of my anger."

Prasad nodded. "Let's just say we had a bad day on the same day. Now we can start over."

"Deal," Fen exclaimed, relieved that she had made things right again.

Prasad walked to the refrigerator and retrieved crystal dessert glasses that shimmered with multi-colored globs. "And, for dessert, we have Jell-O! I understand that you always have room for gelatin," Prasad beamed as he thrust one glass toward Fen for inspection.

"They look beautiful. Here, I'll help you." Fen grabbed a tray for the goblets. Together they entered the dining room just as Chance and Kai were placing drinks on the table. "Prasad made Jell-O for all of us," Fen announced as she helped distribute the shimmering desserts.

Darrius glanced at Prasad who looked delighted as everyone eagerly dug into the yummy jewels. "Looks like everything has turned out just fine, my friend," Darrius said. Prasad stole a glance at Fen as he sat down. Darrius took note of the action. Prasad, usually a very private and stoic individual, was now chatting and laughing with Fen.

Chance inhaled his dessert and eyed Kai's. "Are you going to finish that?"

Kai grabbed his goblet and stood up before Chance could snatch it. They both laughed. The mood had lightened considerably since Hilly's episode. Everyone ate, drank and chatted. Darrius closed his eyes and breathed in the positive energy. He knew the days ahead would be rough, perhaps dangerous, and he was comforted that the family was acting as one cohesive group.

Chance turned to Darrius. "What else should we know?"

"Don't you think you've heard enough for one day?" Darrius replied, his eyes still closed.

"What's the plan for tomorrow?" Chance pushed. "Since our parents didn't really die, there's no reason to read a will, right?"

Prasad overheard Chance's question and rose. He responded in a deliberate tone, "Tomorrow, your father will talk to you about the future and how you must prepare for what is coming."

The mood in the room shifted from gaiety to seriousness in a matter of seconds. It was as though a heavy weight fell onto the table and shattered everything beautiful. "Dad will *talk* to us?" Chance asked, incredulous that a man who was no longer on Earth would be able to chat with them.

"Your parents prepared for this day over a year ago when they realized danger was imminent," Prasad announced. "Your father created a series of movies and compiled notes into a book. Over the upcoming days, you'll view and read what was in his heart and mind. It's their legacy for all of you."

"Tomorrow will be like reading your parents' will," Darrius added. "It's all about respecting their wishes and accepting what they left for each of you." Darrius glanced at his watch. "It's getting late so I suggest that we retire for the evening and meet here for breakfast at eight o'clock tomorrow morning."

"Wait," Fen interrupted, "I need to call my friend, Phyllis. I told her I would call with regular updates. I'm sure she's been texting me, and if our cell phones don't work here, she's probably frantic because I haven't responded. May I use your phone?"

Prasad jumped to his feet. "Absolutely, please follow me to the foyer. You'll be able to sit and chat with your friend with no interference." He opened the door to the study, and Fen walked through. "Does anybody else need to use the phone?" Chance, Hilly and Kai shook their heads. Prasad politely nodded at them and exited.

"Does anybody else need anything before we adjourn?" Darrius asked.

"There's still the issue of retrieving Fen's car by the fountain," Hilly said. "I have a tow-rope and would be happy to get her car in the morning if everyone else can help me."

"Sounds like a family affair," Chance responded. "Let's eat breakfast and then get that old clunker. Does that work into your schedule, Darrius?"

"Yes, that will be just fine. Until tomorrow morning, may you all have a good night's sleep."

Darrius stood as the Kemps filed out of the dining room. He gazed out the window and mused about the days' events. The Kemps reacted better than expected. He sensed that Chance remained skeptical and Fen feared the unknown, but Hilly and Kai appeared intrigued by the history of their family. *Ted and Freda would be proud of their children,* he thought.

Prasad returned to the dining room and closed the door. He joined Darrius at the window and peered into the stormy night. "Fen is chatting with her friend, and the others poured themselves another drink and went upstairs."

Silent minutes passed before Prasad continued, "Time is growing short, isn't it?"

Darrius sighed. "Yes, my friend. I've felt Stygian's energy all day. He must be close. He attempted to look through my eyes and snatch my thoughts. He's growing strong. I'm no longer sure our protection field around the house will prevent him from reaching the Kemps. We may need to reinforce the spell with additional magic."

"Yes," Prasad agreed. "The Cererian Prophecy was clear. We must do everything within our power to keep the Kemps alive. They must survive if peace is to return to this world."

The storm neared the shore, lashing the coast with wind gusts and rain bands. The blackness of a new moon coupled with the thick cloud cover generated an oppressive darkness that descended over the estate. Black shadows danced in the inky landscape. In the distance, near the ruins of the fountain, glowed two bright orange orbs—cat eyes gleaming in a sea of black. The large creature with four white legs sat atop Fen's RAV4, its black fur slickened from the relentless rain. Mr. Spatz glowered at The Nine Muses, scanning the distance for any movement. Tomorrow, he would find Hilly. He grinned at the thought of reuniting with his mistress.

# Chapter 10

# Stygian's Arrival

BREAKFAST AROMAS WAFTED THROUGHOUT the kitchen: scrambled eggs, bacon, citrus and toast. Prasad found cooking to be meditative, a serene outlet for any tension or problem, and with the Kemps back at The Nine Muses, there was plenty of both. Creating meals from simple, raw ingredients provided an immense feeling of accomplishment, and if he stumbled upon a solution to any of his problems, then it was a bonus. Stygian preoccupied his thoughts. He worried the Kemps may not be prepared if the Yfel leader arrived. He was especially concerned for Fen. Although befuddled by her behavior when she first arrived, he found himself attracted to her quiet strength and energy.

He prepared a glass carafe of chilled orange juice and brewed enough coffee to fill a two-gallon urn. Darrius had advised that humans love their coffee and wanted to ensure there was enough for all of them. Curious about the roasted bean's attraction, Prasad tried a cup and immediately spat it out; and scraped a dish towel across his tongue to remove any remnants of the bitter fluid. He might as well brew dirt—it would probably taste the same. Satisfied with the meal, he wheeled the breakfast cart into the dining room and arranged the food on the sideboard just as Hilly strolled in.

"Good morning, Prasad," She chirped. "I do believe I saw a ray of sunshine this morning before the rain clouds smothered it again." Hilly's cheeriness cloaked her intense dread. Another sleepless night fighting a shrieking dragon in her dreams left her exhausted and vulnerable. *Be happy and happy will find you,* she told herself.

"Good morning, Miss Hilly. I understand there's a large storm swirling off the coast. I'm afraid it will be another dreary day."

"I don't mind the rain," Hilly responded as she poured a mug of coffee. "I love gray, stormy skies. There's an energy that bounces before a storm, and it energizes my creative juices. I'm so happy." *Happy*, there was that word again, as if saying it aloud made it real. She heaped eggs and fruit onto her plate, grabbed her mug and sat by the window. Although the sun had risen two hours earlier, a murkiness filled the room as if the light had been sucked away by the deep darkness lurking outside. Kai and Chance shuffled into the room disheveled and holding their heads as if to prevent them from tumbling off their necks.

"Looks like someone shouldn't have taken the liquor bottles back to their rooms!" Hilly shouted, hoping to irritate her brothers. The two men winced in pain. Chance whirled a slice of toast at Hilly which she easily dodged.

"Ah, you two are suffering from, what I believe you call, a hangover," Prasad observed.

"Yeah. We enjoyed our reunion a little too much last night," Kai whispered, as he stared at Prasad through bloodshot eyes. He clumsily maneuvered two coffee mugs under the urn, but missed the spout. A large black puddle spread toward the edge of the sideboard. "Oops. Sorry."

"I'll take care of that. Why don't you and Chance sit down and I'll bring coffee to you," Prasad offered as he dabbed at the spill with a dish towel.

Chance and Kai slumped into chairs opposite Hilly. Their heads drooped, their chins resting on their chests. They squinted as though even the dim light in the room stabbed their pupils with needles.

"Meditation hour for drunkards," Hilly giggled. They ignored her remarks and leaned forward over the coffee. They hoped the steam would magically kill the pain in their skulls.

Fen entered and stared at her brothers, then looked at Hilly who scrunched her face and circled the side of her head with her finger. "Boys be crazy. They decided to drink the bar dry last night."

"Morning coffee prayer, guys?" Fen asked as she piled food onto a plate, clattering the china and cutlery intentionally as she worked her way along the sideboard. The brothers grimaced.

"Okay, okay, we get the picture, Fen," Chance moaned. "Sit down and be quiet. Please?"

"I'll give you ten bucks to eat silently for the next half hour," Kai added.

"You're on." She joined Hilly. The girls peeked at their brothers, spoke in hushed tones, and giggled.

"Good morning, Miss Fen," Prasad greeted. "I trust you had a wonderful conversation with your friend last night."

Fen smiled warmly. "Thank you, Prasad. Phyllis was overjoyed to hear from me. She was on the verge of calling the police because she hadn't heard from me in seven hours. Imagine the police storming this house and putting me in handcuffs. My crime? Because I hadn't called Phyllis in hours. Officer, I must be punished." The girls giggled again. The boys held their heads and moaned.

Darrius appeared in the doorway. As usual, he was impressively dressed. He wore a dark gray suit accented by a bright white shirt, and a bold orange tie and pocket square. Hilly raised an eyebrow. "Wow, Darrius, we're not eating at The Plaza. Aren't you concerned about dripping bacon grease on that gorgeous tie?"

"Why thank you for noticing. I prefer the tailored look as you can see." He glanced at Chance and Kai who grunted a greeting in unison. "Hmm, you look under the weather. Could it be the vodka and bourbon you drank until the wee hours of the morning?"

Kai peered through one puffy eye. "Yeah, maybe that was a mistake." Chance muttered in agreement.

"Well, let me see what I can do about that." Darrius walked behind the brothers. Chance raised a hand to stop him, but Darrius ignored his feeble protest and placed his hands on top of their heads. He cupped their skulls and closed his eyes. A soft white glow appeared under his hands and drifted around the Kemps who whimpered softly. After several moments, Darrius opened his eyes and patted the boys' shoulders. "There, you should feel better now."

They slowly lifted their heads, their eyes wide in amazement. Kai spoke first, "My headache is gone. What about you?" Stunned by the miraculous cure, Chance silently nodded.

"Wonderful, now we can eat breakfast and plan the day," Darrius announced. "Prasad, did you make a lot of coffee for the family?" Prasad nodded and pointed to the coffee urn. "Excellent, I suggest you fill your cups and let's discuss today's agenda."

"What did you just do, Darrius?" Hilly asked. "You healed my hands yesterday in a similar fashion. Is it one of your powers?"

"You might say that we, Prasad and I, have a gift for healing. However, our abilities are limited. When we minister to others, we absorb the ailment or injury which naturally processes through our bodies. But we require time to rebuild our energy. So, if many people require help, we would be forced to choose who receives our gift."

"What would happen if you tried to heal too many people?"

"If we overextend ourselves, we die."

"Does that mean your life force, your energy, would die with you, or would the Cererians create another body for you?"

"We would no longer exist in any form," Prasad answered. "We would be giving the ultimate gift of our life so another can live."

The room grew quiet. Death and sacrifice was a sobering topic for early morning discussion.

Darrius prepared a plate for himself and sat down. He silently sipped orange juice while glancing around the room. Prasad grabbed some fruit and joined the others at the table, sitting cross-legged on a chair near Fen.

Five minutes ticked by before someone finally spoke.

"Thank you for giving us your gift, Darrius. I haven't felt this good in a long time," Kai admitted.

"I feel crappy about some of the things I've said about you guys. I'm sorry. And thank you for providing the best hangover cure ever." Chance managed a quick smile before he continued sipping his coffee.

"Now that we love one another again," Hilly added, "How about finishing breakfast so we can collect Fen's car before the rain gets any worse."

Chance peered outside. Dark gray clouds swept by accompanied by a constant drizzle. "I think we're going to get wet no matter what time we go."

"Let's be mindful that we have important business to attend to today," Darrius cautioned. "It's currently eight thirty. I want to start the reading of the will at ten this morning and need everyone in the study at that time. How long will it take you to bring the car in?"

"It should be a snap. No longer than thirty minutes. So, we'll have plenty of time," Hilly replied.

"Excellent. While you have fun in the rain, Prasad and I will prepare everything here for our meeting."

The Kemps decided to meet in the foyer at nine. They finished breakfast and headed back to their rooms to change into clothes suitable for getting wet and dirty. Always prepared, Fen remembered her rain boots and tossed them into the car just in case there was a need. Now there was a need but, alas, the boots were still in the stranded car. She huffed at the irony.

Hilly marched downstairs dressed like the Gorton's fisherman in her yellow slicker and hat. Chance wore a red North Carolina T-shirt and baseball cap. He toted a blue windbreaker. "You know that's going to get soaked through, don't you?" Hilly noted.

"Yeah, but it's all that I've got so it will have to do."

Kai appeared, wearing tight blue jeans and a casual button-down shirt. What he lacked in suitable clothes he made up for in ingenuity. He held a black, plastic garbage bag he had taken from the kitchen. A large hole was cut out of the bottom, just big enough for his head, and two smaller openings on either side allowed his arms to poke out. "Behold. Beauty and creativity," he proclaimed. Everyone giggled.

"Your garbage poncho is not a bad idea," Chance admitted. "Where did you get that?"

"This, my dear, is a one-of-a-kind Kai Kemp creation. But, follow me into the kitchen and I'll show you quick tips for making a cheap knock-off." Fen and Chance joined Kai and soon emerged with their own homemade raincoats.

Antsy to get moving, Hilly scolded, "Is everyone done with the fashion show? I'd like to get this *show* on the road." She twirled dramatically and walked to the front door. "Please walk this way." With hands poised artistically in the air Kai, Chance and Fen strolled through the door like models walking the catwalk at New York Fashion Week while Hilly serenaded them with, "I'm too sexy for my garbage bag..."

They assembled under the overhang. The relentless rain dampened their mood but they had a job to do. "You guys wait here and I'll grab my truck," Hilly said. She sprinted to the carriage house, leaping over puddles which caused her oversized rain hat to flop around on her head like a floundering yellow fish. She climbed into the truck cab and slowly backed out to the porte cochere. "Chance, I suggest Kai and Fen get into the jump seats.

They're both smaller than you are. If you attempted to sit back there, your knees would be in your mouth."

"What are you saying, Hilly?" Chance complained.

"Oh, come on, Chance. Look at you. You're twice their size. That's what college football does to a body," Hilly placated.

As they squabbled, Kai climbed into one jump seat. Fen hesitated, waiting for Chance to make a decision. "Chance, if you *really* want to get in there, you're welcome to it," she said pointing to the narrow seat opposite Kai.

Chance peered into the cramped rear compartment. His eyes widened with surprise. "Nope, if Hilly wants this seating arrangement, let's not disappoint her," he said as he helped Fen climb in.

"Ha, he's making me out as the tyrant, but he just saw the crowded leg room in the back. There's no way your big old legs would fit back there," Hilly teased. With everyone finally settled, she steered down the driveway. The relentless rain had transformed the path into a rutted obstacle course. The truck bumped and lurched from puddle to puddle as she navigated the short drive to Fen's stranded RAV4. "Hold on, I'm going to pass her car and make a U-turn so I'm facing the right way." Hilly inched forward, careful to leave plenty of room between the vehicles.

"Hilly, STOP!" Fen shouted. "What the hell happened to my car?" Hilly slammed the brakes and everybody lurched forward. Fen pointed out the window. "It looks like a crazy person keyed my car from top to bottom!" Despite the dim daylight and drizzle, silvery scratches shimmered all over the car.

"Wow, this vandalism is something you might see in a big city, but not here in the peaceful countryside," Hilly added. "Hang tight, I'm going to turn around." She drove further down the road, U-turned, and guided the truck just in front of the car. "Okay, let's get out and see what's going on."

They piled out and circled the car. The RAV4 was brutalized as though it had just emerged from a car wash specializing in barbed wire polishing brushes. Scratches crisscrossed the paint on the hood and sides. Chance jumped into the truck's bed for a better view. "Hell, they even scratched the roof, too, Fen."

Hilly's stomach churned as she examined the marks. An uneasy feeling quivered up her spine, and goose-bumps pebbled her skin. She was very familiar with these markings and the little voice in her head screamed a warning. In the distance, a low growl of thunder rolled through the countryside. "Guys, these aren't just random scratches, these are magical symbols. These are sigils."

"What are sigils?" Fen asked.

"They're stylized characters used in ritual magic and carry great power, especially for the practitioner, Hilly replied. "Sigil magic is the art of using symbols to manifest a specific intent or outcome. When grouped with other sigils, the magician's intention is usually for creating or breaking a complicated spell."

"Why scratch them on my car? My car sucks, and magic can't help it anyway."

Kai whipped out his cell phone and snapped photos of the symbols. He tossed the phone to Chance who got shots of the scratches on the roof. "Do you know what they say, Hilly?" Kai asked.

"I'm afraid not. Sigils are personal to the magician," Hilly replied.

Chance butted in, "How do you know so much about these?"

Hilly swallowed hard. She was uncomfortable with the question and didn't respond. Questions from folks from her past often led to misunderstandings, resulting in accusations and lies spread by petty, small-minded people.

Chance repeated it a little louder, "I say, Miss Hilly, how do you know so much about these symbols? Are you some kind of magician?"

Annoyed at Chance's insistence, she snapped back, "Gee, how do I respond? Umm, yes, I'm kind of a magician, in a way. My husband, Curtis, and I are pagan."

Chance ignored her brusque reply. He jumped down from the truck bed and confronted her. "What the hell is a pagan?"

A half smile twitched on Hilly's face. Her siblings stared at her, expecting an answer and it better be the *right* one. She hated confrontations that put her on the spot, like now. There were too many in the past, many with nasty results. She shouldn't have answered Chance, but he had pressed her. Besides, what's wrong with telling the truth? *Fuck them all if they don't like it. I'll be rid of them soon enough after this weekend so what does it matter what I say.*

"I'm a witch. A good witch," she blurted. My husband and I honor all the elemental beings and we practice green magic. Good magic." Her words tumbled out like multi-colored scarves streaming out of a magician's gaping mouth.

Chance laughed out loud. "Hell, we have so many witches in Asheville, they have their own Halloween balls. Our neighbors are witches and they've invited us to their gatherings where they have tons of food, drinks and dancing around bonfires. Perhaps you know them—"

"Just because we share a belief doesn't automatically mean we know each other," Hilly interrupted. They both chuckled, and Hilly relaxed. No nasty outcome this time.

"Stone Mountain has several covens," Fen added. "My husband, Lance, and I used to join one for their full moon gatherings. They would share food and have a drum circle. We enjoyed their company." Fen dipped her head and whispered, "I haven't been since Lance died."

"Aww, Fen, I'm so sorry." Fen allowed Hilly to hug her, but didn't return the gesture. She stood limp in Hilly's arms. The mention of her husband's name pricked the scab of a painful memory. Chance and Kai also wrapped their arms around their sisters.

"Group grope," Chance joked, hoping to lighten the mood. Then he added, "I'm sorry, Fen."

"Me too," Kai added.

"Okay, that's enough," Fen said as she wriggled out of the threesome embrace. "I appreciate the concern, but let's focus on something else."

"I have something to share," Kai teased. "This world is really tiny. My husband, Jeff, is a witch. I guess you would call him a warlock. Looks like we have a witch reunion within our family reunion."

And, just like that, the seriousness of the vandalized car disappeared. Except Hilly wasn't laughing. Deep down, she knew evil was at work, dark magic had been cast by someone (or something) and the spell would soon be revealed. Not wanting to frighten the others, she kept her concerns to herself. "This is great catching up, but we don't have much time to get Fen's car back to the house and get ready for the will reading at ten. Besides, it's cold and wet out here," Hilly said as she grabbed the tow rope from her truck, knotted it around the hitch and kneeled to affix it to the undercarriage of the stranded car.

"Let me help you with that," Chance offered as he crawled onto the ground beside her. Hilly chuckled as he wriggled under the car. His makeshift garbage bag poncho stretched, exposing his neck and shoulders to the rain. He looped the rope around the frame and secured it with a bowline knot, making sure it was tight with a couple of good tugs. "Thank goodness we don't have far to go. I think this rope will snap if we put too much stress on it. Fen, get into your car and steer it while Hilly pulls you along. Hilly, you and Kai get into the cab and I'll keep an eye on the towline from the truck bed."

Kai climbed into the cab. "Sorry about getting the inside of your truck wet and dirty."

"She's seen much worse, Kai. Don't worry about a thing," Hilly replied as she turned the ignition. She inched forward until the rope tightened. Chance held his hand up and motioned to move slowly. The truck strained for a few minutes until the car finally lurched forward. The potholes gripped the wheels as the caravan crept toward the house. When one wheel dropped into a puddle Chance was sure the rope would break from the sudden yank. But Hilly quickly responded, expertly easing off the gas at the right moment. It was skilled teamwork getting both vehicles back to the house.

Hilly dragged Fen's car under the overhang and stopped. Chance crawled under the truck, untied the rope from the frame, and then the trailer hitch before tossing it into the bed. "Fen, grab what you need," Hilly suggested. "There won't be any issues leaving your car here for the time being. I'll park the truck in the garage and will see you all in the study later on." Hilly climbed in the cab and drove to the carriage house.

Prasad met the drenched travelers in the foyer with large fluffy towels. "Please take one and dry yourself off. Just a reminder that you have thirty minutes to prepare for our meeting. We're on a tight schedule. Please be on time. And, don't forget the handwritten cards that were left on your beds. You will need them today."

"So organized," Fen remarked. "That reminds me of my arrival yesterday. Your words don't sound as curt today for some reason." Prasad nodded and smiled warmly back at Fen.

Darrius roamed the study, deep in thought about his friend, Ted Kemp. He glanced around the room and recalled the many meetings that were conducted there. Most revolved around the children's futures and possible deaths at the hands of Stygian. Ted had confided that the survival of his children was paramount to anything else in the world, yet he was fearful that he had done too little, too late. Darrius promised his friend that he and Prasad would do everything in their power to save the family. But he was still concerned about how the siblings would receive today's information. The truth might shatter their world to pieces for the last time.

Prasad entered the room. "The Kemps are upstairs getting ready. Is there anything you need?"

Darrius regarded his old friend. "Everything is in order. I think we'll break for lunch around one o'clock unless we're deep in discussion or the Kemps flee the house." Darrius smiled at Prasad, who didn't understand the joke.

"Very good," Prasad said as he turned to leave. He then added, "Remember, everything will unfold as The Cererian Prophecy dictated." Darrius nodded.

The Kemp's animated chatter floated into the study. Darrius' eyes brightened at the pleasant sound. Just yesterday the siblings were at odds, and now they were a united family, as it used to be. Chance and Kai entered first and went straight to the liquor. Darrius positioned himself in front of the bar. "Might I suggest that you resist drinking alcohol at least until we get through this morning? I have no desire to treat any more hangovers."

Chance and Kai feigned shock before they grudgingly took their seats. Fen and Hilly strolled arm-in-arm into the room, their hair still wet from the morning's deluge. Darrius welcomed them and gestured toward the chairs. He pushed a button on the wall and a large screen descended from the ceiling while an antique, two-reel projector rose from a table across the room. Always concerned about individuals hacking into his computer system, Ted prepared his "will" using an old-school method: his vintage 35mm camera. Over one hundred reels rested in the family vault behind locked doors.

Darrius took his seat in the same red leather chair Ted always occupied during their meetings. It felt strange to sit in his friend's chair.

Hilly noticed Darrius' quiet manner. "Is everything okay, Darrius? You seem lost in thought."

"I was just remembering the last time I was in this study with your father. We discussed the details of the will, the presentation and all the possible questions you might have. He was extremely organized, outlining specifics for every detail. I consider him to be a close friend. and I truly miss him," Darrius replied.

"I miss Dad, too," Hilly noted. Soon, everyone echoed how much they missed their father and mother. Feelings toward their parents had shifted from animosity to   empathy since the Kemps had learned about their parents' efforts to protect them from the Yfel Brethren. The banishment from the estate had occurred out of love, not hatred for the children. Despite the feeling of optimism in the room, it promised to be a somber day.

"Before we get started," Darrius commented, "I'd like to know what everybody thought of yesterday. Have you had a chance to consider what I shared? Do you have any questions?"

"It's a lot to soak in," Kai noted. "It's not every day you learn that you have supernatural powers and are descended from a magical family. And, let's not forget the important part—we are being hosted by aliens from a planet called Ceres." Everyone burst out laughing.

Fen raised her hand. "I have a question. When will we remember the powers that we possess?"

"Good question," Darrius responded. "Your memories will return. Be patient. I dare say you've all experienced some of your powers over the years but likely dismissed them as coincidences. Like a foreign language, if you don't use your abilities, you lose them. The knowledge is still there, hiding beneath the surface, so you need some gentle nudges to allow them to float up. Today, you'll learn more about who you are and about your gifts. You'll understand more about how you are all connected."

Chance added, "This morning, while getting Fen's car, we did learn one big connection we all share. In one way or another we are either pagan or associate with witches. That's something we didn't do as kids, but naturally gravitated toward as adults." Everyone nodded in agreement.

Darrius leaned forward. "That's interesting. How did you realize that connection?"

"Someone vandalized Fen's car last night and I recognized the scratches as sigils," Hilly offered. "One thing led to another and that's how we discovered the witchy connection."

"Sigils?" Darrius asked.

"Yes, they covered the entire body of Fen's car," Hilly replied.

Darrius stood. Concern clouded his eyes. "And, where is the car now?"

"Just outside under the overhang," Fen said. "That way, I can retrieve—"

"Show me. Show me now!" Darrius demanded as he exited the study and walked swiftly to the front door. Exchanging confused glances, the Kemps quickly followed. By the time they caught up to Darrius, he was already inspecting the car. Examining the symbols, he urgently yelled for Prasad. "Prasad! Prasad, I need your help, now!"

"What's wrong, Darrius?" Hilly asked. She recalled her feelings of foreboding earlier when she examined the markings. A shiver of dread raced up her spine.

He ignored her question and dashed into the foyer. "Prasad!" he yelled again.

Prasad emerged from the kitchen wiping his hands on a towel. "What are you yelling about, Darrius?"

"Stygian is here!" Prasad's eyes widened and he trotted after Darrius. They circled the car clockwise, holding their hands over each symbol, their faces dark and serious. They mouthed inaudible words, reciting Cererian protection incantations.

The Kemps exchanged nervous glances but dared not interrupt the men as they inspected the car. After three passes around the car, Darrius turned to the Kemps. "Stygian has broken through our first layer of defense with his vile conjuring. He used Fen's car as a way to break through. He knew you would eventually retrieve the car and drag it through the veil. Unwittingly, you allowed him to penetrate the protection field that kept him from entering the grounds. You are all in danger. Get into the house, now!"

The Kemps quickly filed into the foyer and nervously waited for Darrius and Prasad who remained outside conferring. Fen sat down in the overstuffed chair. "Good grief, what have we done? What are we going to do? That damn car! I wish I had never come here!"

"No one is at fault, Fen," Hilly consoled as she rubbed her sister's shoulders.

"How bad can this Stygian be?" Chance asked. "There's six of us and only one of him."

"He can kill each of you easily," Darrius emphasized as he approached the group. "Don't *ever* underestimate what he can do. If you had your full powers, it might be an even playing field. But, right now, you are powerless humans, with bones that can break and flesh that will bleed."

Prasad bolted the door and drew invisible protection symbols around the door frame with his hands. He then left to reinforce the many windows and doors throughout the house.

Turning to the Kemps, Darrius continued, "We placed another layer of security against Stygian: a protection incantation on the entire house. It's urgent that we start the reading of the will. There's so much to learn and your survival is dependent on you receiving this knowledge. Quickly, into the study and we'll get started."

Hilly collapsed to the floor, screaming in pain.

She opened her eyes but she was no longer in the house, she stood on the beach. Storm-driven waves crashed against her legs that were anchored into the sucking sand. It felt like rough hands holding her hostage. The sky swirled black and menacing. Torrential rain pounded her as she tried to free herself, to get away from the beast she knew would soon arrive. It always did. A piercing shriek filled the sky just as lightning illuminated the clouds. The black creature approached. Oil-black wings beat effortlessly against the gales. The beast *was* the storm and it delighted in its maelstrom punishing the coast below. Another shriek lifted into the air. Only this time it was Hilly. She didn't scream in fear—no—she howled at the beast and raised her hands in defense. Her hands pulsated and glowed red hot. The rain sizzled as it struck her palms. She yelled words into the wind, unintelligible words.

"Hilly, wake up, wake up!" Darrius urged. He carried her into the study and placed her gently into a chair. Her body stiffened, her arms straight in front of her, blood-red palms facing outward. Darrius shook her violently to break her from the nightmare. Finally, in desperation, he slapped her across the face.

Hilly opened her eyes, blood-shot and full of fear. She stared at Darrius who stood poised for another strike if needed. She lifted her hands, glowing red with intense heat, and stared at them like they were foreign objects at the end of her arms. Darrius enveloped her hands with his in an attempt to reduce the heat before she harmed herself or the others. Tears welled in her eyes and she collapsed back into the chair sobbing from fear and exhaustion.

Fen wrapped a blanket around her shoulders. "Hilly, are you okay?"

No response.

Darrius lifted Hilly's chin and stared directly into her eyes. "You were speaking the ancient language of your family, protection words that you shouldn't know. What were you fighting?"

Hilly scanned her sibling's worried faces and turned away. Embarrassed, she felt like a monster and everyone got a free ticket to watch the freak show.

*Step right up, ladies and gentlemen, and see, with your very own eyes, The Amazing Hilly. Gawk as she babbles in tongues. Be mystified as she cooks your hotdogs with her amazing hand irons (hotdogs cost extra)!*

Nope, it's best that she didn't speak about her nightmares, talking about them would only make them tangible.

Darrius gently directed her gaze back to him. His eyes pulsed with different hues of green. She instantly felt safe and warm. She drifted as though lying on a cloud, high in the sky, safe from all danger. "You've had other visions like this before, haven't you?" He asked with concern in his voice.

"Yes," she responded hoarsely as though in a trance.

"What are you fighting in the visions?"

"A black beast flies over a storm-tossed ocean while I stand on the shore."

Darrius poured a glass of water. He carried it over to Hilly and cupped her warm hands around the cool glass. "Here, drink this." Hilly shook her head to clear the sleepy cobwebs and took the water. She sipped slowly, enjoying the coolness on her hands and her tongue.

Darrius glanced at the others. "Stygian has managed to gain entry into Hilly's mind. She is doing her best to fight him, but it's a matter of time before he may win. We need to get started immediately." Everyone took their seats, first stopping by Hilly to reassure her with a pat on the head.

Darrius closed the study door and powered up the film projector which roared to life with a *click, click, click* as the celluloid streamed through the sprockets and gears. A flickering light bathed the screen and a collective gasp filled the room as Ted Kemp welcomed them.

"Hello, my children. How I wish I could be physically with you right now."

# Chapter 11

## Revelations, Part 1

FEN'S EYES MISTED. SHE missed her father. Hearing his voice reminded her of all the lost years, and the time they hadn't spent together. Despite what she had told Darrius and the others, she did care about her parents. Relieved they weren't dead, she looked forward to the day she would see them again.

*Hopefully*, they would see each other again.

On-screen, Mr. Kemp sat at his mahogany desk. The image was life sized and clear; and it appeared as though he was actually in the room with them.

He folded his hands on the desk and began, "Let me start at the beginning. Your mother and I love you very much; and devoted our lives to keeping you safe from the Yfel Brethren. I'm sure Darrius and Prasad have informed you of their brother, Stygian, who leads this evil group of Cererian soldiers.

"You're probably wondering why the Yfel want anything to do with you. The Cererian Prophecy identified each of you as the chosen ones. You are the four magicians who will restore peace to the world, vanquish the Yfel, and clear the way for the Chronicle to ascend to the throne." Ted paused and stared into the camera. His eyes shifted left then right as if he was actually peering into the faces of his children.

Stunned silence filled the room.

Darrius paused the film. "Let me explain about the Chronicle and The Cererian Prophecy that your father mentioned. The Cererian Prophecy was created two millennia ago. At that time, the Earth was ruled by magic. There were no wars, only peace. A foreshadowing of a bleak future emerged. The world's shamans received disturbing visions predicting chaos and death. They met with all the tribal leaders to discuss the implications of the alarming dreams. The Cererian Prophecy was the result of that meeting. Though ancient Cererians had yet to visit Earth, the visions indicated that the arrival of a Cererian exploration party would plunge the world into lawlessness. Therefore, the sacred text was titled The Cererian Prophecy. Since its inception, events have unfolded as they were preordained.

"The Chronicle is a supernatural human who possesses mystic powers beyond the capability of any other magician. This individual is the embodiment of The Prophecy, and uses the sacred Word to ensure balance and peace is maintained throughout the Earth. There has been one other Chronicle. He lived one thousand years ago before Stygian claimed his life, and plunged the world into fear and darkness. While Prasad and I are aware of the second Chronicle's existence, we don't know his or her identity."

Hilly's brow wrinkled in thought. "Our lives have been dictated by words written down thousands of years ago?" She asked.

"Yes. All of our lives have been directed by the holy Word," Darrius replied. "There are no coincidences regarding your arrival here at The Nine Muses as children, nor your return as adults. Prasad and I were made aware of these events through the Prophecy."

"Then if you know what's going to happen, why not tell us? Why do we have to go through these charades?" Chance demanded.

Darrius glanced at Prasad. "Because we, Prasad and I, have not been granted access to the entire text. We are allowed to know only that which is deemed critical to our own involvement."

"Very few individuals are privileged to know the entirety of the holy Word," Prasad added. "I'm aware that Earth's spirits, a few shamans, and the Chronicle are included in that elite group."

"Let's continue watching the film," Darrius interjected. "Ted has more he needs to share." Darrius flipped the switch on the projector and Ted's image flickered on the screen.

Smiling, Ted continued. "Each of you possess amazing powers that Stygian wants. You have innate magic that will continue to grow as you each embark on your quests. You are extraordinary people who are descended from powerful shamans. I witnessed your supernatural abilities, skills that I'd never seen before. It will be these talents that will help you defeat Stygian and his soldiers. I'll share more on this later."

Ted shifted in his chair. "Allow me to explain the events leading up to our difficult meeting in 1992 when we banished all of you from The Nine Muses. When each of you left home and established new lives in other cities, Darrius and Prasad used Cererian magic to cloak your whereabouts so that the Yfel Brethren wouldn't be able to locate you. The protection spell was deployed without your knowledge because we wanted you to live a normal life, one without constantly looking over your shoulder or fearing the future.

"This strategy worked well until my actions drew attention to The Nine Muses. I traveled the world searching for artifacts related to your families and tribes. Many priceless relics reside in the underground vault directly beneath your feet. During one of my adventures, Stygian stumbled upon me in Great Britain. I thought I had successfully thrown him off my trail but he managed to follow me back to The Nine Muses, hoping to find all of you there. Fortunately, Stygian couldn't break through the protection field Darrius and Prasad had erected. But we knew it wo be a matter of time before he would eventually succeed. uld be a matter of time before he would eventually succeed.

"Our sanctuary had been discovered. That night your mother, Darrius, Prasad, and I made the decision to enact an exit strategy."

Ted paused and sipped water; and then cleared his throat. "Our plan was bold. All of you would return to The Nine Muses. Prasad and Darrius would cloud the memories of your magical abilities and family connections. In addition, they would seed your minds with suggestions—new memories that would urge you to relocate to towns that we deemed safe from the Yfel. All of these cities were built on or near energetic formations that naturally fortified the area with powerful magic. Manipulating your future was the only way we could ensure your safety in the present. Please forgive us for controlling you that way. But we needed to keep you safe. It was critical for you to break all ties with the family and with each other. All links in the chain needed to be broken if we were to succeed. We planned to restore your memories when the time was right.

"And, that moment has arrived.

"Once Stygian located The Nine Muses, he made our life miserable in the hopes that our suffering would compel us to divulge your whereabouts. It wasn't worth the effort to kill us since we were mere humans and didn't possess magical powers that he could consume."

Ted grimaced as he explained. "He infected your mother with a virus so vile that boils exploded all over her body, creating constant agony. Still, despite her pain, she urged me to stand my ground. Nobody was going to coerce us into endangering our children. Our stubbornness further enraged Stygian who, along with some of his soldiers, destroyed Apollo's Fountain. He was fully aware that it was a gateway to other portals all over the world yet he chose to obliterate it in pure spite, because of his intense hatred for us."

Darrius paused the film.

The Kemps traded puzzled glances.

Fen drifted back to her childhood when she played in the fountain waters with her siblings. She remembered staring up at Apollo's four horses, each facing a different direction. Apollo tightly gripped the reins as he stood defiantly in his chariot. Water gushed from the horses' mouths sending froth cascading down into the marble pool. There were occasions when the water stopped flowing and a bright light would illuminate the sky. Fen couldn't recall why this occurred. But, now, with her father's revelation, she wondered if visitors were dropping by from a different country or world.

Chance stretched and strode to the bar. He poured a shot of bourbon, tossed it down his throat, smacked his lips, and poured another.

"Chance, better fill my glass. I have a feeling that it only gets weirder from this point on," Kai said as he joined his brother at the bar.

Fen studied Hilly who shivered despite being swaddled in a thick blanket. "You okay, Hilly?""

Hilly wanted to scream. *How the hell do you think I feel? It's not every day that an alien pops in and takes over my body. Gee, Mr. Alien, thank you for visiting, we must do this again another day when the others can't stop you.* She wanted to yell and take her frustrations out on Fen, her brothers, anybody.

But, she didn't.

She needed to remain the strong and powerful Hilly. But, slowly, she was crumbling inside. "I'm fine, just tired," she mumbled.

Kai poured glasses of wine and placed them on a side table between Hilly and Fen. "Just in case you feel the need," he chirped. Then he and Chance took their seats.

"Before we continue," Darrius started, "Does anyone need a break or are you ready to hear the rest of your story? If you're hungry we plan to stop for lunch around one."

The room was silent.

Hilly sulked, still upset that Stygian had found a way to penetrate her mind. It frightened her. She didn't like losing control and wished she could simply download all her powers into her body right now. She snapped.

"Let's just get on with it, Darrius!" Then she checked herself. "Sorry, I'm a little unnerved. I wish we had our powers right now."

Darrius nodded. He understood her concern. Stygian had found an open door. It was a matter of time before he would barge in unannounced. He started the film again.

"So many times, I rehearsed where I should start and what I should say. Finally, I decided to talk to you from my heart. Now you will learn about who you are, where you were born and the significance of your original families. It's critical you understand your past so you will be prepared for your future. Danger lurks around you, ready to pounce and destroy you. Only by embracing who you are will you be able to fight Stygian and the Yfel Brethren. So, let me explain how you came to be my children.

"In the ancient world, each of your families belonged to tribes that existed around the globe. Within each tribe were individuals who had specific powers and those who had no powers at all. Darrius and I had many conversations about why everyone didn't have special abilities. He believed that we had common ancestors and that people from his race intermingled with humans. Therefore you have some individuals displaying powers and others who don't.

"I want to be clear on this topic. If you were human and didn't have powers, you were not considered different or lower class than those with gifts. You were simply part of that family. For instance, not everybody could be creative like your mother or Kai, or play a musical instrument like Fen, but that did not lessen your importance in our family."

Ted smiled weakly at the camera. "Anyway, your mother and I did not possess beautiful powers like what we saw developing in each of you. Throughout history, many gifted humans perished at the hands of the Yfel Brethren, who feasted on them and stole their powers. Those of us without powers were vulnerable to Stygian's evil influence, so Darrius, Prasad, and their benevolent brothers protected and guided us through some very difficult times.

"That brings me to you, my precious children. You each came to us as the lone survivor of Stygian's murder spree. Four orphaned children from four different magical families. The benevolent Cererian brothers rescued you and brought you to our sanctuary, The Nine Muses.

"Your mother and I could never have children of our own. Raising special children became our life's mission and gave us purpose. We loved each of you for who you were. Chance came to us first."

Chance sat up. He had been nursing his bourbon but suddenly paid attention. He appeared both nervous and excited to hear more.

Ted waved and tears welled in Chance's eyes. "Our oldest boy, Chance. You were born in the town of Amesbury on the southern fringes of the Salisbury plain in England. Your home was near Stonehenge, an ancient site to which you must return one day. Your family was an incredible group of people who shared the gift of earth power. Members of your family typically displayed incredible strength, much more than an average human; and could converse with animals, persuading them to do their bidding.

"You also have personal powers. I once witnessed your ability to levitate and was the victim of your telekinetic tricks many times. I remember one time when you were just shy of two years old, and we were walking along the beach, your favorite activity. You ran away from me and right into the waves. You disappeared and reemerged further out in the ocean on the back of a dolphin. You squealed with delight. You were fearless. But I was terrified. Who lets their baby ride the back of a dolphin in the middle of the Atlantic? I was sure your mother would see you and punish both of us." Ted softly chuckled and looked to the side savoring the memory. He then faced the camera with tears in his eyes.

A tear rolled down Chance's cheek. He couldn't recall that specific moment on the beach but hearing the tenderness in his father's voice and seeing him cry meant so much to him.

Ted cleared his throat and swiped at his eyes. "That's just one example of how special you are. When you became a teenager, full of hormones, stubborn and a know-it-all, you frequently jumped from your bedroom window to the ground to explore Manchester-by-the-Sea. The strength in your legs kept you safe from injury, thank goodness. I tried many methods to alert me when you would go on your escapades: tiny bells, metal cans, anything that would make noise. But you always found a way to avoid them and race away on your adventures.

"Hopefully you brought the card I wrote for you," Ted said before pausing. Chance fumbled in his pockets and finally produced the vellum card with purple cursive writing. Instinctively he held it up to the screen to show his father. His siblings chuckled. Embarrassed, Chance blushed. "Let me read it back to you," Ted offered.

> *Keeper of the records, a warrior stands.*
> *From Amesbury the bugles blow.*
> *And, the light casts its shadow on bluestone.*
> *The time is nigh. The battle approaches.*
> *Gather the troops and reclaim the forgotten throne.*

"I'm sure you were puzzled when you read these words. I would be. It was my way of welcoming you back home with gentle hints about your life, past and present. Let's start with the first line.

"'Keeper of the records, a warrior stands.' In Old English, your first name means *keeper of the records*; and our last name stands for *warrior*. The history of all the world's families and tribes spans a millennium. It is your mission to maintain and protect these records. This is a huge responsibility and is not to be taken lightly. Without history, memories of the families and tribes will disappear and be forgotten by future generations.

"But, before you accept this responsibility, you need the assistance of one of your siblings. Each of you is reliant on each other in the journey yet to come."

Hilly shivered, conflicted by her father's statement. Her nightmarish visions had always shown her alone except for the dream where three armored figures plunged their swords into her body. She worried that she would ultimately have to fight the beast by herself.

Ted continued, "The next line is self-explanatory since I've already shared where you were born, Amesbury. But, the third line, 'And, the light casts its shadow on bluestone' drills down to your origins near Stonehenge. The very large standing stones at Stonehenge are sarsen, a local sandstone, but the smaller ones are known as 'bluestones' and come from the Preseli hills in the Pembrokeshire Coast National Park in Wales.

"One day, you will visit this place to collect a significant family artifact that will be used to restore peace to the world. Stonehenge lies along ley lines including one that also runs under The Nine Muses. We directed you to relocate to Asheville, North Carolina, which also sits atop ley lines. The energy was with you when you were born, blossomed as you grew and remains strong with you now. When you return to these sites, this information will serve you well.

"The next two lines are common to everybody's cards, 'The time is nigh. The battle approaches. Gather the troops and reclaim the forgotten throne'. My children, your resolve will be tested as you battle your adversaries in the near future. You are the troops, our warriors. When you vanquish the Yfel Brethren, the Chronicle will ascend the throne, and peace will be restored to our world."

Darrius noticed concern on everyone's faces and paused, stopping the projector. "Is everyone okay? This is a lot of information to process."

"I think we all need a break," Chance said as he stood and poured himself another drink. He sipped this one slowly as he mulled over what had been shared. He felt violated by his dad and Darrius for stealing his past, and his precious childhood memories. He was furious that his new life in Asheville was the result of mind manipulation and not of his own free will. He wondered if Janet was also part of their devious plan. How far had their suggestions gone? He turned to Darrius, "I'm just a puppet in this mad theater. We're all puppets!"

"I don't see it that way, Chance," Kai interjected. "For so long, I've had mental gaps in my life, moments when I was on the verge of remembering something yet it wouldn't come close enough for me to see it. It bugged the shit out of me, but I chalked it up to brain fog. If it was preordained that I move to Sedona, I'm not complaining. I met my husband there, my art flourished, and my community welcomed me. I'm extremely happy and wouldn't change a thing. I think all this talk about magic, super powers, and traveling to strange lands is just overwhelming. Of course, Dad telling us that we are the 'chosen ones', and that we will soon go to battle is shocking and scary, to say the least."

Fen swiftly added, "You can't change that which has been preordained. I'm not a religious person, but I've sensed evil coming for a couple of years. I have received visions of disturbing scenes that are foreign to me. I could be walking down the sidewalk, shopping in the grocery store, or playing in the park, and I would reel from malicious images flooding my mind. Since arriving here, I've been very cautious. Things are not as they appear anymore."

Hilly listened to the banter. Despondent, her eyes drooped and she pouted as though she was attending her parents' funeral, standing graveside and preparing to toss flowers into the large hole. Only Mom and Dad weren't in the coffin, she was. Her life laid out in a pine box ready to be covered by the damp earth. But, like the phoenix, a new existence was emerging. She turned to Darrius. "I reckon we need to eat now. We need a change of scenery so we can chew on this new knowledge." She smiled weakly at her lame joke.

Darrius nodded. "Agreed. I'll see if Prasad has finished making lunch." He left the study. An awkward silence remained, the air heavy and uncomfortable. Each person withdrew, deploying a protective bubble, letting no one in and preventing emotions from leaking out. Chance and

Kai continued drinking in silence. Chance paced back and forth while Kai leaned against the bar and studied himself in the large bronze-framed mirror. Fen instinctively reached for Hilly's hand, which was ice cold. Shocked, Fen wrapped both of her hands around Hilly's. The two sisters looked at each other with eyes full of fear and uncertainty.

Darrius entered the kitchen as Prasad removed a tray of cold cuts from the refrigerator. "My friend, the Kemps are taking the Revelations quite hard. Chance responded poorly to what his father shared. I wonder now if removing some of their memories was wise. They all seem adversely affected by that action."

Prasad set the tray on the counter and faced Darrius. "Place yourself in their shoes. They've had so many distressing situations in their lives: childhood memories erased, banishment from the home they loved; and, now, demands placed upon them by a parent who is living on another planet. I don't know if humans can tolerate extreme changes like that."

Darrius considered Prasad's words. "Indeed, humans are very fragile. I must remind myself of that. But we are running out of time. Their resistance to Ted's information concerns me. I wonder if they will ever accept their fate as it was dictated by The Cererian Prophecy. If they don't, they will surely die."

Prasad placed his hand on Darrius' shoulder. "Your concern is warranted. I have a suggestion. We originally planned to restore everyone's memories tomorrow after Fen and Hilly received their family history. I think it is critical that we recover the remembrances for both Chance and Kai at the end of today. Chance is the leader of this family, and we need him to be at full capacity and supporting the others now that Stygian has made his presence known. I think that is the missing piece—that connection to the past. He's trying hard to learn the new information, yet he struggles to piece the two worlds together."

"Yes, the plan needs to be altered," Darrius agreed. "I'll tell them at lunch. I think it better that we share this update immediately."

The Kemps filed into the dining room. Hilly and Fen sat while Chance and Kai stood by the window staring at the gusting rain. The future was so uncertain for all of them. They struggled dealing with the expectations heaped on them by their father. After all, they had no allegiance to him, he was the one who banished them from the estate and has now informed them they will go to battle. Days ago, they were all in their comfortable homes with their own families. Their only concerns were paying the bills and complaining when the TV went out.

Prasad and Darrius entered the room carrying the tray of cold cuts, bread and condiments. "Lunch has arrived," Prasad cheerily announced. Nobody responded nor looked at him, not even Fen. He added, "I apologize for the meager offering. The storm has thwarted our efforts to have food delivered to the estate."

No response.

Darrius took his seat and glanced around the room. The energy that was so positive in the morning had been swiftly sucked away. Feelings of gloom and doom replaced the gaiety. He sighed audibly.

"Prasad and I have reconsidered, and are modifying our original plan for restoring your memories. This change will have a more positive impact on your outlook." Their curiosity piqued, Chance, Kai and Fen looked at Darrius. Hilly continued staring out the window, lost in her thoughts. "We will restore the memories of Chance and Kai at the end of today after Kai has received his family's history. Originally, we were going to perform this task tomorrow after everyone had received their Revelations. We recognize that it might be easier to cope if you can connect the past with the present."

Fen softly spoke, "Why can't you do that now, with all of us?"

Prasad moved toward Fen and touched her hand lightly. "It is a logical process. You must first understand the importance of your family history before adding the layer of your powers and memories. Like making the perfect layered Jell-O, you must be patient and let the first layer set before adding the next." Fen nodded in acknowledgment.

"What's involved in this restoration?" Chance asked. He had moved to the sideboard and was busy piling meat onto his bread.

Darrius responded, "It will take about thirty minutes with Prasad working on you while I will work with Kai. We need complete quiet in a darkened room. We can do that in the study. The process to reconnect memories is complicated and, once begun, must not be interrupted. Fen and Hilly will stay outside the room. Tomorrow, we will repeat the process for them."

Kai grabbed some bread and sprinkled salt and pepper on each slice. He carefully joined the pieces and then cut them in half at an angle. He sat at the table, took a big bite and looked up. Chance and Fen stared at him with wide eyes. Anticipating their question, he explained, "What? You've never seen this kind of sandwich before? It's called a mock turkey sandwich. If you close your eyes, you can almost imagine it's full of leftover Thanksgiving Day turkey. When I first moved to Sedona, I didn't have much money so I ate on a low budget. You might scoff, but even Jeff likes to have a mock turkey sandwich every now and then."

Fen chuckled and Chance raised an eyebrow muttering, "If you say so, bro."

Darrius could feel the mood nudge in a positive direction. Three of the Kemps were now chatting and gently teasing each other. Hilly, meanwhile, continued to gaze outside lost in her own world, her face expressionless.

Darrius exchanged glances with Prasad. Using telepathy, the two Cererians discussed ways to help Hilly cope with her situation.

Hilly suddenly turned and announced, "I won't lie, I'm scared to death. I used to trust my instincts but now I don't even know if they're mine or if Stygian is poking at me. I don't know about any of you, but I'm sick and tired of this little prick interfering in my life. If there's a way that will prepare me to get rid of him, I'm all for it."

The return of their fiery sister buoyed the Kemps. Fen threw her arms around Hilly's neck and kissed her cheek. Chance and Kai grinned at their spitfire sister who was roaring to life again. Chance rose. "Then it's agreed. From this point forward, we will stick together, no matter what occurs."

Hilly jumped up and joined Chance. "Agreed, big brother. Since Stygian wants to use me as a window to The Nine Muses, I suggest we use that connection to our advantage."

"Our future will not be easy," Kai warned. "But if we rely on each other's strengths, we'll get through this."

"Hopefully," Fen whispered. "The thought of battling a Cererian who is more powerful than any of us is daunting."

Hilly wrapped her arm around Fen and pulled her close. "I won't let you down, Fen. I promise. And, I know you'll always have my back."

*The family stands strong. We must complete their Revelations,* Darrius noted to Prasad via mental telepathy.

Lunch continued full of laughter, bravado and camaraderie. Hilly pulled herself from the depths of despair, and her determination rallied her siblings around her. The mood was so lighthearted that even Prasad and Darrius relaxed and joined in the animated discussions. Darrius was aware that time was short, but he felt compelled to allow the family to revel in the joyful moment as long as they could.

He finally announced, "I wish I could allow you to enjoy your conversations longer, but we need to finish the Revelation for Kai, and then we'll unlock the memories for him and Chance. Are you ready to begin?"

The Kemps nodded in agreement and filed out of the room. Fen lingered behind with Prasad. "I'll stay and help clean up this mess we made."

Prasad shook his head. "I appreciate your offer, but we both have important business that demands our attention." A shadow of disappointment darkened Fen's eyes, and Prasad added, "But I will see you later."

His reply lifted her spirits. She stopped in the doorway as she exited, and turned. Prasad gazed at her. She raised her hand and waved. Prasad nodded and returned the gesture.

Everyone assembled in the study. Chance and Kai poured themselves drinks and sat down. Fen and Hilly hadn't touched their wine from the morning's session. They sipped the tepid alcohol, grimaced at each other, and then shrugged as they reclined back in their seats, glasses in hand. Everyone was ready to proceed.

Darrius turned the switch on the projector and the film flickered to life.

Ted appeared on screen and waved. "Now, it's time to talk to my creative kid, Kai. You may have noticed that I kept many pieces of your artwork in your bedroom. You started painting before you could walk. Mother placed cups of watercolors on the floor and you plunged your hand into each one and swirled the paint all over the canvas she placed on the floor. By the time you finished, paint was all over you and the room, but the results were amazing. I kept those precious early pieces with the rest of the family history. Once Chance opens the vault, you'll be able to see for yourself, the talent that flourished in you at an early age.

"You were only a few months old when the benevolent Cererian brothers delivered you to The Nine Muses. The Yfel Brethren butchered your family while you slept in an upstairs room. Darrius, himself, snatched you from Stygian's claws."

Kai and Darrius exchanged quick glances.

"You were born in the city of Mount Shasta in northern California. Mount Shasta is one of the world's most sacred mountains. It is steeped in ancient Native American history. It is part of the thousand-mile Cascade Range and is part of the chain of volcanoes that comprise The Ring of Fire. While it is dormant today, it will roar again one day, and when it awakens it may be catastrophic. As with Stonehenge, Mount Shasta has powerful connections with other ancient sites around the world. One day you will return to Mount Shasta and walk the path of the Siskiyou Trail, an old Native American path from Oregon to California.

"Your family shared air power with the tribe. Members could fly, manipulate the weather and control winged creatures. Astral travel—journeying while asleep or meditating—is a special family trait, and you will use it often to collect much-needed information. Like Chance, you have personal powers. Most prominent is your ability to read minds. You always seemed one step ahead of me, and I'm sure it's because you knew what I was thinking.

"An endearing example of this ability is when you were three years old. I had been advised by Darrius that another child was coming to The Nine Muses, little Fenna. I sat in the study pondering how to tell you and Chance about the arrival of your sister. You were playing in the foyer, using pastels to draw your rendition of the painting above the fireplace. You suddenly strolled in with a very serious face and announced, 'If I can't be the baby anymore, I want to be the big brother instead of Chance!'

"I burst out laughing. You stood there with your little hands on your hips giving me the stink eye because you already knew what I was going to say next. I told you Chance will always be the big brother, but that you were the second-in-command. Fenna would have two capable soldiers watching over her. You seemed satisfied because you twirled around and marched out of the room."

Kai grinned at the story. Although he couldn't recall the specific moment, it sounded like something he would do. How sweet that his father saved his artwork. He was anxious to get into the vault and see them. He was slightly concerned, though, to hear that his family's power was control of the air. He detested flying and was convinced there was some mistake. Surely, he wasn't an ancestor of this family.

Ted continued, "Now, about the words on your card. You probably figured this out as I spoke since you saw how I handled the card for Chance. Here is the full passage for everyone to hear:

> *Keeper of the keys, a warrior stands.*
> *Shasta beckons the mystics and the shamans.*
> *Electric, magnetic and balanced, the vortex opens.*
> *The time is nigh. The battle approaches.*
> *Gather the troops and reclaim the forgotten throne.*

"The first line, 'Keeper of the keys, a warrior stands' represents the meanings of your name. You already know that Kemp stands for warrior. Your first name, Kai, is Welsh for keeper of the keys. You are responsible for keys that unlock the doors to many important places. Some keys are physical and some can only be found in the ethereal realm. It is important to note, that only you can access the celestial keys. They can only be obtained through the proper process.

"Don't worry, once your memories are restored, you will gain access to this information. You will also become aware of which key is needed for which situation. Chance is reliant on one of your keys to open the vault and gain access to the family history."

Kai whispered to Chance, "Looks like big brother needs the second-in-command to do his job." They chuckled.

Ted continued, "The second line refers to your place of birth, Mount Shasta. As I've already mentioned, this land has ancient roots in the Native American shamans and mystics. Your quest will lead you back to this ancient land so you can retrieve an important family artifact. The third line speaks to your current home in Sedona, a sacred and powerful place pulsing with energy as ley lines cross beneath it. Cosmic forces emanate from the red rocks and vortexes offer healing and reflection.

"The impending battle is real, and you will take your place beside your brother and sisters in restoring peace to the world. Once your recollections are restored, many doors will open to you, and you will finally understand your full powers and your purpose."

Darrius stopped the movie and scanned everybody's faces. This time he saw hope instead of fear. "We have reached the end of the film for Kai and Chance. You now have all the information you need about your past and present. Once Prasad and I restore your memories, you will attain full awareness."

"Darrius, I have a concern," Kai said in a serious tone.

"Oh?" Darrius responded.

"I think there's been a terrible mistake. Dad mentioned my family shares air power with the tribe and members typically fly. Darrius, I hate to fly. I need to get drunk just to get on a plane. I think I was switched at birth. Do you have any families whose power is creating fashion?"

Everyone burst out laughing including Darrius.

Hilly blurted, "Oh, yes! The House of Kai, exclusive fashions for the elite non-flying people."

Kai added, "Parachute apparel for those afraid to fly solo."

The Kemps joked back and forth. Their loud laughter attracted Prasad, who could hear the ruckus from the kitchen. He tip-toed to the door and carefully placed his ear against it. Darrius suddenly swung the door open. Prasad leapt back in surprise, his hands up in defense.

"SURPRISE!"

Prasad stared, wide-eyed, at the mob. The Kemps giggled and Darrius smiled broadly at his friend. Stone-faced, Prasad glared at each person. His dispassionate reaction concerned everyone and they stopped laughing. Fearful their antics hurt Prasad's feelings, Fen offered an apology, "We meant no harm. We were only playing around."

No response

Darrius added, "I'm sorry, my friend. We were lost in a moment of insanity and got carried away."

Still no response.

With hands raised like bear claws, Prasad suddenly jumped toward the crowd yelling, "Got you!"

Everyone jumped back in surprise. Kai tripped over Chance's leg, causing him to tumble to the floor. Hilly stopped Kai's fall but got pulled off balance. Fen grabbed at Hilly but was also yanked off her feet and they all tumbled like a line of dominoes. Darrius and Prasad chuckled as they watched the squirming Kemps laugh and roll around on the floor. The house had not heard the echo of this much laughter in decades.

Darrius was satisfied. He could feel the natural, care-free energy flowing between the siblings as they helped each other from the floor. They may have arrived as individuals but were now performing like a cohesive family force. The next phase—restoring memories—would propel two of them into a different level of consciousness. He knew it was the right decision. He could still sense Stygian was nearby, stalking the home, waiting. Thankfully the protection field around the house was strong enough to keep him out.

But, for how long?

Darrius interrupted, "Now that everybody has blown off steam, Prasad and I have an important duty to perform. Chance and Kai, if you're ready, please go back to the study. Hilly and Fen, it is critical that you remain outside the room. We must not be disturbed until we emerge in about thirty minutes. If you talk, please do so at a low whisper. Do not leave this house for any reason. Are there any questions?"

The siblings traded glances and then shook their heads.

"Wonderful," Darrius said. "As you say, let's get this show on the road." The four men walked into the study and shut the door. Darrius invited Kai to sit in a chair opposite him while Prasad motioned for Chance to do the same.

"Just relax and, when prompted, gaze into the eyes of your partner. Breathe deeply as if falling asleep. But, keep your eyes open the entire time," Darrius instructed.

"Like this," Kai whispered to Chance as he demonstrated the gyan mudra by touching his forefinger with his thumb and extending the remaining fingers straight out as if flashing the "okay" symbol with his hand. Meditation and deep breathing were second nature to Kai. His therapist had suggested the practice to alleviate the bitterness he harbored toward his parents. Chance rolled his eyes but followed his brother's lead. "Keep the mudra while resting the back of your wrist on the tops of your knees, with your feet flat on the floor. Like this. Now just breathe."

Chance shook his head. This mudra shit was total nonsense to him. But he understood the seriousness of the situation. He didn't want to let his brother down nor disappoint his sisters. He sighed heavily and copied Kai. Soon, the brothers breathed in unison.

Satisfied that Chance and Kai were ready, Darrius and Prasad began humming a melodic mantra: single-syllable words escaping their lips in soft whispers. The pace gently increased until the room pulsed with a comforting buzzing like the wings of a million honeybees. The hypnotic droning ebbed and flowed throughout the room.

Kai and Chance gently swayed to the rhythm. The time had come. Prasad and Darrius continued the chant while slowly leaning forward until they were mere inches from Kai and Chance. Widening their brilliant, green eyes, Darrius and Prasad stared directly into the souls of their partners, reaching into the deep recesses of their consciousness, searching for the clouded memories carefully hidden decades ago. Their eyes brightened then shimmered as a probing emerald beam pulsed and reached forward, seeking the recipient's eyes. Soon, a dazzling green shaft of light flickered between the partners, and the connections were established.

Fen and Hilly moved to the sitting room so they could chat freely. They chose a plush sofa that provided a great vantage point in which to keep an eye on the study door, just in case anyone should emerge dazed and confused, which is how Hilly envisioned Chance.

"have an idea about our secret powers," Hilly suggested. "So far, Chance is earth and Kai is air. Those are two of the four natural elements so it only makes sense that you and I are fire and water." Fen agreed, noting that water was more in tune with her calm nature while fire matched Hilly's explosive energy.

The sisters shared their handwritten cards hoping to decipher the cryptic phrases. "I feel guilty doing this without the others present," Fen said.

Hilly scoffed, "Who would ever know? Besides, if we're wrong, we're wrong. We're only messing around, wasting time until Prasad and Darrius finish brainwashing our brothers."

"What? Do you believe that?"

"Nah, I'm just kidding. I'm a little antsy just sitting here while Chance and Kai finally get their memories restored. I'm a little jealous"

"Look, I'm the guardian of peace and you're the guardian of battle. How cool is that? We're the yin and the yang of our family," Fen said, changing the subject.

The girls continued analyzing their cards. Hilly recognized the word *Denali* on hers and guessed that meant she was born in Alaska, but Fen was puzzled by *The Big Wheel* reference on her notecard. While she had no clue where she was born, she was convinced it was connected to Native Americans. The third line revealed aspects of where they currently live and Fen was not surprised her card mentioned healing and atonement. She was quite familiar with the ley lines and powerful energy surrounding Stone Mountain, Georgia. Hilly, on the other hand, shivered at the words on her card: *The beast rips through the vortex.* She immediately envisioned her nightmares and the shrieking beast bearing down on her.

"Maybe we should stop interpreting the cards," Fen said as she saw that familiar worried look creep across Hilly's face. "We should leave some surprises for tomorrow."

Hilly nodded. "You're right, Fen. No reason to worry about things we can't control. Let's put the cards away and spend time catching up, I'm sure there's been a lot of changes for both of us."

"Excellent idea. But I need to make a quick trip upstairs first, if you know what I mean," Fen said, winking at Hilly.

"Okay, I'll wait for you here. I hope everything comes out okay." Hilly winked back.

They both giggled.

Concerned they may have disturbed the memory restorations, they looked nervously toward the study door. Nobody emerged so Hilly gave Fen a thumbs up. All was clear. Fen crept up the staircase to take care of business and Hilly was alone. She leaned back against the comfortable cushion and listened to the rain fall. The wind nudged the boxwoods against the window. *Scratch, scratch, scratch.* Hilly thought of Fen's vandalized car as the branches brushed against the glass. Then she heard a different sound.

*Meow*

Hilly sat up. *Was that a cat?* The sound was distant. She cocked her ear toward the window and listened again. All she could hear was the frenzied scratching from the bushes. Convinced she imagined the noise she relaxed back against the cushion.

*Meow*

She bolted upright. She did hear it. It was a little closer this time. She stared out the window searching for a cat but was met with blackness punctuated with flashes of lightning. She leaned closer. After several minutes, she shook her head and grinned. *You're losing it, Hilly.* She slumped onto the sofa and glanced at her watch, Prasad and Darrius should be almost done with the boys. She furtively looked up the stairs and wished Fen would return. She couldn't shake the uncomfortable feeling that she was being watched.

*Meow*

The sound was much louder and closer. A cat was outside. *Maybe it's Pyewacket*, she thought. *I haven't seen him since yesterday morning. Poor thing is locked outside in this horrible storm.* She rose to investigate and then remembered Darrius' warning: "Do not leave this house for any reason."

*Meoooow*

She glanced at the door, then to the study and, then up the staircase. Nobody. She agonized over what to do next. *I know I should wait for someone, but Pyewacket is getting soaked and cold. What could hurt if I just opened the door and allowed the cat in? Darrius and Prasad would thank me for looking out for their cat. After all, I'm not technically going outside the house, I'm just opening the door.* That sounded feasible.

Certain of her decision, Hilly went to the door, placed her hand on the doorknob and slowly turned it. The massive door suddenly swung open as though unseen hands forcibly pushed it. She jumped back and peered outside but there was no sign of a cat. Leaning over the threshold, she scanned the area under the overhang and the driveway to the carriage house. Still no cat.

*Meow*

Hilly froze. "Mr. Spatz, is that you?" On top of Fen's car sat Mr. Spatz. He casually licked one paw and ran it over his ear, then stared at her. "How did you get away from Curtis?" The cat sat back on his haunches and waved his white legs in the air, his familiar antics for attention. "Oh my god! It is you! Come here, Spatz, and get out of the rain." The feline didn't budge, he stared at Hilly with his bright orange eyes.

Caution nagged at Hilly, and she turned around to see if Fen had returned or if the boys had come out of the study. Nobody. She carefully considered her next step. The cat meowed again and playfully waved his paws. Enticing the feline to come inside, she clucked her tongue and slapped her thigh. Spatz remained on the car and glared at her. It was a stand-off made more miserable by the frequent gusts of chilly, damp breezes pushing through the doorway.

"Fine," she grumbled. "I'll come get you, you lazy beast."

She left the door open and inched toward the car. The cat's eyes grew larger and brighter, sunburst orange orbs with flecks of yellow gold. It purred loudly, or was it a low growl? Hilly almost reached the car when Prasad yelled, "NO, HILLY, STOP! DON'T TOUCH IT!"

Hilly froze midstride. Mr. Spatz screeched. Prasad raced down the steps, encircled Hilly's waist with his arm and pulled her close. The cat snarled a rumbling growl. Prasad backed up locking eyes with the enraged feline, which glared at him with oil-black eyes, the orange completely erased.

"Prasad, what's wrong? That's my cat, Mr. Spatz," Hilly protested.

Prasad yanked her over the threshold while scolding her. "We told you *never* to go out because of the danger. That is *not* your cat. It is Stygian. The imposter has fooled you into believing he is a simple feline. Thank goodness our protection field prevented him from reaching you, or we would have lost you forever."

Mr. Spatz shrieked with rage. The cry reminded Hilly of her nightmares and the sound of the beast as it flew closer to the shore. A blur of black rushed by Prasad and Hilly. In a few bounds, Pyewacket reached the top of the car and howled his distaste for Mr. Spatz who immediately lashed out with claws the length of eagle talons. The two felines crushed together in battle—biting, clawing and, screaming. Mr. Spatz sailed off the car into the darkness followed by Pyewacket. The yowls and screeches echoed in the deep darkness as the blood battle raged.

Prasad slammed the door and dragged Hilly into the foyer. She sobbed, confused and scared. Suddenly a flickering bright light illuminated the room as lightning stabbed the grounds near Apollo's Fountain. Thunder reverberated off the walls as if Apollo was thumping the house with his own hands.

"The fight is over," Prasad announced.

# Chapter 12

# Stygian Attacks

PRASAD HUGGED HILLY IN the middle of the foyer. Soaking wet and in shock, she shook violently. She was furious with herself for not listening to her intuition or to Darrius. How could soft, cuddly Mr. Spatz be Stygian? For over three months, that creature prowled her home, listened to her conversations, and slept in her bed. She shivered. To think he could have easily sliced her open at any time. But he didn't. Instead he used her, waiting patiently until she unwittingly led him to her siblings.

Fen, Kai, and Chance exchanged worried glances. They hadn't witnessed the chaos outside but understood the seriousness of the situation. Hilly was fearless and strong, yet Stygian lured her beyond the protection boundary and almost into his waiting claws.

"If we were a minute longer in the study, I shudder to think what might have happened," Chance said as he gently rubbed Hilly's shoulder, soothing his baby sister just like the old days.

"Now would be a good time to pour a drink," Prasad suggested. Chance nodded and left.

"What happened, Prasad? I was upstairs for only a few minutes," Fen asked as she wrapped a towel around Hilly and dabbed her wet face.

Prasad didn't answer. His mind was on a different matter. He scanned the area, intently searching for something. He narrowed his eyes on a small object moving along the baseboard in the sitting room. Tiny and gray, it appeared to be a mouse.

Chance returned from the study and gently maneuvered a glass of wine into Hilly's shaking hand. She sipped slowly. He tossed back the bourbon he had brought for himself.

Prasad turned to Kai and Chance. "Both of you now have your memories restored and need to allow your brains sufficient time to process the many images shuffling through your minds. The last layer, your powers, will be more apparent by tomorrow morning. It's time for you to take charge of your family. Take Hilly and Fen into the study and lock the doors. Stygian is stronger than we anticipated. He's a ruthless adversary determined to find and kill all of you at any cost."

Fen gently touched Prasad's arm. "The bright light and thunder, what was that? That wasn't normal for a storm. It came from the direction of Apollo's Fountain."

"Please don't be concerned. Darrius left the house to inspect the surrounding grounds, and to ensure that we are safe," he responded, preoccupied with scanning the sitting room, and looking for the creature he'd seen earlier.

Hilly softly spoke, "Pyewacket. I saw Pyewacket attack Mr. Spatz...er I mean Stygian. Is he okay?"

"I'm sure he is. He's a very tough cat."

"I hope so," she replied as she leaned into Chance's side, his arm wrapped around her waist to steady her.

"Come on, guys, let's go," Chance said as he led Hilly into the study.

Prasad called after them, "Be prepared to stay there for the rest of the night. There are blankets in the large chest in the corner. I don't know when I'll return and need you all together while I secure the house."

Prasad walked to the sitting room and stood in front of the window. Moving clockwise, his hands fluttered around the window frame ensuring the protection spell was still in place. He heard the soft *click* of the study door, and glanced to make sure the Kemps were gone. He turned his attention to the mouse he saw earlier.

"Now, where did you go, little fellow?" he whispered. He moved the sofa and found a trail of blood dotting the floor, paralleling the baseboard. He followed the blood trail until it stopped at the coffee table. Atop the table sat a box of tissues, tiny dots of blood peppered the side. Carefully lifting the tissue box, Prasad peered inside and found a small, gray mouse curled on its side in the folds of white tissue. Blood trickled from a gash on its right side. "Poor fellow, I'll take care of you." The tiny creature lifted its head and gazed at Prasad with brilliant, green eyes.

Inside the study, Chance led Hilly to the couch and helped her lay down. He lifted the wine glass from her hand and set it on the end table. Fen covered her with a blanket and stroked her hair until Hilly slowly closed her eyes and drifted into a deep slumber. Kai locked the study door behind him and secured the one leading to the dining room. Then he folded into one of the leather recliners. Fen tossed him a blanket and then curled up in the recliner next to him. Chance wrestled a large oak chair to the door and slumped into it. He surveyed the room, and all was in order. They were ready for anybody, or anything, to come their way.

"The only thing missing is my shotgun. Would it have mattered? Can shotgun shells kill a magical being?" he mused.

"Chance, do you feel any different since the session with Prasad?" Kai asked, eager to change the subject.

"My brain hurts. It's not exactly a headache, it's more like a tremendous pressure. Remember those stress balls shaped like a head with two eyes that bulged when you squeezed it?"

Kai laughed out loud. "That's exactly how I feel!"

Fen jumped in, "I always said you lunks were just a bunch of fat heads."

Kai swatted at Fen and Fen snapped her blanket at Kai as they both chuckled. Chance grinned at their antics but something suddenly snatched his attention.

"Hey, look at Hilly."

Still asleep, Hilly twitched and jerked, mumbling unintelligible words. She thrust her hands toward the ceiling as if pushing something or someone away. Chance bolted from his chair and raced to her side. Remembering what happened earlier, he was concerned about her hands, which now glowed fiery red. "She must be fighting that black beast again...or Stygian!"

Kai joined Chance. "We should wake her up like Darrius did before. She could hurt herself, or hurt one of us."

Hilly fired off a string of foreign words, the language of the ancients. With each incantation, her hands pulsed and glowed with increasing heat.

Fen joined her brothers. "Wake her up. She's casting a spell and we don't know what will happen if she finishes it while she's asleep. Stygian could be working through her to break through the protection field surrounding the house. WAKE HER UP NOW!"

Grabbing her shoulders, Chance and Kai shook Hilly, nudging her softly at first, then violently when she refused to wake. Suddenly her eyes shot open, oil-black orbs stared at them.

"It's Stygian!" Chance yelled as he pulled the blanket over her face to prevent the beast from seeing anything in the room.

"WAKE UP, HILLY!" they all screamed in unison.

"Kai, you can read minds. Get into Hilly's and get that asshole, Stygian, out of there!" Chance barked.

Kai was reluctant. "Prasad said that our powers wouldn't return until after all our memories—"

"Bullshit, you know you can do this. I've seen you do it before!" Chance bellowed

Kai stared at his brother, puzzled by his claim that he'd used his mental gifts in the past. It was obvious Chance's memories had returned, but Kai's remembrances were still murky. Chance knew Kai could penetrate Hilly's mind. Now he needed to convince Kai that he could actually do it.

"Kai, do it now!"

A low chuckle emanated from Hilly, a guttural growl much like a rabid wolf. Kai knelt beside Hilly and wrapped his hands around her forehead, his thumbs pressing on her third eye chakra. He closed his eyes. Instinctively, Fen joined him and placed her hand on Kai's shoulder as she, too, closed her eyes.

"NO, STOP, YOU'RE HURTING ME!" Hilly screamed.

Kai immediately lifted his hands, frightened that he was hurting his sister.

"Put them back, that's the bastard, Stygian, not Hilly!" Chance yelled.

The brothers locked eyes. Kai was unsure about his next move and Chance's anger unnerved him. Chance sensed Kai's hesitancy and urged him forward. "It's okay, Kai, you've got this. You can do this."

Kai returned his hands to Hilly's forehead which was slick with perspiration. He began humming. The words tumbled rapidly from his lips, creating a continuous buzzing mantra that sounded like a million honeybees flying within the room. Fen joined in, and soon fell into Kai's rhythmic pace.

Hilly fought back ferociously and struggled to place her searing hands on all of them, but Chance grabbed her wrists. *My god, she's strong*, Chance thought as he fought to keep her still. Hilly thrashed beneath them as Kai and Fen continued chanting their mantra, and Chance pinned her arms.

Kai and Fen's eyes flew open as they shouted together, "You are banished forever!"

The work was done. Hilly's arms grew limp and she ceased struggling. Exhausted, Kai and Fen collapsed to the floor, arms wrapped around each other. Chance removed the blanket from Hilly's face and was relieved to find no black orbs staring back at him. He gently shook her. Her eyes fluttered before she collapsed into a deep sleep. Chance inspected her hands, which still glowed red and hot.

"Fen, please grab some ice from the bar. We may not be able to heal her hands like Darrius but we can cool them down a bit." Fen scooped ice into a towel and carried it over to Hilly. Very carefully Chance placed her hands on the ice. Steam hissed into the air.

"I could use a drink, how about you two?" Before anyone answered Chance strode to the bar and poured bourbon, vodka and wine. Kai and Fen joined him. Glasses in hand they faced Hilly, who slept peacefully on the couch.

"A toast," Chance announced as he raised his glass, "To the chosen ones!"

Prasad tenderly carried the tiny rodent to a secret room on the third floor, accessible by a secret doorway near the bookcase in the hallway. The Nine Muses had many secret passageways that led to hidden chambers. He and his precious cargo were safe in this room, hidden from any disturbances.

Pushing the large, wooden door aside, he entered the space, a sanctuary bathed in voluminous, flowing white linens drifting gracefully from a skylight in the middle of the ceiling. The window framed dots of starlight in the pitch blackness of the raging storm, and somewhere in the heavens above, Ceres looked down. Prasad gazed up, as he did each night, and wished he was home. He lit several sticks of patchouli incense and watched the curls of smoke rise, delivering healing scents throughout the room.

He carried the mouse into the bathroom and carefully placed the tissue box beside the bathtub. He looked down, the creature panted in pain and its wound oozed blood. "Hang on, little one," he soothed. "Time for a little alchemy."

Prasad reviewed the multi-colored bottles on the shelf, lightly brushing his fingertips across each one, sensing the contents. Intuitively selecting the proper mix of potions, he collected three bottles with liquids that, when combined, would produce the desired outcome. He turned on the faucet and held his hand under the spout until warm water flowed into the tub.

As the water gushed, he added the three liquids: an amethyst-colored potion, coral-tinged crystals and a dark-blue fluid with the consistency of ink. After each addition, he used a copper rod to mix the potions thoroughly with the water. When six inches of water collected in the tub, he turned off the faucet and placed a large cushion in the middle of the water. The fabric immediately soaked up the healing concoction.

Careful not to hurt the mouse, he gently lifted it from the box and cradled it as he placed it onto the pillow, which was now saturated with the potions. Its gray fur changed to a purplish, blue-brown as the potions made their way onto and into the rodent's body. It did not stir or open its eyes. It lay on its side and breathed heavily. Prasad gently stroked the creature. "All will be well, my friend. All will be well, Darrius."

# Chapter 13

# Calm Before the Storm

THE DAWN FLED FROM the advancing storm. Menacing thunderheads moved onshore and smothered the sun with driving rain, strong winds, and vicious lightning. Fen tip-toed into the darkened dining room, her fuzzy pink slippers scuffing the floor. Now that morning had arrived, she didn't see any reason to remain locked in the study. The dining room was empty, so she padded into the kitchen expecting to see Prasad busily making breakfast. She blinked in the dim light. No Prasad. She shrugged, switched on the overhead light and began making coffee.

Kai and Chance grunted awake shortly after Fen left them in the study. They woke tired and sluggish, having drank too much celebrating their defeat over Stygian.

Kai rubbed his swollen eyes and snapped, "Yeah, well you don't look like the queen of the ball either, Chance!"

"What the fuck, Kai? I didn't say anything. I may have been *thinking* it, but I didn't say it out loud."

"Hey, our powers are back, big brother," Kai said. "Show me what you can do. Levitate something. Take the blanket off my chair." Chance massaged his temples. He wasn't in the mood to perform for Kai today. "Come on, bro. Just give it a try."

"Leave me alone, Kai. I need coffee."

"You're afraid to try, aren't you?"

"You're such an ass!" Chance hissed, fed up with Kai's pestering. He pushed his palm toward Kai. "See, nothing happened."

"You're trying too hard. Relax and let it happen naturally."

"Give me a fucking chance! It's been over twenty years since I've done this!" He closed his eyes, took a long, deep breath, and then exhaled slowly while pushing his hand toward the blanket. The fringe twitched as if teased by a sudden breeze, then the corner lifted as if someone pinched it tightly. Seconds later the blanket skyrocketed toward the ceiling before gently drifting toward Chance, sweeping the carpet as it moved slowly through the air. Finally, it settled into his outstretched hand and he snatched it.

"Aha. Gotcha!"

"Bravo!" Kai cheered, clapping his hands together. The ruckus woke Hilly. She stretched the full length of the couch and ran her fingers through her matted hair. "Sorry to wake you, Hilly, but Chance just used his powers to levitate the blanket."

"Couldn't he have just walked over here and grabbed it?"

"What's the fun in the mundane stuff? Chance, do it again for Hilly, and, this time, be faster."

Hilly stood and yawned. Hands on her hips, she leaned backwards. She grimaced as she wiggled from side to side until several vertebrae snapped and popped. She cupped Kai's cheek in one hand.

"There, there, Kai. You and Chance can show off later after we've all cleaned up and eaten. I really need a shower." Then she embraced Chance's face with both hands. She gently pulled it close to hers and kissed him on the forehead. "Now put away your toys and let's get changed."

Chance blurted, "Your hands are like ice. How are you feeling?"

"Are they?" She responded as she regarded her brother. Her mouth twisted as she wrestled with her next comment. "I'm good," she declared before she whirled and exited the study.

Chance and Kai exchanged puzzled looks.

"You're right, Chance," Kai added. "When she cupped my cheek, it felt like the hand of death cradled my face. Hilly doesn't like to dwell on things, especially bad shit. Perhaps she's already moved on from last night's close call with Stygian." Chance nodded but wasn't convinced. He would keep an eye on her throughout the day just in case remnants of Stygian remained.

Prasad heard the Kemp's conversation as he dressed. "The Kemps are up." He walked to the bathroom and peered in. "How are you feeling this morning, my friend?"

Darrius lay in the bathtub, a soaked green pillow under his head, his right leg dangled over the tub's edge. Sweat ran down his face and glistened on his dark brown arms and legs.

"I still feel feverish." He lightly touched the ribs on the right side. "The wound is almost healed but it's still very sensitive to the touch." Prasad knelt beside Darrius and placed his hand on his forehead. "What are you doing?" Darrius asked as he gazed up with sleepy eyes.

"Feeling for a temperature. At least, this is what humans do when they're ill."

"Do I have a temperature?"

"I'm not sure. What would be a normal temperature for you?" Prasad playfully tousled Darrius' hair and stood up. "I think you're doing just fine. At least you were able to transform back into your human body. I was concerned you expended too much energy fighting Stygian.

"Shape-shifting into a mouse not only allowed you to gain easy entrance into the home but permitted me to fully immerse you in the healing potions. I fear I would have lost you had I not been able to cover your entire body with my powerful tincture. My magic isn't strong enough to heal your wounds and transform you back."

"I will never doubt your magical concoctions ever again," Darrius proclaimed as he struggled to stand. Prasad rushed to his side and steadied him as he rose.

"You should relax here for the morning and regain more of your strength. I'll go downstairs and prepare breakfast. I'm late but I've become accustomed to humans being more relaxed about things like eating at a certain time."

"The Kemps are having an impact on you, aren't they?"

Prasad finished dressing. "I must admit, I didn't expect to grow so fond of them. They have a carefree love of life that draws me to them. Fen, in particular, has a peculiar effect on me."

Darrius chuckled. "I noticed. You share the same temperament. I've seen how you gaze into each other's eyes."

Prasad blushed. "Enough of that, Darrius. I'm leaving now. I'll inform the Kemps that you'll join them later for the session. I told them last night that you were ensuring the house was protected so, if they ask, I'll just mention you were out late and needed more rest."

Prasad opened the door to leave, but then turned to his friend and warned, "Darrius, please behave yourself today."

Darrius walked out of the bathroom and stood naked in the middle of the room, a towel hugging his shoulders. His muscular, dark brown body was smooth and hairless like melted dark chocolate. "Put something on, Darrius, you'll catch a cold walking around wet."

Darrius nodded. "Okay, my friend, don't worry about me. I'll stay here and rest." Satisfied, Prasad headed downstairs. Darrius walked in front of the full-length mirror and studied the wound on his right side. Once a deep gash, it was now an angry red welt tracing the full length of one rib. The wound drove deep, bruising soft tissue from his rib cage to his spine, which had been nicked during battle. He was fortunate Stygian hadnt punctured his lung with his long talons. Darrius recalled the scenes of the battle. All Cererians can shape-shift, but Stygian had transformed into a hybrid animal, one he had never seen: a cat with claws the length of an eagle's talons. If Stygian can transform into hybrid creatures, the Kemps will need to know, and prepare.

Fen raided the refrigerator and found some eggs, cheese, green peppers and mushrooms. *Perfect for an egg scramble surprise,* she thought. She diced the vegetables and grated the cheddar. After cracking all the eggs into a large ceramic bowl, she added spices and a dash of cream before whisking them together. She slathered a cast iron skillet with butter and lowered the heat to medium. Prasad entered from the back staircase.

"Good morning, Miss Fen."

Fen jumped and almost spilled the egg mixture all over the stove. "Holy cow, Prasad, warn a girl when you're going to sidle up to her."

"I'm so sorry, Miss Fen. I didn't mean to startle you."

"A good scare in the morning certainly gets the blood pumping," She playfully tapped his nose with the back of the spatula.

Prasad was confused by human emotions. First, she was angry and now she was fun-loving. He wasn't sure how to behave with Fen sometimes.

"You're just in time to help with breakfast," Fen continued as she turned back to the stove and added the vegetables into the mixture. "By the way, where have you been? It's not like you to be late."

Prasad wanted to tell her everything—about their ability to shapeshift, Darrius' injuries, and how he was healed. He trusted Fen, but he dared not share. There was a place and a time. He needed to stick to the plan.

"Darrius and I stayed up late ensuring the protection spells held against Stygian. I'm afraid I overslept. Thankfully, I have you to fill in for me." He smiled deeply at Fen, hoping she wouldn't detect any deception.

"It was a crazy night for everyone," she said as she swirled the egg mixture. "We had our own drama in the study last night. Hilly had another episode with Stygian. We were sure he was conjuring magic through her in an attempt to break the protection spell. "You would have been proud of how we all worked together."

"Stygian channeled through Hilly?"

"Calm down, Prasad. We got it all under control," Fen said nonchalantly as she scooped the eggs into a serving bowl and sprinkled the cheese on top.

"Tell me what happened, Fen. Every detail."

Fen sensed his serious tone. "We were going to tell you at breakfast. Everyone had a hand in helping Hilly. Kai even used his power of telepathy to break Hilly free from Stygian's grasp."

Prasad felt frantic, but he didn't want to frighten Fen. He needed to hear the entire story, and right away so he could inform Darrius. He collected himself, grabbed the coffee and calmly suggested, "Then let's go into the dining room and eat. I'm anxious to hear about your adventures."

When Prasad and Fen entered, Chance teased, "Well, it's about time. I'm *hungry*. Bring me my food." Kai laughed but noticed Prasad's pensive mood and instinctively scanned his mind for a clue on his behavior. Penetrating Prasad's brain was like slamming one's head against a concrete wall, entrance was forbidden. Kai felt Prasad forcibly push him away.

Fen circled the table portioning out the eggs. "We're short on supplies so you'll eat what I give you. I hope you like my scrambler surprise."

"Smells great," Kai raved. "Is there any toast?"

"Oh, damn. I knew I forgot something." Fen set the dish down and dashed back into the kitchen.

"Coffee, anyone?" Prasad filled everyone's mug. As he circled the table, he analyzed each person's mood. Chance and Kai joked about their special powers, Hilly sat expressionless in her chair, eyes glazed as if in a trance.

"Fen tells me you had an exciting night."

"That's putting it mildly," Chance said as he shoveled eggs into his mouth.

"It was a little scary," Kai interjected. "But we all jumped in to handle the situation. I was surprised my telepathy returned so quickly."

"I had to push you to do that," Chance barked. Food food flew out of his mouth and scattered onto the table.

"Nice, Chance. Really pretty," Kai teased. "We're all impressed that you took charge last night."

Fen entered with the toast. Chance grabbed a slice from the platter and whirled it at Kai.

"No, no, no!" Fen howled. "No food fights. We don't have much food left."

The guys continued teasing each other while Fen circled the table offering toast and butter. Unfazed by her brothers' antics, Hilly gazed out the window. She took a piece of toast and chewed it slowly, her thoughts a million miles away. Hilly stared at the rainy weather, pausing now and then to sip her coffee.

"Now that Fen is here, please tell me the rest of the story from last night. I heard you had quite an adventure." Prasad's request was lighthearted, but anxiety churned inside as he awaited the details about Stygian's visit.

Chance started explaining how the events unfolded, but Kai broke in with his version, only to be interrupted by Fen who offered a summary.

"Stygian appeared to be casting a spell through Hilly, Kai was able to penetrate her mind, Chance held her hands from harming us, and I joined Kai in freeing Hilly."

Fascinated, Prasad approached Hilly. "Do you remember anything?"

Hilly munched her toast and gazed out the window.

"Hilly, did you hear me?"

Slowly she turned her head toward him. She smiled and replied, "I heard you." She returned to gazing out the window.

The Kemps and Prasad exchanged worried looks. Kai immediately began scanning Hilly's mind for any trace of Stygian. Prasad pressed on, "Is there anything you would like to add to what your brothers and sister told me?"

"I don't think it was *that* bad. They make it sound as though they performed an exorcism on me, complete with head spinning and green vomit everywhere."

"I can't find any trace of Stygian in her mind," Kai proclaimed. "Is it possible he could enter her body and go undetected?"

Furious, Hilly cried out, "Don't talk about me like I'm not here!" She stood and faced Kai. "And, stop screwing around with my thoughts. I don't appreciate the intrusion. After last night, I wanted a quiet morning. Yet, all of you act as though I'm the enemy and not your sister."

Fen ran to Hilly's side. "Hilly, we were concerned. Last night was hard to watch. Your eyes were black as coal. Stygian was attempting to see through your eyes. And, the words you spoke...hon, you were casting a spell. Your hands were hot and red. We were worried that you were trying to break the protection spell around the house."

Hilly's face softened. "I know you were only looking out for me. But I don't like to dwell on these damned events. They upset me because when they occur, I can't control what's happening." She forced a grin. "Believe me, I'm fine. I just need a peaceful morning."

The room quieted. Chance and Kai settled into eating breakfast. Hilly returned to nibbling her toast, sipping her coffee, and staring out the window. Fen sat beside Prasad and shot him a sideways glance, indicating she had more to say but not here, not now. "I'm going to make more coffee," Fen said as she rose from the table.

"I'll help you," Prasad offered.

Kai watched them leave. "I think something is developing between the two of them. Have you seen how they look at each other?"

"Give it a rest, Kai. You must miss your soap operas," Chance joked.

Fen led Prasad to the far corner of the kitchen so they wouldn't be overheard. "Something is up with Hilly. She looks and speaks like Hilly, but her demeanor and behavior are very different. Even her eyes are different. They used to be hazel, but now they're a bright green. Something happened last night, and I thought we banished Stygian, but now I'm worried that he's found a way to secretly inhabit her body."

"I know what you mean, Fen. It's as though we lose a piece of Hilly after each episode. I must tell Darrius what occurred last night." Prasad turned to go up the stairs.

"Where is Darrius? I thought he would be down by now."

Prasad stopped. He invited Fen to sit beside him on the stairs. He collected his thoughts and then explained the fantastic tale from last night. "Fen, what I tell you is confidential. I prefer that you not share any of these details with your siblings. At least, for now."

Fen took Prasad's hand and squeezed it. The serious tone in his voice frightened her. "Okay. Please continue."

"Last night, Darrius transformed into Pyewacket—a form he typically assumes when he needs to move undetected throughout the house. During his battle with Stygian, he was severely wounded and shape-shifted into a mouse so he could easily enter the house. Darrius was critically injured and required one of my magical concoctions in order to heal the wound, and to allow him to transform back into his human body. He is currently resting upstairs and gathering his strength."

Prasad stopped talking. Fen looked down at the floor. Finally, she looked at him. "I knew this weekend was going to be different, but every hour brings something stranger than before."

"Please keep this between us. Darrius should be the one to inform the others."

"It will be our little secret," Fen said as she patted Prasad's hand. She gazed into his emerald-green eyes. "Thank you for trusting me."

Prasad wrapped his fingers around her hand and leaned close. They gazed intently into each other's eyes. Fen flushed and felt an intense warmth spread through her body. The first line of John Denver's "Annie's Song" popped into her head: "You fill up my senses like a night in the forest."

Suddenly the kitchen door burst open and Chance bellowed, "Is there more coffee?" Prasad and Fen jumped, the spell broken. Chance grinned. ""Sorry for interrupting you two, but I need more coffee."

Fen scurried to her feet and shoved by her brother. "You really are something else, Chance."

Chance stared at Prasad and winked. "I guess Kai was right."

"What do you mean?" Fen asked as she grabbed the coffee maker.

"Oh, nothing. How long will it be, Fen?"

"About five minutes, Chance. I'll bring it out when it's done."

Fen didn't look at Chance. Embarrassed, her face flushed bright red and she didn't want to answer any more of his questions. She wished he would just leave.

Chance finally headed for the door. "Cool, I'll tell the gang." He stopped and winked at Prasad one more time before exiting.

"Humans are funny," Prasad observed.

"Don't pay Chance any mind. He likes to stir things up."

"I'm going to check on Darrius. He needs to know what happened to Hilly. I'll see you later for your session. Are you excited to have your memories and powers restored?"

"I'm excited, but there's a little piece of me that is nervous about restoring Hilly's full powers. What if Stygian has managed to invade her body and remains hidden from us?"

Prasad lightly placed his hands on Fen's shoulders. "Everything will be fine. Please don't worry."

Fen hugged Prasad and buried her face against his chest. Startled, Prasad slowly raised his arms and hugged her back. He lowered his face into her hair, which smelled of flowers and herbs. Minutes passed. He then pushed her back and looked down into her eyes. "I'll be back, I promise." He swiftly turned and trotted up the stairs.

Fen watched him go. She held her hand up to her heart which galloped just like the first time she laid eyes on her late husband, Lance. She grinned and grabbed the coffee urn. Another lyric from "Annie's Song" came to her: "Come let me love you, come love me again."

Prasad found Darrius deep in meditation on the bed. Still nude, he sat cross-legged, eyes closed and hands draped over his knees. Enshrouding his body swirled a blue mist smelling of roses and gardenias, the remnants of the healing waters evaporating from his skin. Prasad sat down and waited for Darrius to finish.

A half-hour passed and the blue mist dissipated. Darrius slowly opened his eyes. They flashed a brilliant green with specks of gold. He turned to Prasad. "I feel better, old friend."

Prasad rose and inspected Darrius' side. All remnants of the wound were gone. Only smooth dark brown skin remained. "Excellent," Prasad said as he ran his finger the length of the rib. "A full recovery."

"I owe my life to you, Prasad," Darrius said as he slid off the bed and wrapped a white bathrobe around his body.

"I'm sure you would have done the same for me," Prasad replied.

"I don't possess your talents for alchemy," Darrius said as he strode into the closet. "You'll need to teach me one day." He returned with a dark gray suit, a white shirt and a lavender silk tie. Holding them against himself in the mirror, he nodded his approval.

# Chapter 14

# Revelations, Part 2

HILLY SIPPED HER COFFEE and watched the storm's fury through the dining room window. Flashes of lightning illuminated the ancient cedars swaying violently as they battled the gales and torrential rain. She sniffed the air, sweet and pungent. Despite being inside, the aromas of the thunderstorm teased her senses as though she was outside, wet and wild. She closed her eyes and breathed deeply, the storm excited her, energized her. She longed to be outside and be part of the chaos, hunting like a predator, killing like a monster.

The primal urges tugged at her brain. Adrenaline rushed through her veins and her pulse quickened. She glanced around the dining room narrowing her eyes on her brothers and sister like a tiger stalking her prey. She considered how easy it would be to kill all three.

She gasped. These thoughts were wrong, not the feelings of a sister toward her family. She immediately thought of Stygian. Had he left traces of evil on her soul? Despite what she had told her siblings, she did remember the attack. She was fully aware that the evil being had joined her as she slept. She remembered everything—her siblings holding her down as they tried to banish Stygian, and the incantation—ancient words from a distant land.

She felt unclean and violated. Yet, she was tantalized by the strength of Stygian's abilities, how he crept into her body and fused with her soul, embracing her in a hypnotic hug, gazing into her mind's eye. His presence was comforting, familiar and seductive. He whispered ancient words and she had swooned. Yet, she had fought for control, choosing, instead, to feign submission so she could know him and discover his weaknesses.

"Fen was wrong," she whispered to herself. "The incantation was not Stygian's, it was mine. Had they left me alone, I would have overpowered him."

She took another sip and smiled. "I know how to catch him now."

Darrius appeared in the doorway. "Good morning, everyone."

Kai held his breath and gawked, mouth agape, at Darrius. The Cererian's beautiful white teeth gleamed in a flawless mocha face accentuated by dazzling green eyes. The tailored gray suit and crisp white shirt hugged his trim, firm body. And, that tie, that luscious lavender tie. "Well, hello, handsome."

"Kai, you're married!" Fen scolded as she rose to greet Darrius. "What would your husband say?"

"He would say the same thing. We both appreciate fine art when we see it." Kai winked at Darrius.

Darrius blushed. "Sounds like everybody is relaxed and ready to start the day. Stygian's attack on Hilly yesterday is a reminder that our time grows short and we need to move quickly with our plans to restore Fen's and Hilly's memories."

Preoccupied with her thoughts, Hilly stared at Darrius. She envisioned slicing his throat open with the butter knife. She jerked and blinked. A shiver crept up her spine as she realized Stygian had just entered her body for mere seconds. The bastard was devious. She needed to keep her wits about her, she must stay strong. She bit her lower lip and a thin line of blood trickled down her chin.

"Hilly, you're bleeding," Fen exclaimed as she rushed to her side with a napkin, and dabbed her lip. "What happened?"

"Damn, I hate when I bite myself." Hilly assured Fen she was fine and stood to join the others. She quickly dismissed Stygian's brief visit and turned her attention to the morning's activities. "I'm looking forward to today, Darrius. I hope Dad's revelations shed light on what's happening to me...to us." Hilly's slip up caught Darrius' attention. He peered intently at her as she glared back with slitted eyes. Darrius' brilliant green eyes pulsed and shimmered. A minute passed and no words were spoken as the two friends eyed each other.

Hilly broke the awkward silence. "My god, Kai is right, you *are* handsome." Hilly playfully adjusted the knot in Darrius' tie and then whirled and left the dining room. Fen followed her.

Chance and Kai refilled their coffee mugs. Chance couldn't resist showing off his levitation power by propelling his cup midair ahead of him, a big smirk on his face.

"Show off!" Kai yelled as he grabbed the mug and dashed to the study dripping coffee all over the floor.

"Asshole!" Chance shouted, running after him.

Darrius watched the family leave. Something troubled him. There was something unusual about Hilly, a foreign connection, an ancient energy lurking beneath the surface which reminded him of Ceres and...of Stygian. Closing his eyes, he mentally alerted Prasad. *Be on high alert, nothing is as it seems. Trust only your intuition, your eyes will betray you.*

Fen and Hilly settled into comfortable chairs closest to the screen. They wanted the best seats when Dad spoke to them. They squirmed like excitable young girls awaiting Santa Claus on Christmas morning. Passing the bar, Chance gazed into his half-empty coffee mug and then to the Woodford Reserve bottle.

"Take it easy today," Hilly urged. "We need you at one-hundred percent if Stygian returns."

"I'm always at my best with a little extra bravado in my cup," Chance said as he poured a shot into his coffee and sat down.

Kai gently tapped his head to disrupt the cacophony of voices drifting into his mind. His telepathic powers had not fully returned and he was struggling to control the noisy interference.

Darrius sat tall in the red leather chair, his fingers laced and resting on the desk, appearing much like a contemplative detective facing suspects of a crime. But no wrong had been committed. He surveyed the room, locking eyes with each Kemp, especially Hilly, before he finally announced. "Let's begin." The projector clicked as the reels pulled the footage through the machine. Ted flickered on the screen.

He looked down at his papers, shuffled them, then looked up. "My beautiful, quiet Fenna. My studious child. You showed an early interest in advanced studies, so I encouraged you to read college textbooks and resource books. You demonstrated a fascination for alchemy, and I even caught you staring at my ancient Egyptian texts, tracing the hieroglyphics with your finger. You especially loved reading *Gray's Anatomy*. You were fascinated by the human body and medical terms. We spent hours together, I would point at medical illustrations and you would rattle off the names, definitions, and relationships to other parts of the body."

Fen's eyes misted. She recalled the many times she and her father would sit and read. Even at only nine years old, her father chose advanced books, volumes that spoke of mathematics, science, and ancient poetry. She sat on his lap scanning the text as Ted's finger underscored each line. She would ask, "What does that mean, daddy?" and Ted would patiently explain while Fen nodded in amazement. They spent hours curled up together. The alone time with her father was special and so missed.

Ted continued, "You were very keen on how the cells healed, even after vicious wounds or viral attacks. I knew in my heart you would become either a doctor or a researcher because of your intense interest in everything medical."

"Hey, Fen, that's what you ended up doing, right?" Hilly asked.

"Yes." After finishing college, she joined a laboratory as a medical researcher with a specialty in studying pandemic viruses. Her work focused on the unique qualities of each virus—how it attacked the body and how the body reacted. She was responsible for successfully developing vaccines for some of the world's deadliest viruses.

"Your innate healing ability will surface as you regain your memories and powers. Do you recall the spring ice storm that caught the Northeast by surprise? You found a bird frozen dead on the ground. You gently lifted its feathered body, instinctively cupped your hands around it and gently blew while humming a mantra. A soft white light enveloped your hands. After a few minutes, you opened your fingers, and the little bird chirped and darted into the trees."

Eyes wide with disbelief, Fen stared at her hands. She didn't recall the moment at all.

"You're lucky the little bird didn't leave a little poopy prize in your hand," Chance quipped.

"Shut up, Chance," Fen barked as she turned back to her father who continued speaking. She wanted to hear more, and to find out everything about who she is. She didn't need a pestering brother to interfere.

"We were not surprised at your ability. You come from a long line of healers. You were born in Lovell, Wyoming near the Bighorn Medicine Wheel, a sacred Native American site. The medicine wheel has been used for generations for health and healing. It embodies the Four Directions, as well as Father Sky, Mother Earth, and Spirit Tree—all of which symbolize dimensions of health and the cycles of life. One day, you will return to this sacred site as you embark on your quest to find your family artifact that will contribute to the restoration of world peace.

"Look at the card Prasad left in your room. Follow along as I read:

*Guardian of peace, a warrior stands.*
*The Big Wheel turns again.*
*Healing, atonement, and visions, the quest begins.*
*The time is nigh. The battle approaches.*
*Gather the troops and reclaim the forgotten throne.*

"Your first name is Dutch for peace and, of course, you know your last name means warrior. Leaders of your tribe have always been the peacemakers in the global community. While all the tribes lived in harmony, petty squabbles eventually rose. It was the responsibility of your people to maintain the agreed-upon rules. In essence, they were the judges who determined the outcome of disagreements. Known for their impeccable integrity, honor, and negotiating ability, members of your tribe were held in high esteem.

"The next two lines on the card reference where you were born and your quest. You'll follow the paths of Native Americans and embrace the ancient ways, the shamanistic way.

"Your family shared the power of water. Members could control any water including rain, waterfalls, rivers, oceans and even the polar ice caps. They also communicated with the creatures that lived in these waters. You even have the unique ability to breathe underwater."

Fen's heart raced and her face reddened. She was terrified of water unless she could easily stand like she could in the Apollo Fountain. The thought of immersing her head underwater was unnerving.

Ted continued, "When you were four years old, you went outside to explore for wild creatures. It was a beautiful summer day. Your mother sat on the patio watching you dash among the rhododendron in search of lizards and frogs. A bright light flashed in the sky temporarily blinding your mother. It lasted only two seconds, but when she turned back, you were gone. She frantically called your name but you didn't answer. Convinced something horrible had happened, she ran to get help. As she passed the pool, she noticed bubbles roiling on the surface. There, at the bottom of the pool, in the deep end, sat you with three large frogs. You frolicked with them as they leapt just out of your reach. Each time you giggled, bubbles escaped to the water's surface. She soon realized your amazing gift to breathe underwater. Freda was so upset with you, Fen, but she later admitted giggling at your underwater ballet."

Fen shook her head in disbelief. She didn't recall that moment with her mother.

Ted quickly added, "And, like Kai, you can read minds. What a team you two will make."

"Wait a minute," Hilly interrupted, signaling Darrius to stop the movie. "Dad said a bright light flashed in the sky. He didn't explain anything about its origin nor did it appear he or Mom were concerned about it. Why was that?"

"Yeah," Chance agreed. "If it was a nice summer day, it couldn't have been lightning."

Darrius was impressed by their curiosity. "Your parents were accustomed to arrivals and departures via the portals: the one located on the patio that led to Ceres, and the global gateway located in Apollo's Fountain. Portal activity is signaled by flashes of bright light. I was not present that day, but considering Freda was not frightened by the light, I would assume someone had just dropped in, so to speak." Darrius grinned, amused at his joke.

"That's it! I'm no longer surprised by anything I hear anymore." Kai leapt from his chair and poured himself a drink. Chance saw the opportunity and freshened his mug as well. Kai gulped a shot and continued, "Fen swims with the fish, I fly with the birds and Chance runs with the animals. I can't wait to see what Hilly can do. You really can't make this shit up."

Everyone burst out laughing. Hilly snorted. "I know what I am. I'm related to insects and can irritate the shit out of you." She threw a cushion at Kai and hit him in the forehead.

"Ow! So that's how you're going to play, eh?" Kai jumped up and playfully batted at Hilly.

Chance laughed so hard, he grabbed his belly, fearful he would soon burst.

Undetected, Fen slipped out the study door.

Overwhelmed and near panic, Fen hurried into the foyer. Scenes invaded her brain: The Medicine Wheel, breathing underwater with frogs, the rhythmic beat of Native American drums, a warm glow from her hands, frozen birds coming to life. *Too much...this is too much for me to comprehend. I want my peaceful life back! I want Lance back!*

Fen squeezed her hands hard against her temples, trying to push the images from her mind. Or, an attempt to contain her sanity. She wandered the foyer aimlessly, panting, trying to regain control and soon found herself at the mantel. The cold, unlit fireplace gawked at her with an unwelcome sneer.

She looked up at the ancient painting: the ancestor, clad in armor, standing bravely on the beach. The helmeted warrior stared back. A gust of wind howled and savagely knocked against the front door snatching Fen's attention. When she turned back to the painting, something had changed. She narrowed her eyes and studied the picture. The warrior still stood defiant in the surf, but the helmet's visor had lifted. *Wait, that wasn't there before.* Emerald-green eyes stared back at Fen.

"What's wrong, Fenster?"

Fen jumped. "Jeez, Hilly, warn a body that you're sneaking up on them." Fen nervously glanced back at the painting. "Nothing's wrong."

"Yeah, right," Hilly mocked. She pulled Fen closer and peered into her eyes. "Look at me, Fenny."

Fen shoved her away. "Leave me alone. I mean it. I want to be left alone. Weird things are going on."

"You're scared!"

"No, I'm not!" Fen bellowed as she glared at Hilly. Fen looked away. She felt confused. Did the painting change? No, it couldn't have. It was created hundreds of years ago. It was just a trick of the lightning. There's too much going on and she's imagining things.

"Fen, it's okay if you're scared."

Deep down, Fen knew Hilly was right. Fen was scared. Petrified was more accurate. There were so many changes happening all at once. She couldn't make sense of everything. She was secure in the logic of science: black-and-white proven facts and predictable outcomes. Magical people, mumbo jumbo and quests...these were outside her realm of understanding. Yet, Dad just informed her she comes from a lineage steeped in mystical and shamanistic ways. She just needed some time. Time to process all this information.

"Just give me some time, Hilly. I'm having a hard time adjusting."

"We don't have time for you to analyze everything right now, Fen." Hilly gently grabbed Fen by the arm and began leading her back to the study. "We need to hear the rest of the story. I'll pour you some wine and you can relax while Dad reveals I'm the queen of the dinosaurs."

"What?" Fen stopped and looked at Hilly, half believing what she said.

"Gotcha! Come on Fenster, let's get this done, then we'll eat and get reacquainted with our *new* selves. Whatcha say?"

The study door creaked open, and Darrius stepped through. "Is everything okay? We're ready to start again."

"Everything is peachy," Hilly said as she stepped toward the door, her hand still on Fen's arm. Like a stubborn dog, Fen wouldn't budge. Hilly tugged gently. "Come on Fenny, I'm with you and won't let anything happen to you."

Chance barged through the study door. "Come on, girls! We got things to do and places to see! I've poured you some big glasses of wine." He winked at Fen and Hilly.

Fen grinned at her big brother. Chance could always chase away her demons. "Okay, I'll come. But I don't want to hear that Hilly is actually the queen of the dinosaurs."

Darrius and Chance exchanged puzzled looks as the girls trotted into the study. Hilly passed them, walking stiff-legged, her fingers curled into claws like a T-Rex. "Grrrrr!"

Kai swirled his drink as Hilly and Fen strolled by. "Glad you could join us ladies. Chance and I need more fodder for our jokes."

Hilly smacked Kai across the back of his head. "Go ahead brother. You lob them, and I'll throw them back. But remember, I throw harder than you do.'" She winked at Kai and sat.

Darrius looked around the room. "It appears that we're ready to resume." He flipped the switch on the projector, and Ted began talking.

"Form a strong alliance with your siblings, Fen. You'll be instrumental in keeping the balance and peace within the family, and within the tribes. The Egyptian book on alchemy will serve you well. It lies in the vault with the family records. Once Kai has produced the key, you will have access to many amazing healing secrets that only you will understand."

Ted took a long drink of water and gazed out the window. He moved a new folder on top of the desk and looked up at the camera. Weariness crept into his eyes. He forced a smile to his lips and began, "Hilliard Kemp. Where do I start?"

Hilly straightened in her chair, eyes wide with attention.

"You joined our family at the tender age of one. An age when babies are laughing, learning to talk, and creeping along the floor on new adventures. While you later learned to laugh and talk, you spent the first few months in our home healing and recovering."

Hilly's face turned white as she stared first at Darrius and then at her siblings.

Gently, Ted continued, "My precious Hilly. Stygian and the Yfel Brethren viciously murdered your family. And, you did not escape unscathed. Stygian plunged his long claws into your arms, raised you over his head, and was poised to consume your life essence when Prasad intervened." Hilly absently stroked the faint row of scars on her left arm. Mom had told her she had fallen into a hedgerow of holly bushes when she was a toddler.

"Prasad can create doppelgangers, duplicates of a living person. He created a duplicate of you and shape-shifted into the persona of one of Stygian's trusted brothers. In this form, he confronted Stygian and convinced him that you were a doppelganger. Outraged that he was tricked, he threw you against a wall and snatched the duplicate baby from Prasad. There wasn't much time before the truth would be known, so Prasad grabbed your broken body and slipped into another dimension before Stygian realized what had happened."

Expecting questions, Darrius stopped the film.

Prasad suddenly stepped from the shadows of the far wall. "Excuse my intrusion." Everyone jumped at his sudden appearance. Kai spilled his drink and Fen instinctively grabbed Hilly's arm.

"Holy cow, Prasad," Chance barked as he wiped Kai's drink off his pants. "You've got to warn people when you sneak into a room."

"My apologies. Darrius suggested that I be present for this moment in case there were inquiries about what happened." He turned to Hilly. "Miss Hilly, I, and my brothers, had hoped to save your entire family but..." Prasad's words trailed off as he wiped away a tear remembering the massacre.

Hilly rose, still stroking the dotted scars on her arm. She stood speechless, looking first to Prasad and then to Darrius. Finally, she moved to Prasad and enveloped him with a bear hug.

"Thank you, my friend. Thank you so much." Hilly said. Prasad gripped her tight, and returned the embrace.

Darrius added, "Prasad found safe passage back to The Nine Muses. He feared you would perish in his arms. Not only were you bleeding profusely, but you had a concussion, and many fractured bones. You spent your first two days swaddled in gauze moistened by the healing potions Prasad applied constantly. While I focused on healing your concussion, Prasad worked on your fragile body, carefully aligning your bones. Despite your agony, you would smile at us, and touch us reassuringly."

The room grew somber. While everyone had unusual beginnings at The Nine Muses, Hilly's arrival was extraordinarily shocking. Everyone reeled from this revelation.

"Way to kill the mood, Prasad." But Chance's joke fell flat, and the room remained silent except for occasional sniffing.

Kai touched Hilly's hand, smiled and mentally reached out to her. *I love you and won't let anything hurt you again.*

Hilly mouthed, "Message received."

Darrius continued, "Despite your beginning, you have blossomed into an incredible individual. You grew strong in the arms of your loving family. They hoped that any lingering memories, if any, would soon fade along with your scars." Darrius' demeanor turned serious. "But they, along with me and Prasad, could never have known the significance of your birth and your arrival here at The Nine Muses."

Prasad held up his hand and stopped Darrius. "Not now, brother, not until the will reading is complete."

Darrius and Prasad exchanged penetrating gazes, mentally discussing their next steps. Kai attempted to sneak into their mindful conversation, but their power was much stronger than his. Darrius finally spoke, "You're right, Prasad. One step at a time." Darrius turned to the Kemps and smiled warmly.

Hilly pushed Darrius, "What were you going to say?"

Prasad interrupted, "The matter is important, but there is a time and a place. You must have the completion of your history before you will understand." Prasad gently guided Hilly to her seat and then turned to the others. "The next few hours are very important. Please remember why you are here. You must learn who you are and support each other." Prasad and Darrius exchanged glances once again.

Darrius spoke, "Thank you, dear friend. We will continue with Hilly's history, and then break for lunch. Do we have any food left in the house?"

"I managed to scrounge up a few items."

"Thank goodness, I'm starving," Chance whined as he dramatically grabbed his throat and feigned passing out.

Darrius cleared his throat. "Is everybody ready?" Hilly straightened in her chair, grabbed Fen's hand and nodded for Darrius to continue.

The screen flickered to life.

Eyes tearing, Ted continued, "If it hadn't been for Darrius and Prasad, we would have lost you. They stayed with you for two days, healing your battered body. You will discover, if you haven't already, that you feel a closeness to both of them. They gave you the gift of life and you retain elements of their precious gifts. Despite your injuries, I never heard you cry. You were the ultimate warrior even as a baby.

"The poem on your card echoes that description:

> *Guardian of battle, a warrior stands.*
> *Denali rises, ancient and sacred.*
> *The beast rips through the vortex.*
> *The time is nigh. The battle approaches.*
> *Gather the troops and reclaim the forgotten throne.*

"Your parents named you Hilliard. An appropriate name since it means "guardian of battle" in German. "Hilliard" evokes a vision of a strong woman with long braids, a Viking hat and a metal shield. But, as you grew up, your blonde wispy hair turned to dark brown and you preferred gelled spikes to long locks. We shortened your name to Hilly, which resonated better with your perky personality.

"Your family provided the gift of fire to the tribe. Known informally as firewalkers, your family members could open and close portals, manipulate the sun, fire and other light sources, and move between dimensions." Ted grew serious. "Families with your gift were instrumental in shepherding all the tribes to locations around the globe to escape Stygian and his soldiers. Firewalkers saved thousands from certain death."

Hilly thought back to her childhood memory of dancing on the patio by the fire pit, singing an unfamiliar melody and watching light emanate from her hands. Why had she remembered when Darrius and Prasad erased everybody's memory? She kept that thought to herself as she continued to listen.

"You were born in Anchorage, in the shadow of Mt. Denali, Athabascan for The High One. You may know the mountain as Mount McKinley, the highest peak in North America. The mountain possesses powerful supernatural energies and is home to many spirits. It lies on the energetic grid crisscrossing the globe and is a strong vortex linked to Mount Shasta, Kai's birthplace. One day, you will return home to Denali and retrace the steps of the ancients who roamed that land before you. Your presence in that land will begin a chain reaction or extraordinary events.

"All of you were born in places of mystical and magical properties, locations of vortices and portals. Your birth families arranged this by design, using the earth's energy highway to evade Stygian. When Prasad and Darrius clouded your memories, they implanted the new locations to where you would each relocate. These, too, are part of the energy system so that you would continue to stay within that protective boundary of positive energy, and not be detected.

"Now, for the meaning of the line *'The beast rips through the vortex.'* Stygian intends to destroy you all and will eventually penetrate the magical walls Darrius and Prasad erected to keep him out. It is only a matter of time before he accomplishes this because you all share one link...Hilly. Hilly is the key."

Ted cleared his throat. "Hilly, you put the others at risk because Stygian will find them through you. Like a bloodhound on the scent of a wounded rabbit, he will sniff you out because..." Ted paused and sipped his water. Hilly scooted to the edge of her seat as the tension rose in the room. "Because you share his DNA. You are a descendant of Stygian."

A loud gasp filled the room. Hilly sank back into her chair, and gawked wide-eyed at her siblings. No one said a word but Hilly sensed their judgement. Stygian would find them because of her. Fen patted her hand and recoiled. Hilly's skin was like ice.

Ted continued, "Don't let this news make you fearful or disgusted with your heritage. You are who you are and you cannot change that. You are a hybrid human who has many of the Cererian abilities exhibited by Stygian,

Prasad and Darrius. Because of these powers, we could not erase all of your memories.

"If he hasn't already tried, Stygian will use this familial connection to reach out to you and attempt to enter your mind. Be wary, my child, for his abilities are a hundred times more powerful than yours or Darrius' and Prasad's. Stygian learned, quite by accident, that the supernatural gifts of deceased magicians can easily transfer to him. He embarked on his blood lust with the help of the Yfel Brethren. With each murder, he consumes the individual's powers and grows stronger. His thirst for ultimate control has driven him to hunt you, his descendent. That's why it will take all four of you to win the battle. I wish there was a different way to accomplish this, I really do.

"The time is nigh, my child, to gather your siblings and draft a battle plan. Stygian will pounce at any time. Darrius and Prasad will now prepare you for what you must do next."

Ted paused and surveyed the room as if he could actually see his children. "My precious children, once your powers are restored, you will be able to face Stygian. Do not hesitate to act, for if you do, all of you may perish. Remember, you are the chosen ones. The Cererian Prophecy has identified the four of you as the magicians who will restore peace to the world.

"I love you all and hope to see you one day." Ted blew a kiss toward the screen and the film abruptly stopped.

No one dared to speak.

"Well, fuck me!" Chance shattered the quiet. "What the hell are we supposed to do with that shit? How do we know Hilly is not luring Stygian here at this moment? He's been able to slip in and out like a thief. She hasn't controlled it at all!"

"Fuck you, Chance!" Hilly yelled as she stood in front of him, and glared up into his face. "I had Stygian right in my hands last time, but *you* didn't allow me to beat him. That was *my* incantation, not his. I was close to beating him at his own game, but *you* had to interfere!"

Fen jumped between Hilly and Chance, separating them at arm's length. "Stop it you two. We're getting too emotional. We need to take a breather."

Kai joined Fen and reassured Hilly and Chance, "Look guys, like it or not, we have to work together now. We *are* a family first and foremost."

After many tense moments, Chance blurted, "Shit, I didn't mean anything, Hilly. You know I have a big mouth."

Hilly's face softened "Yeah, and you're always sticking your big fat foot in it." They hugged. But, deep down, distrust festered.

"I hate to interrupt," Darrius said. "But Prasad and I have urgent work to do with Fen and Hilly. We need to restore your memories while Kai and Chance eat."

Prasad entered the room. "Cold cuts are now available in the dining room."

"Food. Finally!" Chance exclaimed. He dashed out of the study, nearly knocking Prasad into the wall.

"Sorry, Prasad," Kai apologized. "You know how Chance gets around food. His stomach, not his brain, is in complete control. I think we could vanquish Stygian if he was actually a medium-rare steak. Chance would consume him in five seconds."

Kai looked at Darrius and saluted. "I leave Hilly and Fen in your capable hands, sir."

"Why, thank you, Keeper of the Keys," Darrius replied. "Please make sure we're not disturbed until we have restored Hilly and Fen's memories. And, remind Chance about that as well."

Kai nodded and left the study shouting, "Chance! Leave some food for me!"

Darrius turned to Fen and Hilly. "Please take a seat. Prasad and I will now fully restore your powers and memories. Prasad will work with Fen. Hilly, I will work with you. Please be quiet and patient. This process will take about thirty minutes."

Hilly balked. "Darrius, is there any chance that Stygian will try to enter my mind while you're doing this?"

"Not while I'm with you. I guarantee it," Darrius reassured. "Now, both of you, begin breathing deeply and relax."

Darrius sat opposite Hilly and peered into her eyes. Prasad did the same with Fen. In unison, Prasad and Darrius hummed a mantra in low, whispers that quickened into a buzz as if a multitude of busy bees had flown into the study. Static energy permeated the room, electrical charges skipping off Hilly and Fen causing the hair on their arms to rise in protest. Soon a pulsing green beam penetrated their eyes.

The process had began.

Lightning flashed across the blackened sky. Even though it was one o'clock in the afternoon, the ferocious storm obliterated the sun, bathing The Nine Muses and the surrounding area in a deep murkiness. Another stab of lightning thundered its arrival. The flickering light bounced off the white marble of Apollo's Fountain, and illuminated a lone figure. A tall, blond man with pale features stared intently at The Nine Muses. His green eyes sparkled like gemstones in the torrential downpour. "Hilly," he whispered.

# Chapter 15

---

# A Meeting Between Brothers

BY THE TIME KAI reached the dining room, Chance had devoured an entire sandwich and heaped meat for a second. "Good grief, Chance, ease up and leave some food for all of us," Kai scolded.

Chance rolled his eyes and squirted mustard with a loud *FRAPP*. "What do you think about Hilly's history?"

"An unexpected revelation."

Chance leaned closer to Kai and whispered, "I know she's our sister, but I can't shake the feeling that Stygian can use her like a revolving door. I don't know if I can ever completely trust her."

Kai glanced around the room. "Why are you whispering? Nobody's around. Let's not be so judgmental. When she receives all her abilities and memories, we might discover that she possesses skills to prevent him from entering her mind."

Chance shrugged. "I don't know, we'll just have to see. I'm keeping a close eye on her. As the big brother, it's my responsibility to know everything that is going on."

Kai punched Chance in the shoulder. "Well, as the second-in-command, it's my job to keep an eye on you so you don't get into any trouble. And, to make sure you don't eat every bit of food left in the house." Kai snatched the tray of cold cuts, and darted for the kitchen. "I'll make sure these are safe in the refrigerator for the time being."

"Kai, bring my food back." Chance protested, chunks of bread flying from his mouth.

Hilly tumbled in a free fall, drifting on currents of air. There was no fear, just an immense calm as she glided, arms outstretched to either side. Aware that she remained in the study with Darrius, she willingly sank into a slow-moving current of warm water.

Flashes of pleasant images zoomed by: her childhood, her husband, visions of a home in another world. The waters darkened and the current quickened as nightmarish scenes materialized: Mr. Spatz and Stygian, swirling portals, and the screams of dying people.

Darrius floated above her and soothed her with ancient words. He whispered secrets in a foreign tongue, yet, Hilly understood and relaxed. She drifted farther down the stream, away from the familiar, still waters and directly into the raging rapids—roiling water roaring its disapproval of the intruder. She tumbled over boulders and smashed against the gravel bottom before clawing her way to the surface in a panic. She bobbed violently in the churning waters and clutched at passing branches as the swift current propelled her toward the open sea.

A shriek ripped the air and she trembled. A familiar sound, she knew the evil beast had returned and hunted for her. She glanced into the sky which swirled black like the waters that clutched her. The oily-black beast hovered overhead, the downdrafts of its immense wings buffeting her, pushing her underwater, drowning her. She lashed out, grabbing onto anything to hold her afloat, one last attempt to fight the creature and to save herself. The blackness shrieked again.

"Hilly! Hilly, wake up!" Darrius sat opposite her and held her hands which glowed red hot. Hilly's eyes fluttered open, and she sputtered river water out of her mouth. Struggling to breathe, she gulped in the fresh air and stared wide-eyed at Darrius.

"You're safe. You're in control. You're home." Darrius repeated the soothing words again and again until Hilly's breathing calmed, and the panic subsided.

"Where am I?"

"You're in the study of The Nine Muses." Darrius dampened a towel with cool water and wrapped it around her burning hands. The soft hiss surprised Hilly and she stared, dumbfounded, at the rising steam.

"No, I was somewhere else, some other world and the dragon was forcing me underwater." Darrius offered a cool glass of water, and Hilly sipped it while glancing around the room, ensuring she was no longer near the river or the creature. The storm raged outside, casting dark shadows throughout the study. "Was it real?"

Darrius considered her question and carefully responded. "The images were very real." He grabbed her hands; they were cool to the touch. "You've been having visions of the beast for some time, haven't you?"

"Yes. The nightmares started six months ago, but now they're almost daily and are much more violent."

"What do the images tell you?"

"I've never been afraid of dragons. I believe that they're friendly elemental beings. They represent strength and protection. I'm confused why this creature would attack me in my dreams. But I've noticed that the beast morphs with each visit, becoming something new and more terrifying every time I have the dream."

"Enough for now. Allow your mind to settle and accept all that has been given to you. Don't press for answers, allow them to come to you."

"The dragon is Stygian, isn't it?"

"Perhaps, or maybe it's an image of a future event. You mentioned that the dragon symbolizes strength and protection, but for whom? The dreamer or for the nightmare?"

Hilly was convinced Darrius was withholding something from her. Exhausted, she chose not to press the issue. She needed to rest and think.

"Yes, perhaps that's what it is. I'll take some time to dwell on it," she said as she stood up. Darrius took her elbow and guided her to join the others who awaited them in the dining room.

Fen and Prasad had finished their session earlier. Disoriented and woozy, Fen asked to leave. Prasad led her to the comfortable chair in the foyer. He knelt beside her, worried.

"You've been through a lot. This must be overwhelming for you," he said.

Fen gently touched his cheek. "I'm glad you were my guide on this journey. I feel so incredibly powerful and yet so weak, like a day-old kitten."

Prasad flushed. These emotions were foreign to him, they were both confusing and yet so welcoming. "You will have a slight headache for a while. Would you like me to remove that pain?" he asked, moving his fingers up to her temples.

Fen nodded and closed her eyes, allowing Prasad to stroke her forehead. His fingers barely skimmed the surface as they followed the strands of hair down to each ear and then back up again. He hummed a low and soothing melody. Fen swayed in time with Prasad's voice, soft notes caressing her heart.

"Hello you two," Darrius interrupted as he led Hilly out of the study.

Fen jerked and Prasad withdrew his hand. "I was removing Fen's headache. Is that better, Miss Fen?"

"Yes, yes...that's much better." She jumped up and joined Hilly. "How are you doing?"

"I'm a little confused," Hilly replied.

"Let's go into the dining room," Darrius interjected. "I hope Chance and Kai left some food for you two." Wrapping his arm around Hilly, he guided her forward while glancing back at Prasad. He flashed a quick smile at his friend.

Prasad feigned puzzlement.

"May I show you the way?" Prasad asked Fen as he offered the crook of his arm, which she gladly accepted.

When they entered, Chance snored loudly on the sofa and Kai sat cross-legged on the floor in deep meditation, mouthing a mantra.

"Hello!" Darrius called out. Chance snorted and Kai fell over. "I Didn't mean to startle you but Hilly and Fen are done with their session and are hungry. I hope you left something for them to eat." Kai sprang to his feet.

"Well, of course, we did!" he said and bounded into the kitchen to retrieve the cold cuts.

Chance sat up and grudgingly made space for Hilly who plunked down beside him and leaned into his shoulder. "Are you okay, sis?"

Eyes closed, she nodded. "Uh, huh. I'm just very tired."

Chance encircled Hilly with his left arm and invited Fen to snuggle under his right arm, which she willingly accepted. He felt like a big brother again as he hugged his sisters to his body, a protective shield against the evil in the world. Soon, both girls drifted to sleep.

Kai entered carrying the tray of food. "Good grief, I leave for a few minutes, and all of sudden, we have a family moment and I'm not invited?"

Chance grinned, reveling in his brother's jealousy. "I've still got room on my lap, Kai. You can scrunch up here and put your head on my chest."

Kai laughed out loud. The girls stirred but didn't wake up.

A psychic disturbance compelled Prasad to dash to the window. Inaudible alarms rang within his head. He frantically searched the blackness, looking for the entity who triggered the protection force field. He turned to Darrius and whispered in his ear.

Darrius closed his eyes for a moment, mentally searching, probing outside. Unhappy with his findings, he addressed Chance and Kai. "Please excuse us, but Prasad and I need to take care of an important matter. Do not leave this room under any circumstances."

Darrius and Prasad abruptly left and closed the door. Standing in the foyer, he addressed Prasad, "Stygian is near, our brother grows bolder."

"Yes, I can sense him trying to break through our protection field. What do you plan to do?"

"I'm going to call Stygian out of his cowardly shadows. It's time we had a meeting."

"No, brother. He's becoming more powerful. You've seen, and felt, what he can do."

"Exactly, and that's why we must meet. We were once friends, close friends. If I can reach that side of him, perhaps we can—"

"He's already here!" Prasad cut him off.

The front door flew open propelled by unseen, violent forces. Wind-driven rain swirled throughout the foyer; and the lights flickered in response to the lightning stabbing the grounds. In the dim light, a young blond man filled the entryway. He cocked his head and smiled—a wicked grin somewhere between insanity and murderous intent.

"Hello brothers." Stygian glared from the threshold as Darrius and Prasad ran forward, arms outstretched casting protection spells.

Stygian laughed, a guttural sound starting low in his belly then rising high into a screeching cackle. He pushed his pale, bony finger through the invisible protection shield barring his entry. Sparks flew and the magical barrier rippled around his finger as though he had penetrated a thick pool of viscous fluid. He quickly drew it back, the skin sizzling and sloughing off. "That's an interesting spell."

"What do you want Stygian?" Darrius demanded. "You won't penetrate this fortress. It's been sealed by our benevolent Cererian brothers."

Stygian smiled, brilliant white teeth in a flawless translucent face, thin blue veins crisscrossing his alabaster skin. Wisps of blond hair blew across his icy green eyes. "I just want to chat, Darrius. I miss our late-night debates."

"Don't trust him," Prasad warned, his hands outstretched, prepared to fight.

Enraged, Stygian's eyes turned oily-black, and he glared at Prasad. "I'll deal with you in due time, Prasad. But right now, I'm here for Darrius. I want to discuss our options. After all, we were friends at one time."

Prasad mentally implored Darrius to walk away. *Brother, don't trust him. You've seen how he's stolen into Hilly's mind. You witnessed how strong he's become during your battle with him. He intends only to inflict harm.*

*Yes, but he's also vain. I may trick him into divulging his plans.* Darrius turned to Stygian. "Okay, let's talk. I'm curious what you have to say."

"Alone," Stygian hissed, sneering at Prasad. "What I have to say is only for you."

Darrius sensed Prasad's anger and held up his hand.

"Be still, my friend. No harm will come of me. Please stay in the dining room until we're finished."

Stygian smirked. "Yes, leave us. Tell Hilly I'll see her soon."

Furious, Prasad rushed Stygian, but Darrius grabbed him in a tight embrace. He struggled to be free. "Let me go, Darrius, let me deal with this monster!"

Darrius leaned close and whispered, "Don't show emotion. Enter my thoughts and monitor my conversation. You'll be with me every step of the way." Prasad relaxed in Darrius' arms and nodded. His friend was right, the best strategy was to remain calm and not be provoked. Without another word, Prasad left.

Stygian watched him exit and then turned to Darrius. "What happened between us Darrius? We always had the best times together."

"You began killing people."

"You've killed before."

"To protect myself. Not for sport, and not to harvest a person's energy."

"Try it. The feeling is incredible...like a rush of energy after consuming Cererian-spiced droge. It's addictive. Especially when you find and kill the more powerful ones."

"Stop, Stygian. What do you want?"

"You know I will eventually kill them all, don't you? You and Prasad won't stop it."

"They will vanquish you. The Prophecy has foretold their victory."

Stygian chuckled. "Do you still believe in those Prophecy fairy tales? Look inside, Darrius. You know I speak the truth. My powers are far superior to the insignificant abilities of your four magicians. You're delaying the inevitable. They will die miserably, and you only prolong their suffering." Stygian's features softened and he appeared childlike, vulnerable, almost believable. "Let me have them now and I will dispatch them swiftly and with no pain."

Darrius shook his head. "No, brother. This I will never allow."

Stygian growled. "I already own Hilly. We are bound by blood, and I've stolen into her soul. I come and go whenever I please. I have the power to turn her against her siblings. They can die by her hands, or they can perish by mine. Either way, their deaths will be your responsibility if you don't turn them over to me now!"

Expressionless, Darrius responded, "I remember the early days, when we were young men on Ceres, when we eagerly volunteered for the mission that led us to Earth. We couldn't have had a better assignment: to observe a population of beings, some with abilities similar to our own. The tribes welcomed us in friendship and invited us to lodge with them. Over time, many became close friends of mine, just like you used to be. There was a woman who caught your eye. What was her name?"

"Shut up!"

Stygian's sudden rage delighted Darrius, and he pressed on. "She was such a talented soul, so beautiful. And, what a warrior. I believe she bested you on many occasions during swordplay, did she not?"

"I warn you...shut up." Stygian glared at Darrius with vacant, black eyes.

"Ah, yes, I remember. Her name was Elizabeth. But you called her Liz."

Enraged, Stygian threw himself against the protection field. Blue light arced from the tips of his fingers as he pushed them into the membrane, trying hard to reach Darrius. Sparks cascaded to the floor as the translucent energy barrier bent inward. Darrius instinctively raised his hands in defense, and stepped backward. The protection spell was too powerful and soon shoved Stygian's hands back through the opening, across the threshold. With a loud *WHOOSH* the force field closed and propelled Stygian ten feet through the air until he thumped against Fen's car pushing a sizable dent into the driver's side.

Stygian slumped under the overhang, dazed, his hands glowed red hot, flesh dripping from his fingers like a melting candle. Darrius neared the threshold and looked at his brother with pity. "You were once my friend, my confidant, but those bonds are now broken and discarded. There's no turning back—you must be destroyed."

Darrius winked.

The ridiculous gesture further incensed Stygian and he howled into the storm, the sound of a tortured, enraged beast. He turned and fled into the night, a wounded creature scurrying away to lick his wounds, rest, and plan his return to kill.

Darrius searched the blackness. A calm descended despite the pelting rain. Satisfied Stygian had left The Nine Muses, he stepped backward into the foyer and closed the door. He turned to face Prasad who rushed from the dining room. "You heard and felt everything?"

"Yes. His power is immense."

"I fear that he was only testing the strength of the barrier, probing for its secrets, looking for weaknesses. The trickster will be back, and it will be soon."

Darrius and Prasad entered the dining room. Hilly and Fen remained in Chance's embrace and all three were in deep slumber. Kai sat on the floor as if in meditation but a low snore proved otherwise.

Darrius turned to Prasad. "You were wise to induce sleep."

"It's what I do," Prasad said with a twinkle in his eye.

"I suggest we rouse them and send them to bed. It will be an early morning for them. The final step in their Revelations is to open the family vault, claim the family artifacts and arm themselves. Stygian will return and I sense it will be soon. Everyone must be prepared."

Prasad circled the room and touched each Kemp lightly on the top of the head. They all stretched and yawned as if awaking from a long nap. "Time for you all to go to bed," he said as he rejoined Darrius. "We need you fresh in the morning so you can unlock the final chapter of your family."

They all rose to leave. As Hilly passed Darrius she casually mentioned, "What an odd dream. A young man knocked on the door and wanted to see me. But he wouldn't come in. Weird, eh?"

# Chapter 16

# Opening the Vault

THE NOR'EASTER LASHED THE coast, pounding The Nine Muses with seventy-mile-per-hour gales and drenching the grounds with over eight inches of rain. Forecasters along the Eastern Seaboard scratched their heads over the phenomenon which materialized just off the Massachusetts coast and stalled over Manchester-by-the-Sea. By their reckoning, the storm shouldn't even exist—two warm fronts surrounded the squall which needed cold air for energy; and it didn't travel northeast like most nor'easters, instead it moved west and chose to remain stationary. It's immense cloud cover smothered the state of Massachusetts like a lid on a pressure cooker.

The atmosphere in the dining room loomed dark and dreary—a combination of the two energies from the storm that raged outside and the somber mood inside. The Kemps hunched in their chairs, heads down over steaming mugs of coffee.

"Good morning," Darrius cheerfully greeted as he entered.

Silence.

Prasad entered carrying a tray of pastries and nodded toward Darrius. "It's a quiet morning."

Darrius sat down, grabbed a scone and surveyed the room as he slowly buttered his pastry. "Have they said anything?"

"Not a word. They shuffled in one by one, grabbed coffee and sat down as you see them now," Prasad replied.

Darrius telepathically communicated with Prasad. *Side effects from your slumber spell?*

*No, I sense something is troubling them, but nobody will talk. I'll mentally chat with Kai and Fen. Maybe they'll respond to me in that manner.*

Prasad sat next to Fen. She didn't glance up nor acknowledge him. *Fen, what is troubling you?*

Her finger twitched. She had heard him.

Prasad pressed again. *Are you ill? If so, I can fix it.*

Kai mentally responded. *We're not the same anymore! We've gone from normal to something that's...something that's totally abnormal! You can't expect us to embrace all of this in just a matter of hours!*

Still staring into her coffee, Fen nodded in agreement.

Darrius overheard the mental conversation and rose. He straightened and smoothed his jacket while he scanned the table of depressed, defeated souls. He pounded the table and shouted, "LOOK AT ME, NOW!"

They jerked, wide eyes riveted on the usually calm and peaceful Darrius.

"What do you see?"

Nobody answered. They blinked in disbelief and stared dumbfoundedly.

He slapped the table again, "WHAT DO YOU SEE?"

Chance whispered, "Dead people."

The macabre answer struck Kai's funny bone and he spit coffee onto the table as he tried to suppress a laugh. "It may have been morbid, but Chance is right. Yesterday we rediscovered ourselves and had fun reuniting as a family. Today we die."

Darrius sighed and walked around the table, hands clasped in front of him.

In a soft, tender tone he continued, "Look at yourselves. Before me sit members of ancient families with incredible powers capable of healing, protecting and fighting. I see representatives whose blood pulses with the magic of powerful tribes that once ruled the world, without war, without strife. I witnessed four individuals arriving at this house, alone and distrustful, but now each has become a valued member of a close, loving family. Where are those fierce warriors, my four chosen ones?"

Fen spoke, "Yes, you gave us the gift to find ourselves and each other. But, today, we may lose all that. We may lose each other. I've experienced love and loss, and I can't bear to do this again. I hate you both for doing this to me." She turned away and cried softly.

Prasad joined Darrius. "We only gave you what you already possessed. These powers were always with you, lurking beneath the surface, waiting to be released. We only unlocked the door so you could embrace them once again. Hate me if you will, but you are now the individual you were always meant to be. Your youthful self was denied these powers to protect you from Stygian, but now you have a chance to survive."

Prasad walked around the table and peered into the eyes of each person. "Life is never easy," he began in a soft tone. "Even for a magical being. But, *each* of you possess the powers and skills of warriors. You are the four magicians identified by The Cererian Prophecy to restore peace to Earth.

"Yes, you may lose. But you have so much to win."

Hilly remained quiet throughout the discussion. Since her Revelation, all of her senses had intensified and she found it easy to be a silent observer to the mindful discussion between Darrius and Prasad, especially when they neglected to cloak their conversation. "Stygian visited last night, didn't he?"

"What?" The Kemps echoed.

Darrius and Prasad exchanged glances, and then Darrius responded, "Yes, he asked for a meeting and I granted it. He demanded we hand you over to him. His abilities are immense but I sensed doubt in his heart. He knows that your powers are restored and that you grow stronger each day. He fears what you can do."

Hilly rose and peered out the window into the murkiness. Angry wind-driven bands of rain pounded the glass. "He watches us now."

Chance bolted out of his chair. "Where is that little fuck? I'll take care of him!" he shouted.

Hilly gently touched Chance's arm. "Not yet. But soon you'll have your chance to take care of him. I promise."

"You have a plan? You know how to defeat him?" Fen asked.

"I do." Hilly faced everyone, her eyes sparkling a vivid green. "And, it will happen later tonight. We need to prepare now. I can't beat Stygian by myself. I need all of you to help me." Thrusting her hand above the center of the table, she asked, "Is everyone in?"

The Kemps exchanged worried, unsure glances. After several moments Chance stepped forward and slapped his hand on Hilly's. "I've got your back, little sister."

"I'm one hundred percent in," Kai said.

Fen looked at Prasad and then at Hilly. "My instincts are telling me to run, but I won't. I'm part of a great family and I will be there for you and my brothers." She stepped forward and slapped her hand on top of the pile.

"One, two, three!" Hilly counted. "Here's to the four chosen ones!" Then the siblings threw their hands into the air.

Darrius and Prasad nodded. The family had united once again.

As the Kemps filed into the study the mood remained serious, but there was also an element of excitement in the air. They gathered for the last step in their Revelations: opening the family vault. Constructed of a Cererian metal alloy to prevent mind penetration and detection, the hidden chamber had been built by the benevolent Cererians for Ted and Freda sixty years ago to safely store and protect familial artifacts.

"Circle around me," Darrius requested. "The time has come for the final stage in restoring your memories—reclaiming your family property. First, the family vault needs to be exposed. Chance, please move the table from the middle of the room and place it against that wall over there." Chance nodded, eager to use his telekinetic abilities.

Like a conductor preparing to direct an orchestra, he stretched out his arms, palms down, toward the furniture. With tense fingers, his hands trembled as one end of the table lifted and then the other until it was a foot above the floor. Chance slid his hands sideways beckoning the table to move. It silently obeyed its master and settled easily against the far wall.

"Very good, now, roll up the Oriental rug and place it by the same wall." Darrius instructed. Chance circled his hands and teased one end of the carpet upward before it quickly rolled into itself. Then he hovered it toward the wall, gently laying it by the table.

The Kemps peered down at the golden oak flooring anticipating hinges or an outline of a trap door, but there were none.

"What are we looking at?" Chance asked as he knelt and brushed his hand along the surface feeling for anomalies in the floorboards.

"Patience, I'll show you," Darrius said, closing his eyes and mouthing an incantation. Groans and creaks emanated from the old oak floor and Chance jumped back, ducking just as a board flew past his head. The Kemps stood wide-eyed as the planks lifted one-by-one and drifted against the wall in a neat stack leaving a square hole in the floor. "Here is the entrance to the vault."

Everyone gathered around the cavity and stared into the chamber, anticipating treasures and family fortunes. The unassuming secret room measured ten feet square with a height of twelve feet. Within the space stood various pieces of furniture. A double-wide cabinet with glass doors and notched shelves held the family weaponry including swords, muskets, and bows and arrows. Floor-to-ceiling bookcases displayed artifacts and relics from around the world. Four stuffed mannequins were outfitted with armor. And along one wall was a vintage Diebold fire-proof safe.

Darrius turned to Chance. "Use your powers to bring the safe up to this level."

Chance flexed his arms like a strongman.

"Good gawd," Kai teased. "Just lift the bloody safe and drop the drama."

"You're one to talk about drama," Chance retorted. He hovered his hands over the safe.

Nothing happened.

He refocused and stretched his fingers.

Again, nothing happened.

He looked anxiously at Darrius. "I've lost the ability to levitate!"

Darrius said reassuringly, "You've only been levitating lightweight items. The safe weighs two thousand pounds so you need to focus. Flex your mental muscles, not just your physical ones."

"Imagine it's a T-bone steak," Kai joked. Everyone snickered.

Chance glared at Kai before turning his attention back to the safe. Closing his eyes, he pushed his hands forward, envisioning energy extending from his fingertips to underneath and around the metal box. Like silken threads of light, the energy ball moved the safe upward through the hole and settled it gently onto the study floor.

"Ta da!" Chance announced, bowing as everyone applauded.

Darrius turned to Kai. "Now, it's your turn. Produce the key that will open the safe."

Kai hesitated. "I'm not sure I remember how to do this. I think you left something out of my Revelation."

"Focus, clear your mind and ask for the key."

Kai closed his eyes and breathed deeply. He thought to himself, *I need the key, I need the key.*

His hands fluttered back and forth through the air while he uttered an ancient language. The fingers of his right hand arched as if holding a writing instrument. He scribbled invisible symbols from right to left at such a speed that the movements soon blurred; and the faint outline of a blue key appeared in front of the safe. Kai pushed his hands forward, gently guiding the luminescent key into the lock until there was a soft click. The door sprang open, and the key immediately vanished.

"Wow!" his siblings yelled.

Sweat pouring down his face, Kai quickly sat. "I don't feel well." Darrius poured him a glass of water which he gladly accepted and gulped. "That's much better, it's like I was on fire from the inside out."

"Your body will get accustomed to this gift. It will become second nature in no time," Darrius assured.

He then knelt in front of the safe, the Kemps huddled behind him, curious to see what was inside. He removed the first artifact gently from its tomb—the family records. The massive leather-bound tome, decorated in gilt on the cover and spine, measured two feet square. Darrius easily lifted the thick book and lofted it to Chance. "I believe this is yours, Keeper of the Records." Chance hugged the precious relic against his chest and carried it to his dad's desk. He sat bug-eyed as he turned the gold-edged parchment pages containing the written testimonies from their ancestors.

Darrius then extracted another book, a curious one constructed with thick cedar covers and interior pages made of animal hide. It was bound with sinew laced through holes punched in the spine. Symbols drawn in red ink covered the pages. Fen eagerly took the book from Darrius.

"Dad's old alchemy book." Fen had instantly recognized the hieroglyphics. She lightly touched the familiar volume she had once studied with her father. "Oh my, I can read and understand everything," she exclaimed.

Kai and Hilly stood, arms around each other, anticipating what awaited them. Darrius extracted a large ebony box with ancient symbols painted in silver all around the sides. He handed it to Kai. "Now, you will understand more about your magical keys." Kai snatched the box and scurried away to investigate the contents.

"What do you have in your magical safe for me?" Hilly asked.

"I saved the best for last," Darrius said as he lifted out an iridescent crystal the size of his palm. The jewel consisted of five flawless sides creating a point at the bottom and angling up to form a multi-faceted top. He held it up to the light and slowly turned it in his fingers. Miniature rainbows cascaded across the floor and walls. Like an activated tuning fork, a soft vibration hummed as the crystal twirled in his hands.

"This jewel is the crystal of your family—the family of fire. Long ago it sat protected within its Guardian boulder where it was energetically connected to three other crystals. Those gems, representing the families of earth, air, and water, were contained within their own Guardians. Together the four gemstones produced an energy so powerful it covered the entire world and joined a network of energy maintained by the other tribes. The resulting positive energy nurtured peace, restored balance and brought all the natural elements and dimensions together in harmony."

Hilly gazed at the jewel, mesmerized by its brilliance. "Do Chance, Kai and Fen have crystals too?"

"Yes and no. Their gemstones are not in the safe, nor in the vault. They were spirited away by family shamans when Stygian and his brothers attacked." Pointing at Chance, Kai and Fen, Darrius continued, "When you embark on your quests, each of you will need to locate and retrieve your family crystal. The day all four jewels are returned to their respective Guardian boulders is the day peace will once again rule the world.”

Hilly cradled the crystal close to her chest prompting the jewel's vibration to increase, a soothing thrum like a gathering of honeybees. She swayed to the rhythm, humming in the same pitch until their two sounds merged into one song. The resulting tune permeated the room with love and tranquility.

“You hold a precious life in your hands,” Darrius acknowledged. “The jewel is a living entity that contains the life force of your ancestors. Protect this crystal from harm, hide it from Stygian until the day you can reunite it with its Guardian boulder.” Tears trickled down Hilly's face. She was suddenly filled with the emotions of a million people who had lived before her—their sorrow, happiness, fear and hope.

“If the shamans of other tribes fled into other dimensions with their crystal, how did my family's stone end up in this safe?” Hilly asked.

“My dear Hilly, you *are* the shaman of your tribe. As you recall, your entire family was massacred by Stygian. Your adopted father kept the treasure secured in the safe, all this time, awaiting the arrival of its rightful owner. The crystal pulsed in Hilly's hand and emitted a warm, inviting glow. “The crystal knows it's home.”

Darrius surveyed the room, satisfied. Everyone was immersed in their artifacts, reading, touching, sensing, becoming one with them.

Prasad announced, “I apologize for the abruptness, but time is not on our side.” The Kemps carefully secured their artifacts and joined Prasad. “I have the honor to present you with your weaponry.” He retrieved four broadswords from the vault and laid them side-by-side on the table. Each measured four-feet long and was covered by a different-colored cloth representing each of the elemental families. “The broadsword is an extension of your family, and your tribe. It wields incredible power. It is an honor to possess this weapon and it should never be disrespected or abandoned.”

The siblings locked hands and stepped closer. The seriousness of their situation was quite clear—the battle was nigh—and the air in the study stilled as everyone sucked in a deep breath anticipating the reception of their weapons. Prasad selected the first sword, treating it with the utmost respect as he gingerly removed the emerald-green covering, revealing a translucent blade that appeared more like milky glass than steel. Encrusted in the pommel were emeralds, lodestone, and malachite while engraved pentacles lined the grip.

"Chance, I present to you the sword of your family who hails from the North, those who command earth power," Prasad said as he lifted the weapon to Chance. Chance received it in both hands and almost dropped it because it was lighter than a feather. Puzzled, he turned to Prasad who explained, "All of the swords are pure energy, so they barely weigh anything. I'll explain more once I've distributed the others."

He picked up the next sword, which was swaddled in light blue silk. Pulling off the cloth, he exposed a blade similar to the first, but the pommel was bejeweled with mica, pumice, and fluorite and wing symbols etched the grip. "Kai, this weapon belongs to your family who rules the East and controls the air," Prasad said carefully placing the broadsword into Kai's hands.

Fen was next to receive her weapon. Prasad removed the purple satin revealing a brilliant sword like the others but it was decorated with amethyst, moonstone and rose quartz. Along the grip were etched symbols of shells and bells.

"Fen, I am happy to present you with the family sword. Your family originates in the West and controls Earth's water."

Chance, Kai, and Fen stood in awe of their lightweight weapons gleaming in their hands as they examined the symbols and stones of their families. Hilly watched them with envy and was eager to have a sword in her hand, too.

"And, now for Hilly," Prasad began as he pulled the bright red cotton sheath off the weapon and placed the broadsword into her hands. Stones of amber, tiger's eye, and garnet crusted the pommel while the grip displayed etchings of the sun and dragons.

"Hilly, please accept the sword of your family who rules the South and controls fire." She traced the image of dragons on the hilt with her fingers. Suddenly it all became clear.

Prasad continued. "You've noticed the swords weigh very little. That's because they're constructed of lightweight metal alloys infused with Cererian crystals making them tools of pure energy. Due to this composition, they are incredibly durable, lethal, and can even channel energy. Let me demonstrate." Prasad pulled a small dagger from his waist. Similar to the swords, it had a milky, translucent blade and the handle was decorated with stones and carvings. He turned toward the study door, leveled his knife at the handle, and focused his thoughts on that point. The dagger responded. A glow pulsed from the blade, then it throbbed like a heart beating faster and faster until a narrow white light struck the doorknob, which melted and fell to the floor.

Darrius sighed. "The demonstration was needed but now we have no way of locking the study."

"Cool!" Chance shouted.

"I want to zap something, too," Kai yelled as he turned in the room looking for a target.

Prasad held up his hand. "Please settle down. I understand your enthusiasm but you wield very dangerous weapons, and we can't afford any accidents. We'll work with each of you, so you understand the power of your swords." He sheepishly looked at Darrius. "I will repair the doorknob right away."

Darrius led the Kemps to a secret room in the basement accessible only through the vault room. "Your restored powers will assist you in learning the techniques for wielding the weapons and for fighting an opponent.

Your sword is an extension of your innate magical abilities, and it will be the tool that you will use to channel those powers to vanquish Stygian."

"How long will we practice?" Chance asked.

"You have a half a day to prepare," Darrius replied.

"A half a day to practice?" Kai exclaimed. "You're joking, aren't you?"

"Stygian will attack, and soon. You must be ready to fight him, or all of you will die."

Darrius ushered the Kemps to line up by one wall. Then, he swung his sword overhead. The weapon sang with energy as it sliced through the air. "Observe my skills as I point my sword at the target, and only use my mind to direct the energy." A padded mannequin awaited his attack. Darrius lowered his broadsword until the tip was parallel to the heart of the dummy. Focusing his thoughts on that spot, he tensed. Sparks flew from his blade as a thin beam of light snaked forward and penetrated the mannequin leaving a charred gaping hole.

"Wow," Kai whispered.

"Now, it's your turn," Darrius instructed. He paired everyone with a dummy and announced, "Focus your thoughts and call forth your powers. I want to see these mannequins annihilated." The Kemps lowered their weapons at their dummies and stared at Darrius, hesitant about their next moves.

"Chance, what power can you call forth?" Darrius asked.

"Um. I'm not sure. I know I can move things with my mind, and I'm stronger than most folks." Frustrated, Chance allowed the tip of his sword to drop to the floor."

"Pick up that weapon!" Darrius ordered. Chance quickly lifted it into the air.

"Never disrespect your sword. It is a living entity. Once it is in your hand, it joins with your energy. Focus, Chance. How can you destroy that mannequin in front of you?"

Chance blushed from embarrassment. As the big brother, he felt he needed to set the example for his siblings and had failed miserably.

"I think I know how," Fen whispered. She pursed in lips and frowned at her dummy. Then she leveled her sword at its heart. Instantly, a shower of sparks ignited from the tip of her sword and a think bright light drilled through the mannequin leaving a clean hole from front to back.

"Very good, Fen," Darrius praised. "Now, how about the rest of you? Show me what you can conjure."

Inspired by Fen's example, the Kemps spent the next hours practicing.

At noon, the exhausted warriors filed upstairs for lunch. On the way to the dining room, Fen felt a strong pull to walk into the foyer.

She wandered to the mantel as if the cold marble fireplace willed her to come near. She glanced up at the painting. The room pulsed like an underwater shockwave rippling through her body. Dizzy, she pressed the heels of her hands against her temples and forced herself to look up at the picture. The image shimmered and shifted. Instead of a lone warrior standing in the surf, there were four and all had their swords pointing upward, light beams shooting from the tips straight into the black sky.

"Are you okay?" Prasad asked, approaching from behind.

Fen jumped in surprise, blinked, and looked back at the painting. The four warriors were still there. "Prasad, look at the painting. What do you see?"

He dutifully glanced up. "A Kemp ancestor is standing on the beach. They have a helmet, so I cannot tell you who they are."

"You don't see four people?"

Prasad looked again. "No, only one. Why?"

Fen shook her head, closed her eyes and then looked back at the painting. A lone person stood on the beach.

"Oh no!" she wailed. She instinctively wrapped her arms around Prasad's waist and hugged him tightly.

"Fen, what's wrong?"

She looked up into his beautiful green eyes.

"I have premonitions. I've always had them, but they've been occurring more frequently since I arrived at The Nine Muses. Every time I look at the painting, I see something different."

Prasad looked into her face. "Tell me what you've seen."

"When I first arrived, I only saw the ancestor you described. But after Hilly had her encounter with Stygian, the painting changed and showed the warrior in the surf but with their helmet visor raised revealing green eyes. Just now, there were four warriors on the beach with their broadswords raised to the sky. What does all of this mean? Am I seeing the future?"

Exhausted, Fen leaned into Prasad and he pulled her closer. He chose not to speak. Instead, he reached out mentally. She closed her eyes and rested her head on his chest, feeling the rise and fall of his breaths. She received his message and smiled as she telepathically answered him. She liked this form of communication, especially with Prasad.

# Chapter 17

# The Battle

"THERE'S HARDLY A SCRAP of food to be found," Kai complained as he rifled through the kitchen cupboards.

"Not much in the fridge either," Hilly said searching the crisper bins. "I've got some veggies that aren't too far gone and something that smells like leftover soup."

"Any eggs?" Kai asked.

"Hmm, I found three," Hilly replied as she laid them on the counter.

"We can make an omelet with the eggs and veg," Kai proclaimed.

"That won't feed all of us," Hilly admitted.

"We can stretch it with this rice milk I found." Kai withdrew a small carton of rice milk hiding in the back of the cupboard. "And, it's not expired."

"Oh, joy," Hilly laughed. "I can't wait to see Chance's face when he tastes this concoction."

"Do you know our brother? He'll eat anything. Besides, what else is he going to do...walk to the store?" They both chuckled.

Storm gales slammed branches against the kitchen window. Hilly and Kai jerked expecting to see Stygian staring back at them. They peered outside into the dark and foreboding thunderstorm. Hilly shivered and hugged herself.

"What's up?" Kai asked while wrapping his arm around her. "Do you feel something?" Like Chance, Kai was concerned about Stygian worming into Hilly's mind again. The brothers agreed to keep an eye on her at all times.

"Please Kai, I know what you're thinking. You forget I have powers like Prasad and Darrius. And, yes, I'm nervous, too, about Stygian. But I don't fear him. Now that we've been together on several occasions, I know his weaknesses and understand his tricks."

"Can you, um, feel him?"

"Yeah, he's on my back like a monkey just winding me up and making me dance," Hilly sarcastically replied.

"That's not what I meant," Kai protested.

"I know, I know. But you're getting too serious. And, I depend on you to keep things light around here because there's some serious shit coming." She looked outside again and frowned. "He is out there, watching...waiting. But he's not able to enter my mind again, not without my permission." She began whipping the egg and milk mixture. She nodded at Kai. "You better get to work on cutting those veggies."

Fen slowly withdrew from Prasad's embrace. "Thank you for being there for me." She turned to go to the dining room. Prasad didn't follow. "Aren't you coming?"

"I have business to attend to. Darrius and I will be with all of you soon." He patted her arm, "Don't worry, everything will work out just fine. I promise."

Fen turned and gave him an impulsive kiss on the lips. They both took a step back, stunned. Then Prasad pulled Fen into his arms and tenderly kissed her. She didn't resist. It had been so long since she had felt passion for a man, and she wanted, needed, this moment to last. They separated and gazed into each other's eyes.

A loud yowl shattered the moment. Pyewacket sat outside the dining room swishing his tail back and forth. Prasad glared at the cat before kissing Fen on the forehead and trotting up the staircase.

Fen lingered for a few minutes reliving the special moment she had just shared with Prasad. As though in a dream, she shuffled toward the dining room, to Pyewacket who yowled again jerking her back to reality.

"You're a demanding boy," she said as she picked him up and stroked his fur. "Pyewacket, I'm falling for Prasad. I can't wait to see him again." The cat purred loudly and rubbed his head against her chin. Fen hefted him onto her shoulder and opened the dining room door.

Hilly and Kai burst into the dining room with their meager offerings. Chance scoffed at the meal Hilly placed onto the table. "Did you make anything for yourselves? This isn't even enough for me," he complained as he leaned forward to scoop up the omelet. Hilly plunged a large knife into the eggs and Chance quickly snatched his hand back. "Are you crazy? You could have stabbed me!"

"Chance, stop whining. I'm just making sure there's enough for everyone." She quickly sliced four portions, which Kai distributed around the table. "There. Now everyone has a piece."

"Hey, I'm bigger than everyone else. I should have a larger slice!" Chance roared. Hilly locked eyes with her brother. "Oh, you want to have a stare-down? You're on!" Hilly's brilliant emerald eyes flashed and shimmered as she moved closer to his face, their eyelashes almost touching. A heavy sleepiness crept over Chance and his eyes fluttered as he rocked side to side. "I know what you're doing, Hilly. You're trying to trance me, but you're not going to win." The siblings continued to stare at each other, fighting the urge to blink. "Okay! You win! I guess I'll make do with this scrawny little piece. Just get outta my face!"

"Make sure you eat slowly...it will last a lot longer." Hilly laughed as she patted Chance's head. Everyone ate in silence. Fen cuddled Pyewacket who sat on her lap purring contentedly. Hilly glanced at her siblings. "I guess we should talk about the elephant in the room."

Kai grabbed a piece of paper and pen from the sideboard, drew some lines and threw it into the middle of the table. "You mean this one?" He had drawn a bloated elephant sitting on its haunches with huge ears and long trunk curling into the air.

Chance grabbed the sketch and studied it. "Yep, that's the one. So, what do you want to talk about?" The table erupted into wild laughter as Chance folded the elephant into a paper airplane and shot it over Fen's head.

The giggling was a nervous release of emotions that had been building since their Revelations.

They soon settled down and Hilly announced, "I know we will need to face Stygian soon. He's prowling the grounds searching for ways to reach us. If we're prepared, he won't catch us unaware."

She paused and sipped her water. "I have a plan. A clever way to defeat Stygian. But you must do what I ask and not deviate from my instructions."

"Aren't you concerned Stygian can hear you," Chance asked as he glanced out the window into the ferocious storm.

"He can't hear or see anything because of the protection field, and because I can prevent him from entering my mind."

Curious about her plan, her siblings leaned closer to hear the details. In a whisper, Hilly described the plan thumping the table with her fingertip to emphasize important details. No one said a word until she was done. "Any questions?"

"No. I won't do it! I can't do it!" Fen shouted.

"Fen, it's the only way. Trust me on this." Hilly glanced around the room. Chance and Kai stared at the table. "Come on, guys. We're a team...we're the chosen ones. We knew this wasn't going to be easy. Please don't let me down."

The whole house shook as if God had punched his fist through the roof. Startled, they all jumped to their feet, hands outstretched in defense, their backs to one another. A high-pitched shriek split the air. It was soon followed by another thump. The house vibrated.

Hilly placed her hands on the window and closed her eyes. She could see him—an immense blackness roiling inside the thunderstorm.

"Stygian is here. He comes alone without the aid of his Yfel Brethren. He wants us all to himself. What a cocky bastard!" Hilly faced her siblings. "I love all of you and trust you to remember the plan. We cannot fail. As in ancient times, the families stand together in battle: the armies of the North, the East, the South and the West."

"Wait, Hilly, I need to see Prasad before we go," Fen pleaded.

Hilly gripped Fen's arms. "Honey, we just don't have time. We need to leave now."

Hilly saw the fear in Fen's eyes and hugged her.

"We have a job to do, Fen. We can't do it without all of us. That includes you. Are you with us?" Fen slowly nodded. "Besides, you'll have all the time in the world once this is all over."

"Okay, Hilly. Let's go," Fen said as she hugged her sister.

"Collect your weapons. The battle is nigh!" Hilly yelled as she burst through the door leading her siblings toward the basement. They didn't hesitate to follow. With their full memories restored, confidence in their powers and belief in their magic propelled them toward the inevitable.

Pyewacket sat in the doorway and switched his tail, watching them go. Then he dashed upstairs.

Prasad unfolded his gambeson, a quilted battle jacket woven with threads of Cererian metal. The prophecy spoke of this day, but he didn't think it would actually arrive. He thought of Fen, their time alone, their kiss.

"Lost in thoughts?" Darrius said as he silently entered the room.

"I saw you crouching by the door watching us. Fen and I."

"Even an old fighter deserves at least one love in his lifetime." Darrius patted his friend on the shoulder. "Drink in the moment and let it be your fuel for what is to come." Darrius gathered his battle gear and began placing the layers on his body. "You felt Stygian's arrival?"

"Yes, I'm sure it rattled the Kemps. Stygian is like a child beating his fists on the house to get what he wants."

"I was able to eavesdrop on their conversation. They have a plan. Hilly conceived of the perfect way to lure Stygian into a trap. But her brothers and sister must not hesitate, or Stygian will win."

They continued their conversation telepathically, cloaked from eavesdropping. Afterward Prasad walked to the window and lowered his head. "Yes, I see that is the only way. We always knew this is how it would end."

"The Kemps are retrieving their swords now and intend to face Stygian. We should hurry. The Cererian Prophecy was clear. As Observers we are not allowed to interfere but we need to bear witness to the outcome."

Prasad nodded. "It's in their hands now."

A long screech followed by a rumbling thump rocked the basement as the siblings dressed for battle. Hilly gazed up, grinning. "He's getting impatient. I like that."

The siblings assisted each other into their fighting jackets, longer gambesons that landed just above their knees. The protective padding looked as if it weighed more than fifty pounds but, because of the Cererian metal fibers, was virtually weightless and incredibly durable. Kai fastened the snaps on his jacket and turned to the others. "Does this make my butt look cute?"

Chance scowled. "This isn't the time for joking."

"I disagree. This is the perfect time for levity. We don't know what's going to happen, and if this is the final time we're together, I want it to be a fucking happy time."

Fen grabbed Hilly's hand. "I trust you Hilly. Don't let me down. Now that I've found you again, I don't want to lose you." Fen hugged Hilly, squeezing her tight. Then Chance and Kai joined the group hug.

"Help, I can't breathe!" Hilly laughed.

A flash of lightning followed by a clap of thunder shook the house. The vibrations rolled through the walls for almost a minute.

"Let's take care of this unruly child, shall we?" Hilly said, thrusting her broadsword into the air. The others grabbed their weapons and joined her. Slowly they dipped their weapons until the translucent blades touched, igniting a shower of sparks. "Remember, stick to the plan."

Hilly charged out of the basement followed by Chance, Kai and Fen.

They assembled on the patio. The storm growled its displeasure as black clouds swirled in the sky and relentless rain blew sideways. A gust of wind shoved Hilly backward against Chance who clamped his arms around her before she tumbled onto the flagstones.

*SCREECH!*

The piercing wail sent chills down their spines and shivers throughout their bodies as evil hovered above them.

The four siblings stood abreast with their heads bent into the gales. "Are you ready?" Hilly screamed into the howling wind.

"Yes!" they replied in unison.

"Then, follow me, warriors!" Her broadsword held high, she sprinted toward the beach, to set the trap. The wet sand sucked at their legs while monstrous waves pummeled them, pushing them off their feet.

"Stand your ground!" she screamed. "Stygian will come to us." The Kemps stood in a circle, back-to-back, swords at the ready.

*SKRRREEEK!*

The warriors tensed, looking up into the pelting rain. Hovering just above them, an oil-black dragon pumped its massive leathery wings. A breath caught in Hilly's throat as she stared into the eyes of the black beast that had haunted her nightmares for months. *We finally meet,* she thought.

It shrieked again, an unnatural sound so loud the Kemps dropped their swords and clamped their hands over their ears.

"Retrieve your weapons!" Hilly cried into the tempest. "Don't let your guard down, no matter what Stygian does!" The warriors collected their swords, closed ranks and pointed their weapons at the vile creature flying thirty feet above.

Hilly mentally reached out to Kai, *Now's the time, brother!*

*See you later, sis.* Kai soared into the air, his illuminated sword leading the way like a torch in the night.

Doubts surfaced as Kai approached Stygian. He'd never encountered a dragon before let alone a powerful beast with supernatural powers. His restored memories provided no clues for how to fight the snarling monster. But he had a job to do and he wouldn't let his family down.

"Die, Stygian!" Kai yelled as he maneuvered around the dragon, stabbing him multiple times like a hungry mosquito. Each gash produced a loud hiss as the wounds sizzled from the broadsword's Cererian energy. Kai tormented the creature with ease, deftly flying around the massive dragon puncturing its wings and ripping gaping holes. Kai grew more confident with each wound he inflicted, and became emboldened to fly closer to his adversary.

It was time to initiate his part of Hilly's plan.

*Don't let me down, Stygian,* Kai thought as he approached the head. Stygian growled and opened his mouth. Jagged, pointed teeth filled his fetid jaws reeking of death. The gust of putridness sickened Kai but he flew, undeterred, toward an eye, his sword poised to strike. Stygian swirled his massive scaly tail, the tip catching Kai in the stomach and catapulting him into the distant horizon.

As he disappeared into the ocean Kai mentally reached out to Hilly, *See you soon.*

The Kemps feigned horror as their brother disappeared. Kai had successfully completed his portion of the plan, now it was their turn.

The three warriors regrouped on the beach, back-to-back as the scaly creature landed nearby, rocking the ground under their feet and throwing them off balance. The creature's wings directed vortices of sand and water at them, blinding them as he crawled closer. Chance deflected the debris by deploying a dome of telekinetic energy around them like a shield while Fen diverted the water back to the ocean. Stygian screamed. Opening his mouth wide, he roared at them spewing foul-smelling air that stank of rotting flesh.

"Be brave!" Hilly screamed into the wind.

The code words. Chance and Fen nodded as they swung their swords forward preparing for Hilly's ploy.

Hilly turned to the creature and opened her mind. *Stygian, come to me.*

The beast stopped and snorted into the sand.

*Remember when you visited me? You spoke ancient words, the voice of our family. Come to me my lord. Take me. I willingly offer myself if you will spare Chance and Fen. You've already taken Kai.*

The dragon stomped the earth and snorted again. *You're trying to trick me.* It threw its head back and shrieked. *You are not stronger than me. You never will be.* Stygian roared into the blackened sky. Squalls buffeted the Kemps as lightning stabbed the beach.

Hilly gritted her teeth and glared at the beast. *Do you accept my offer?*

Lightning flickered nearby, temporarily blinding the warriors. In those few seconds of distraction, Stygian vanished.

Hilly gasped and then buckled over as though she had been punched in the stomach.

"Hilly!" Chance shouted as he and Fen whirled to help her. "Are you okay?"

Hilly knelt in the sand and clutched her belly. Eyes closed, she rocked back and forth groaning.

Chance knelt beside her and touched her shoulder. "Hilly?"

Her head snapped upward and she glared at Chance with oil-black eyes.

"Stygian is inside her!" Chance shouted as he and Fen raised their swords and backed away.

Controlling Hilly's body, Stygian stood and smirked. "You thought you could outsmart me. You are weak humans, like your ancestors before you. It will be an honor to erase you from this earth. You've given me the perfect chance to kill you all. How stupid!"

Chance gripped Fen's arm and winked at her. Fen nodded in response. She mentally called, *Kai, join us now!* Kai shot out of the ocean and landed between Chance and Fen with his sword ready to strike a blow.

"What?" Surprised, Stygian faltered, providing Hilly the opportunity she awaited.

Since Stygian had entered her body, Hilly remained subdued, appearing weak and submissive so he would direct his power at her siblings. Kai's distraction broke Stygian's concentration enough to allow Hilly to punch forward and seize control.

The oily black eyes transformed to shimmering emerald-green as Hilly's life force moved forward, and shoved Stygian aside. Her plan needed to be enacted before Stygian fought for control again.

She nodded at her siblings and began chanting an exile spell using the ancient language of her family, mystical words used by her tribe in all banishment incantations. Her siblings encircled her, walking clockwise as she slowly raised her sword into the sky. On her final words, "So mote it be!" The siblings drove their blades into their sister's body.

A burst of white light illuminated the beach as the blades burned flesh and scraped bone as the tips emerged on the other side. Hilly shook violently. An intense beam of light shot upward from her eyes and mouth, stabbing forks of lightning into the dark belly of the storm. Convulsing, Hilly stood her ground until the final moment: a concussive burst of light blew out from her body, throwing everyone to the ground and opening a gaping hole in the raging storm above. An explosion rocked the sky sending rolls of thunder racing toward the horizon.

Silence.

The storm retreated as though a plug was pulled and all remnants of the nor'easter were suddenly sucked away. The ocean swells calmed, and the rain stopped. Wispy white clouds raced through a peach-colored sky. The blast from the energy pulse seared the sandy beach birthing bejeweled glass nuggets that sparkled in the sunshine—a serene aftermath in contrast to the bloody battle waged moments earlier.

The explosion threw Chance, Fen and Kai backward ten feet from the epicenter. Flat on their backs, eyes closed, they appeared as though they were simply enjoying the sunshine. But, upon closer inspection their bruised and bloody bodies told a different story.

Having observed the fight from The Nine Muses, Darrius and Prasad quickly made their way to the beach hoping all the Kemps survived. Prasad found Fen first, and was relieved to see her breathing. Blood trickled down her face from a nasty gash above her eye. He passed his hand over the wound which slowly scarred over. He gently touched her head and her eyes fluttered open.

"Hello," she whispered.

Prasad smiled and gently kissed her. He scanned the rest of her body and found no major injuries.

Darrius reached Kai, who was conscious and struggled to stand.

"Please sit down," Darrius soothed guiding Kai back to the sand. "I need to inspect your injuries."

Kai held his head. "My ears are ringing. But I think I'm okay except for this cut on my arm." Darrius waved his hand over the gash and it healed. He examined Kai for additional injuries. "You'll heal nicely but stay here and rest while I attend to your brother." Kneeling beside Chance, Darrius placed a hand on his chest watching it rise and fall evenly. A quick scan revealed no broken bones, only abrasions and contusions.

"Chance, open your eyes," Darrius commanded, using his fingertips to stroke his forehead. Slowly they opened and squinted in the bright light. He recognized Darrius and grinned widely. "Don't try to speak or get up yet, just lie there and rest while I check on Hilly." Chance nodded and closed his eyes again.

Prasad and Darrius searched the beach for Hilly but couldn't find her. In the distance, seagulls screeched as they dipped and hovered over a collection of boulders tumbling into the sea. Opportunistic scavengers, they patrolled the shore for any digestible tidbit, living or dead, and this flock was particularly interested in one area. Prasad and Darrius raced toward the birds. As they neared, they saw a body draped across a jagged boulder. It lay face-down, and its right arm twisted unnaturally toward the sky as if holding something. A large gull squawked a threat.

"Be gone!" Darrius shouted thrusting his hands toward the bird. The flock scattered, screeching as they flew further up the beach. Something glinted in the sand below the boulder.

"Hilly's broadsword," Prasad said, withdrawing it from its resting spot. "It's still warm and vibrating."

"Help me, Prasad," Darrius urged. "Let's move her onto the beach."

Together they lifted her lifeless body and tenderly laid it down in the sand. Hilly's face appeared peaceful as if in meditation, and a hint of a smile graced her lips. One might assume she was napping if it wasn't for the facial burns and bluish skin. The men examined her body and found almost every bone broken and almost all the organs failing. They exchanged worried glances.

"Prasad, see that the Kemps make it inside and then join me in your room. I'm going to take Hilly back." Prasad nodded as he helped lift Hilly into Darrius' arms. "Join me as soon as you can." Closing his eyes, Darrius mouthed an incantation and vanished, spiriting Hilly to The Nine Muses.

Prasad glanced up the beach. Chance, Fen and Kai stood watching him. He sighed and joined them. "I have unfortunate news..."

"We already know," Kai said.

Chance added, "They've been mentally contacting Hilly and have been met with silence."

"It was more like a nothingness...a black void," Fen whispered as she stepped closer to Prasad searching his eyes "Is there any chance?"

"Darrius rushed Hilly back to The Nine Muses to perform more intense healing work. I must join him as well. Between the two of us, we may have a good chance of reviving her."

"She promised me her plan would be safe! She told me to trust her, and all would be well. What went wrong?" Fen fell into Prasad's arms weeping. "What did we do...what did we do?"

Prasad hugged her tightly. "Nobody is to blame. Hilly's plan was an excellent scheme to catch Stygian. The explosion of energy proved too much for her body which sustained the bulk of the concussion. Her body succumbed to the intense heat and shockwaves."

"What do we do now?" Chance asked as he collected the broadswords from the sand.

"We go back to The Nine Muses, and then I'll join Darrius."

"Let's get moving," Kai urged.

With Prasad leading the way, the siblings limped back to the estate and took refuge in the study. "You'll be comfortable here," Prasad said as he helped ease Fen into a recliner. "And, you have access to the alcohol, which I'm sure you're in great need of."

"Don't mind if I do," Chance said as he walked to the bar. He stopped and stared at the bottle of bourbon. He twirled and addressed everybody. "But, I won't drink until my baby sister gets back."

"We'll do the best that we can. I promise you that," Prasad said hurrying away. A sad and uncomfortable silence filled the room.

Fen grabbed Chance's hand. "I'm not religious but I feel that we can help Hilly by sending her as much positive energy as possible. Kai, come join hands with us, clear your minds and only think of Hilly." Kai hummed a melodious mantra followed by Fen and then Chance until a loud thrumming filled the room. A magical soft glow encircled the trio.

Joining Darrius in the sanctuary, Prasad grabbed potions off the shelf in preparation for the healing bath. "How is she doing?"

"Her injuries are extensive. I've restarted her heart and lungs but they're weak and try to shut down whenever I move to another part of her body."

Prasad opened the faucet and ran warm water into the bathtub while Darrius carefully undressed Hilly. A jagged burn ran from her right arm, across her body and exited her hip where the energy pulse left a bloody, gaping hole. A patchwork of bruises criss crossed her skin and a blackness filled her belly as a collection of blood pooled underneath the surface.

As with the injured mouse, the master alchemist added the healing medicine to the water while thoroughly stirring the concoction with a copper rod.

"Darrius, I fear that I don't have enough tincture to heal a human. I'm concerned we won't be able to save Hilly."

"We must try, dear friend," Darrius said gently lowering Hilly into the purple water.

As her naked body entered the mixture, a blue mist lifted into the air surrounding her with a veil of azure droplets. Prasad and Darrius channeled their Cererian healing energy on her broken body—Prasad focused on knitting her spine and hips while Darrius mended her pulverized organs.

After an hour, they had successfully healed her heart and lungs which helped sustain her, but her poor body was too damaged and they soon realized that even their efforts would not be enough to save her. The men grew weary, having expended all their energy in keeping Hilly alive. Their limitations showed in their labored breathing.

"Darrius, we can't continue like this," Prasad said gasping between words. "We don't have enough energy to heal her. But I do have an idea." Prasad continued his conversation telepathically finding it less laborious than speaking. Darrius grew somber and hung his head as he listened to his friend.

Finally, Darrius agreed. *It is a great sacrifice. An honorable solution.* The two men hugged while Darrius showered kisses all over Prasad's face. *Continue the fight my warrior brother! As it was in the past, so shall it be in the future and beyond! Our paths may separate but will converge when peace returns to the world.*

Kai gazed out the study window at the Atlantic Ocean. "It's so calm, it's like looking into a mirror." His gaze followed the shore to the beach where they had fought Stygian just hours earlier. Gentle waves lapped the sand, erasing all scars of the battle. Kai studied his arm and hoped his scars would soon vanish as well.

Fen curled up in the recliner, a blanket wrapped around her. Tears trickled down her face. Despite casting their energy circle, she knew Hilly was dead. After two hours she had not peered into her sister's mind or read her thoughts—an ominous nothingness was all that she received.

Kai heard Fen's thoughts and telepathically soothed her. *Yes, Hilly is gone but so is Stygian. She gave her life so many more could live.*

Fen shook her head. *I wish there had been another way.* She turned away from Kai and cried softly into her blanket.

Chance remained at the bar holding a glass of bourbon, the one he poured two hours earlier. "Do you intend to nurse that drink forever, brother?" Kai poked.

Chance stared at the floor. "I refuse to believe she's gone. I expect her to bounce in here and tease us just like she always did."

The door slowly opened and Darrius entered. Everyone stared with hopeful faces, but he couldn't bear to look at them. Kai rushed to greet him but stopped when he saw a trail of tears on his cheek.

Darrius passed Kai and strode over to the bar. He glanced briefly at Chance before snatching the drink from his hand and tossing it back in one gulp. He then joined Fen. With tears in his eyes, he cradled her cheek and soothed her.

"I have very sad news." Darrius took a deep breath. "But I also have extremely good news. One announcement causes me great pain, but that hurt is lessened by the joy of the other message. Today, I witnessed four unlikely warriors band together, follow their destiny, and vanquish evil. In all wars, there are always casualties and today was no different." Fen sobbed out loud and Kai ran to her side.

Darrius continued, "Hilly fell mortally wounded after successfully luring Stygian inside her so you three could dispatch him with your broadswords. It was a clever plan, but a very dangerous one because the timing needed to be perfect to catch Stygian off guard. My warriors...I'm so proud of you for not hesitating and for supporting each other in combat.

"Unfortunately, Hilly's powers could not prevent the tremendous energy pulse from impacting her body. Stygian's power had risen to astronomical levels unbeknownst to everybody." Darrius paused, walked to the bar and reached for the bourbon. Chance grabbed the bottle and poured two glasses. One for Darrius and one for himself. Darrius gulped it and continued, "Hilly died on the battlefield."

Fen sobbed uncontrollably while Kai quietly rocked her. Chance swallowed his bourbon and quickly poured another one.

Collecting his thoughts, Darrius paused and then faced the family. A single tear ran down his cheek. "But, in battle, sacrifices must be made especially when waging war against evil. Today, another sacrifice was made." Puzzled, the Kemps stared at Darrius.

Darrius walked to the study door and held it ajar. "Today, Prasad passed into the light so Hilly could continue the battle." Hilly glided into the room, her feet barely touching the floor while a blue mist swirled around her. She stopped and smiled at her siblings.

"Hilly!" Chance and Kai yelled as they hugged and kissed her.

Stunned by the news, Fen collapsed to the floor. She regained her sister, but the man she loved was lost forever. Sorrow, happiness and anger exploded in her heart. The emotions boiled over. Fen lay on the floor crying. Darrius knelt beside her, placing a comforting hand on her shoulder, urging her to come into his arms.

"Leave me alone!" she wailed, smacking his arm away. But Darrius persisted and eventually she collapsed into his arms. Fen sobbed into his chest, "It's not fair, Darrius...it's not fair."

"Prasad wanted you to have something," Darrius soothed, tilting her chin to look into her eyes.

"Prasad? What?"

Darrius pulled Fen up from the floor and guided her back to the chair. "Hold out your hand." She did as she was told and Darrius gently placed a delicate, iridescent flower onto her palm. It vibrated and pulsed to the rhythm of her heartbeat. She held it up to the window and gently turned it in the light showering the room with a kaleidoscope of colors. "On our planet, this flower is called Granon. It is the flower of union and it represents long life and love. The Granon thrives on a small part of Prasad's life essence, so, in a way, he will always be with you." Darrius looked into her eyes, "Fen, Prasad's last thoughts were of you." Fen cried louder and buried her head into Darrius' chest.

Hilly glided to the bar and poured two glasses of red wine. She joined Darrius and Fen, and pushed a glass into Fen's trembling hand. "Dear Fen," Hilly began. "Prasad was the greatest warrior of all time. He paid the ultimate price, and, for that, I propose a toast: to Prasad, a humble soul who saved the world."

Sniffing, Fen added, "And, a warm individual with a big heart."

The sisters clinked glasses and took long drinks. "I'm so sorry for your loss, Fen, but I will be forever grateful for Prasad's selflessness." Hilly dabbed Fen's eyes with the edge of her shirt. "I'm so fortunate to be with my fabulous family again." Fen smiled as she gazed into Hilly's eyes—emerald jewels shimmering in a serene face. The Granon thrummed and lit up the room. "Look how Prasad's flower glows with your happiness, Fen."

Chance interrupted, "Hilly, what happened to Stygian? Was he vaporized?"

"Not exactly." Hilly sighed and sipped her wine.

"He's dead, right?"

"Depends on how you interpret the word *dead*."

"Stop playing around...just answer the question."

Hilly took another sip. "I sent him to a secure place—an interdimensional cell."

"A what?" Chance asked.

Hilly chuckled. "A prison that exists in a different universe. I learned about these realms from Stygian. Whenever he entered my body, our minds merged. While he was busy trying to gain control, I learned his secrets—all without his knowledge. Stygian now resides in a locked room I created within one of these universes. It's an impenetrable cell generated through my incantation and the magic all of you contributed."

"Son of a bitch," Chance exclaimed. "He can't get out? Ever?"

"Not without my permission." Hilly grinned.

"With Stygian locked away, will his Yfel Brethren continue to kill magicians?" Kai asked.

"Yes," Darrius interrupted. "The Brethren will continue their murder spree, and they will turn their attention to all of you since you defeated their leader."

Chance poured a drink, lifted the glass to his lips, and paused. "We have a target on our backs now," he uttered glumly. He gulped the bourbon.

"Yes," Darrius agreed. "The news about his capture will travel fast. It's critical that you begin your quests as soon as possible."

"Where do we go from here?" Kai asked.

"I'll let your father answer that." Darrius led Fen to join her siblings. He pressed the remote and the screen silently descended from the ceiling. Flipping a switch on the vintage projector, the film roared to life.

Ted appeared on the patio, the tranquil beach and calm ocean behind him. He grinned, "Hello my children. If you are watching this film, you have survived the battle with Stygian which was preordained by The Cererian Prophecy. I'm extremely happy and so proud of all of you. But now you must embark on your adventures. You will gain more wisdom and knowledge as you travel the paths of your ancient families and search for the crystals that, when united with their Guardian boulders, will finally restore peace in the world. Darrius and Prasad will always be there to guide you. Depend on them with your life."

"I already have, Dad, I already have!" Hilly exclaimed.

# Epilogue

"ARE WE MONSTERS?"

Hilly pondered Kai's question as she swirled her wine and gazed at the calm Atlantic. Remnants of Stygian's power stirred within her bones. As a result of her Cererian heritage, her magical abilities were stronger than those of her siblings.

"No, Kai. We're not monsters. We're magicians," she responded.

Hilly faced her siblings. The stress of the recent battle etched their faces. "The Cererian Prophecy identified us as the chosen ones. It's our mission to locate our family crystals, and then reunite them with their respective Guardian boulders.

"Once all four gemstones are placed onto their altars, peace will be restored and the Yfel Brethren will no longer exist. I suggest that we make arrangements to embark on our quests as soon as possible so we can put an end to the Yfel's murder spree."

"Janet won't believe me," Chance fretted. "I wouldn't believe me, and I lived through it."

"I have several gallery openings scheduled throughout the year. There isn't time for me to go treasure hunting for a hidden crystal." Kai crossed his arms and pouted.

Fen held the Granon in her hands and absently hummed a tune. After Kai's statement, she stood up and faced him. "Why did you battle Stygian?"

"What?" Kai stammered.

"Why did any of us battle Stygian?" Fen challenged her siblings.

No one spoke.

"Too soon we have forgotten what was won and what was lost today." Fen held the Granon aloft. A soft white glow surrounded it like a halo. "There are no coincidences. Each of us arrived at The Nine Muses expecting closure, but, instead, we were gifted new opportunities. We are now living our intended lives, existences filled with magic and with purpose.

"We are not monsters. We are magical human beings who have been given the chance to save our world." Fen gazed into the Granon.

"Prasad taught me the importance of love and of duty. He believed in the The Cererian Prophecy. He died defending the holy Word to ensure Hilly would live and complete her destiny. We all have a responsibility to each other and to every person living on this planet." Fen raised her arms toward her siblings.

"Join me," she beckoned. "Hold hands and recommit your souls to the purpose responsible for bringing us together." Chance, Kai and Hilly formed a circle with Fen, and interlaced fingers.

Fen spoke reverently. "By this circle we commit our lives to The Cererian Prophecy and all that it stands for. Let's go forth and restore peace to our world."

"So mote it be," Hilly added.

# Thank You

Thank you for taking the time to read **Beginning of Tomorrows**, book 1 of Chronicle of Ceres.

**Please take a moment to write a review.**

It's so important for a book to have social proof, and I'd love your help sharing this series with others who embrace their magic.

Leave a review or star rating at your favorite book retailer

For new releases, giveaways, and fun info, subscribe to my newsletter by visiting www.cllavigne.com

# Acknowledgements

THERE ARE MANY SOULS who assisted me on my magical journey into the realm of the Kemp family and the beautiful Cererians:

- Chris held my hand, calmed my fears, endured late-night "aha" moments, and ensured wine was always in my glass.

- John, Judy and Steve (my siblings) provided traits for all the characters in the book, but not in the manner they may suspect.

- Jim (aka Super Jimmy) annoyed the heck out of me about rewriting the beginning of the book. And, he was SO right. RIP, James. Your insight was brilliant!

- Brittany helped me realize the value of great editing. Her thoughtful questions and honest suggestions urged me to make this book the best it could be.

- A huge THANKS goes to my friends who supported me as I hid in my cave working diligently on the remaining books in Chronicle of Ceres.

# About Author

Born in Alaska and raised in England, CL is an Elemental Specialist who writes magical realism novels that have witch fantasy overtones. Her stories feature real people and natural magic, all controlled by the Spirits of Nature and otherworldly beings.

Residing in the Sunshine State with her husband, four cats and four goldfish, CL incorporates elements of magic, mysticism and mythology into her writings. It's not unusual to encounter dragons, elemental spirits, Leotes (glowing orbs) and even Big Foot as you follow her characters on their adventures.

Her current fantasy series is Chronicle of Ceres, which will feature 6 books. Fantasy fans loved Book 1 (Beginning of Tomorrow) and Book 2 (Denali Rising) and Book 3 (Shasta Beckons) will release early 2023.

A collection of horror short stories titled Tales From the Crows will release October 2023.

Embrace your magic!

Find the magic and stay informed about special deals, giveaways, new releases and other great updates by subscribing to her **NEWSLETTER**.

**Discover CL's magic:**

www.cllavigne.com

www.facebook.com/CLLaVigneAuthor

www.instagram.com/cllavigneauthor/

# Also By

**Chronicle of Ceres Magical Realism Series**
Beginning of Tomorrows, book 1
Denali Rising, book 2
Shasta Beckons, book 3 (releasing July 2023)

**Tales From the Crows**
Horror short story collection (releasing October 2023)